Others Available by D.K. Holmberg

The Dark Ability

The Dark Ability
The Heartstone Blade
The Tower of Venass
Blood of the Watcher
The Shadowsteel Forge
The Guild Secret
Rise of the Elder

The Cloud Warrior Saga

Chased by Fire
Bound by Fire
Changed by Fire
Fortress of Fire
Forged in Fire
Serpent of Fire
Servant of Fire
Born of Fire
Broken of Fire

The Lost Garden

Keeper of the Forest
The Desolate Bond
Keeper of Light

THE GUILD SECRET

THE DARK ABILITY
BOOK 6

ASH Publishing
dkholmberg.com

The Guild Secret

Copyright © 2016 by D.K. Holmberg
All Rights Reserved
Published by ASH Publishing

Cover art copyright © 2016 Rebecca Frank
Book design copyright © 2016 ASH Publishing

ISBN-13: 978-1536899948
ISBN-10: 1536899941

Disclaimer: The book is licensed for your personal enjoyment only. All rights reserved. This is a work of fiction. All characters and events portrayed in this book are fictional, and any resemblance to real people or incidents is purely coincidental. This book, or parts thereof, may not be reproduced in any form without permission.

ASH Publishing
dkholmberg.com

THE GUILD SECRET

THE DARK ABILITY
BOOK 6

CHAPTER 1

THE SUN'S LIGHT FADED AS IT DISAPPEARED behind thick clouds, casting a haze across the late evening sky that reminded Rsiran of when he Slid to the center of the Aisl Forest. A chill hung in the air. It had been that way all day, even under the day's bright sunshine, and he pulled his cloak tight around him, over the line of knives sheathed at his waist.

"Are you sure that you want to do this?" Valn asked. The dark-haired man crouched next to Rsiran, staring out at the distant city of Thyr with eyes that were a moderate green, his hand resting on the hilt of his sword. His sharp jaw clenched, the tension visible to Rsiran.

"You don't have to come," Rsiran said.

Valn turned and shot him a hard look. Since the attack on Elaeavn, Valn had come with Rsiran often on his scouting trips. Having someone accompany him was the only way that Jessa would really let him go.

"Don't I? After what happened in the city—"

"Are you sure you want to risk yourself again?" Rsiran asked. "The last time…"

"The last time? You mean the time when we caught the three Venass scholars in Eban trying to blend in? The time when you decided to throw around your knives as we caught them, getting the attention of their city watch? That time?"

"I don't throw my knives. Then my aim would be nearly as bad as yours."

Valn shook his head.

Rsiran tried to hide his smile as he patted him on the shoulder. It was easy to get Valn on edge, and Rsiran needed to stop taking advantage of it by making fun.

"Coming so close to Thyr… This isn't our best idea, Rsiran."

He knew it wasn't, but their search for scholars of Venass had only turned up a few stragglers. The more they looked, the more it seemed that Venass had tried to disappear, pulling their people back to Thyr. It was the one place he hadn't risked visiting until now.

"I need to find him."

"It's not *your* fault that Danis escaped," Sarah said. She shifted the ends of the long cloak she wore, dragging it across the hard stone. Valn had insisted on her coming with them this time, especially as they got closer to Thyr. As one of the Thenar Guild, she could detect Sliding, at least those who did so using their talent. Rsiran still didn't know whether she could detect Sliding done the way Venass did. "They had enough people with them who Slide that they were in and out of the Forgotten Palace before we could get back there. Besides, you managed to stop the others from destroying any more of the Elder Trees."

"Still lost the one," Rsiran said.

Sarah's deep green eyes wrinkled as she frowned. "Yes, we did. Father still isn't sure what that means for the alchemists."

"It doesn't mean anything," Valn said. "The trees mattered in times past, but it's been centuries since they played a relevant role."

Sarah looked toward Rsiran, as if searching for answers. He didn't know what to tell her. Should he share that there was still power in the Elder Trees but that he seemed the only one able to reach it? Would that make her feel better, or worse? They hadn't saved the alchemist tree. The tree itself wasn't dead, but the power within it had changed, leaving the tree darkened. There didn't seem to be anything they could do that would restore it.

But he had saved the other that had shown signs of being poisoned, only learning later that it was the smith tree. The Smith Guild had rewarded him for restoring the tree by naming him guildlord, but he still didn't know if it had been a reward or a punishment, especially with all the meetings he now had to attend.

"They still protect the crystals," Sarah said when it became clear that Rsiran wouldn't answer.

"The guilds have them protected," Valn said. "I should know. I have to take my turn on the rotation, watching the entrances to the room. The last time was so boring, I think I would rather have been back in Eban again with Rsiran."

Rsiran smiled. "I think you liked Eban."

"There's really nothing like having a dozen men with swords surround you," Valn said.

"You were never in any danger," Sarah chided. "You can Slide away from swords."

"And the next time? What if they have crossbows?"

"Slide faster," Sarah suggested.

She stalked away from them and stood on the peak overlooking Thyr. Rsiran turned his attention there, as well, watching as the city slowly blinked to life as the sun set completely. He focused on his sense of metals within the city, and with his increased affinity for lorcith, he could practically feel the shapes that had been forged, everything from pots and decorative works to knives. Even two swords. The knives were his work—the act of forging them created an even stronger connection to them for him—but the others were not.

Rsiran focused on heartstone but found none. That he didn't made it less likely that Danis was down in the city. Rsiran still wasn't sure that he was prepared to face his grandfather again. The last time, he had nearly died. Others *had* died. And if not for the cell that had originally been created to hold Rsiran, he might not have survived.

Had he only been more decisive when he'd trapped his grandfather in that very cell, he wouldn't have to worry now about what the man might do next. He'd had him, contained. He could have gone back, finished him off, so that he wouldn't cause anyone else the same harm that he had caused all of Rsiran's family, but he hadn't. At the time, he claimed that it was compassion, but the more he thought about it, the more he wondered if it hadn't been something else: fear.

Rsiran had already lost his mother—killed by his own knives—and still didn't know what had happened to his father. How many more would die because of him?

"Is he down there?" Sarah asked.

Rsiran shook his head. "I don't detect any heartstone."

"And you're sure that's how you'll know he's there?"

"He carried something with him," Rsiran said. "It was his sister's."

"Evaelyn," Sarah said. She didn't mask the anger in her voice. She had been controlled by Evaelyn, Compelled to nearly attack Rsiran. Fear that it might happen again had kept her from getting involved in the last attack. Now she wore bracelets much like Rsiran's and Valn's that were meant to prevent her from being Compelled. "I didn't think they were close."

"Maybe not anymore," Rsiran said. "But Della claims that they once were very close and that he would have done anything for her. Considering how she went to him for help…"

Sarah nodded, her eyes still troubled. "Why are we *really* here?"

"Venass. We need to weaken Venass," Rsiran answered.

Sarah focused on the distant shape of the Tower of Venass. From where they stood, a mist seemed to envelop it. Rsiran could feel the way that Venass pulled on him, as if the lorcith within the tower itself drew him forward. He had stopped wondering how Venass had access to so much lorcith, having discovered that they had access to alternative mines with seemingly limitless veins of the metal. This unending supply allowed Venass to experiment with the metal, learning of uses that those in Elaeavn would have once believed impossible.

"I don't know that we can truly weaken Venass from here." Sarah stared at the tower, likely feeling its pull in some way as well. As a member of the Alchemist Guild as well as the Thenar Guild, she would share a connection, though probably weakened compared to what Rsiran experienced. "Reaching the tower—"

"We're not going to enter the tower," Rsiran said.

She turned her attention to him, glancing briefly at Valn as she did. "You intend to go into Thyr. That is close enough to the heart of Venass."

"We will enter Thyr to demonstrate that we aren't afraid of Venass," Rsiran said.

"That isn't why you're going."

Rsiran shook his head. "There is word of Venass scholars in Thyr."

"I suspect this close to Venass, it would not be uncommon for their scholars to be there," Valn said.

"That isn't the reason, either," Sarah said.

"You don't have to come with me," Rsiran told her.

"I want you to admit the real reason we're doing this."

Rsiran took a deep breath before answering. The more he discovered about his connection to the guild, especially now that he was guildlord, the more he questioned why his father had kept it from him. And now that he was missing… Rsiran had no way to ask. What had happened to him? Could it simply be that his mother's attempts at Compelling his father had caused him to go mad over time, much the same way that Luca had grown increasingly insane during his time in the mine all alone, with nothing other than the song of the lorcith and Venass attempting to Compel him?

"I need to find my father," he answered. "You don't have to come with me if you don't want to, but it's important for me. For the guilds," he added, though he wasn't sure it was convincing.

"Will it change anything?" Sarah asked. Valn touched her shoulder and she shook her head. "No, Valn. That's the question, isn't it? Will finding his father change anything that we do?"

"Not that we do," Rsiran answered, "but it changes things for me. I… I need to know what happened to him."

"Even if that means finding out that he's really gone?" Sarah asked. Her tone had softened, and she brushed a strand of dark hair away from her face.

He nodded. He needed to know.

For so many years, he had believed that his father hadn't wanted anything to do with him once he'd learned of his son's abilities. Rsiran assumed his father had feared his ability to Slide—seeing it as the dark ability from the Great Watcher. He assumed that when the old smith discovered the way that lorcith called to his son, he simply couldn't understand. But it seems his father knew these abilities all too well. Though he might not understand why or how Rsiran managed to Slide, he clearly understood the call of the lorcith… Because his father had the same ability. He was a Master Smith, born with smith blood. The difference was that his father believed one should deny the call of the lorcith, not embrace it. He thought of all the years his father had been tormented by his mother, unwittingly manipulated as she attempted to use him so that she could discover the secret of the guild—the Elder Trees that he'd discovered were the heart of the Aisl.

He'd learned all of the family secrets that day back in his mother's home, overhearing her conversation with Danis… her father. He now saw his own father in a different light. A victim. And a man who maybe wanted to get to know his son. But it was more than that. Finding his father was something that he needed to do for Alyse. She had found happiness with Brusus, something that Rsiran would have thought impossible when she first moved to Lower Town, and he knew there was a part of her that longed for their father's approval. If Rsiran were honest with himself, there was a part of him that longed for that approval as well.

"Night time," Valn said, breaking the silence that had spread between them. "Time to make our visit."

He and Sarah both looked to Rsiran. Valn could Slide himself to Thyr, but doing so risked someone like Sarah with Thenar Guild abilities influencing the Slide. Letting Rsiran take them didn't carry the same risk, especially not when he *pulled* them in his Slide.

He held his arms out and they each grabbed on.

Thinking of where he wanted to go, he Slid.

They emerged inside Thyr, in an alley where he'd once been attacked. Familiarity made Sliding easier, and this was a place that he knew had some protection so that he didn't have to fear harming anyone by suddenly appearing.

Inside the city, the stink of filth rose to his nostrils. Sounds drifted down the street—loud voices and music, likely from the taverns nearby. Valn released Rsiran's arm and held onto the hilt of his sword. Sarah shifted the cloak around her, less eager to grab her sword than Valn, but tension still apparent in her posture.

"Interesting choice," Valn said.

"It's one I knew. I've been here before."

Sarah glanced at him. In the faint glow from the streetlight, he could see the frown on her face. "From when you chased that Hjan here?" She fumbled over the word as most of them did. From Haern, they knew the Hjan were a part of Venass, assassins trained with skills that gave them speed and abilities. Haern had nearly been one of them, taking the first steps with the implant that had augmented his ability as Seer.

"Thom," Rsiran said. He felt no remorse for the fact that he was dead.

"Well, time to work your magic," Valn told him. "Can you detect anything?"

They counted on his ability to discern the lorcith found throughout the city. Not only to discover where it might be, but to find when that lorcith—or heartstone as there had been a few of the Venass they discovered with heartstone implants—had been placed inside of someone. Making that distinction required a greater proximity to the city. His sensitivity to lorcith had improved, but not to the point where he could stand outside the city and discern absolutely everything about the metal he detected.

He hadn't attempted Traveling as a means of detecting lorcith. Though he'd tried the mind-travel several times since discovering his ability, the effort of Traveling still left him weakened unless he returned to the Elder Trees, and he had reservations about relying on their ability to power him.

"There's lorcith all around here," Rsiran said.

Standing in the city, he could feel it in ways that he was unable to from outside the city. As he let his awareness of it stretch away from him, he detected the growing sense of lorcith. Even along the street, there were dozens of items of lorcith.

"Anything stand out for you?" Valn asked.

Rsiran swept his focus through the city. He detected the same items that he had from above the city but nothing that made him think of an implant. "Not like what we need. Maybe the report was—"

A flash of lorcith came to him, one that he recognized. A knife, formed by his hand.

Had it been there before?

Hard to know. There were plenty of knives outside of Elaeavn that he'd made, especially considering how many he'd made for Brusus, who then sold them, shipping them outside the city.

"What about the report?" Sarah asked.

Rsiran blinked, continuing to move his focus around the city, but he kept coming back to that knife. It moved quickly. He would almost think that whoever held it Slid, but there was never a significant jump that would make it clear.

"Do you sense anything?" he asked her.

"Sliding?" When he nodded, she closed her eyes, cupping her hands together in front of her. A moment passed, and then she opened her eyes again. "Nothing that I can detect."

"What is it? What did you find?" Valn asked.

"A knife."

Valn flipped a pair of knives from sheaths hidden up his sleeves. "That's nothing special. I have a few of those."

"You're right," Rsiran said.

He still couldn't shake the way that knife called to him. Even those that he carried, also forged by his hand, didn't call to him in the same way, but he'd grown accustomed to listening when lorcith demanded his attention. And this was something that demanded his attention.

The knife moved again. This time, it seemed even more like it had skipped.

"Rsiran?"

He turned and realized that he had Slid, moving part way down the street as he started to follow the sense of lorcith that he'd detected.

The knife moved again, only this time, it was closer to him. There was no question that it had Slid.

"Wait for me," he said.

Grabbing onto the sense of lorcith that he'd detected, he Slid where he'd last found it.

He emerged on a narrow street. Tall buildings practically leaned into the street, blocking out light from the sliver of moon. No streetlights lit the way here.

Rsiran *pushed* on a pair of knives, sending them flying from him, sweeping down the street, and he prepared to send another pair if needed.

Nothing moved.

Where was the lorcith that he'd detected?

He focused on it, trying to listen, and found it farther down the street.

Another Slide.

When he emerged, he found the knife.

It was plunged into the stone of one of the buildings. Rsiran *pulled* on it, and the knife whipped back to him. As he caught it, he had a flash from the knife, and knew why it had called to him and when he had last held it, a time when he had nearly died.

His heart hammered in his chest. Why should Josun be here?

Better yet, where had he gone?

CHAPTER 2

Rsiran Slid back to the alley where he had left Sarah and Valn.

He emerged to a battle.

Sarah and Valn stood back to back, surrounded by five attackers. Lorcith flared from implants within three of them. He detected nothing from the other two. Did that mean they carried shadowsteel?

Pulling on the lorcith implants, he dragged the three from Venass down. One of them screamed, and the other two fell silent as Valn's knives found their targets.

The two without implants—at least, without those that he could detect—turned toward him, ignoring Valn and Sarah.

One of them flicked something in Rsiran's direction.

He Slid, emerging behind them.

The object changed direction, as if somehow targeting only him.

Rsiran Slid again, this time emerging long enough to grab Sarah, and pulled her with him to the back of the alley. Valn followed.

"What happened?" he asked.

Valn shook his head. "Don't know. Appeared when you Slid off."

The dark object streaked toward them.

Rsiran *pushed* a pair of knives and struck the object—some sort of metal ball, he realized—sending it flying off to the side. Using heartstone knives, he *pushed* them at the attackers.

As the knives neared, the closest man somehow caught them in the air and then threw them down, embedding each blade deeply into the ground.

Rsiran *pulled* on them, but something had changed in the knives, as if when the man grabbed them, he had distorted Rsiran's connection to the metal.

He sent five more knives streaking toward the two men, all lorcith.

This time, he *pushed* with the strength of Ilphaesn, summoning the image of the lorcith within the mountain, and pressing with all of that behind him.

The knives slowed, one or both of the men *pushing* against them.

He should be stronger than they were, but they still managed to slow his knives. The nearest attacker unsheathed a black-bladed sword and sliced it through the air, splitting the knives, and tearing his connection to them away.

"Rsiran!"

He glanced to see Sarah swinging her sword at the black metallic ball. She struck it, knocking it to the side, but the damn thing continued to move, managing to maneuver around her attack.

Did the attackers control the ball, or was it somehow keyed to Rsiran so that it sought him independently?

Grabbing Valn and Sarah, he Slid again, emerging on top of one of the buildings, above the men.

"Why here, Lareth? Just take us back to Elaeavn," Valn said.

The dark ball shot toward him again.

Rsiran took a quick inventory of his knives. He still had a dozen, but each time they touched the shadowsteel, his connection to the knives changed. They could still return to the city as Valn wanted, but doing so would keep him from the answers that he wanted. Josun *had* been here, and had used one of his knives, almost as a calling card. Almost as much as he wanted to find Danis—and his father—he wanted to find Josun. He'd let him run free for far too long.

"Take her back," Rsiran said.

"I'm not leaving you here."

"I can handle this better if I don't have to watch out for you."

"And who will watch out for you? I told Jessa that I'd cover you. Don't want to make a liar out of me, do you?"

They didn't have time to argue. He *pushed* a knife at the ball again, and it collided with the sphere, sending it away from him. It wouldn't be long before it changed direction again and came back at him.

"They're using shadowsteel. When they touch my knives, they distort my connection to lorcith."

"That shouldn't happen," Sarah said. "Nothing should affect the potential of the metal like that."

"I don't know how else to explain it."

He heard the whistling of the sphere as it streaked toward him. Somehow, he had to keep it from reaching him.

Could he force metal around it?

Rsiran *pushed* one of his knives, sending a message to the lorcith within about what he intended. As the knife streaked toward the sphere, he *pushed* on the metal, so that when it reached the sphere, it wrapped around it.

The sphere dropped to the ground.

Rsiran tried *pulling* on the lorcith, but his connection to it was faded. Not absent, but muted, much like it had been when a similar sphere left spikes in his back and almost paralyzed. Was this a similar weapon?

He turned his attention to the men on the street. They watched him, the glow of the streetlight catching their dark eyes. Not green.

Had Venass begun using others?

Or maybe it always had.

"Why are they looking at you like that?" Valn asked.

"Not looking. Studying," Sarah said with a shiver.

Rsiran sent his remaining knives, both heartstone and lorcith, all at the same time. Before holding the crystal for a second time, he wouldn't have been able to use both at once. Since then, his connection to heartstone had improved, and he now managed to sense them both at once.

The nearest man swung his sword, *pushing* against the lorcith knives.

The heartstone slipped past.

One of the knives struck. Rsiran *pushed*.

The other man sliced at the air, moving in a blur as he knocked the remaining knives from the air.

The first man fell to his knees.

Rsiran *pulled* Valn's sword and Slid to the street.

The remaining Hjan made as if he might attack, but jumped back and—with a blur of blackness—disappeared.

Rsiran jabbed at the fallen man and kicked the shadowsteel sword out of his hand.

Valn Slid with Sarah to join him. Rsiran handed him his sword back. "Sorry about taking that."

"You made it, so I guess you have first crack with it. Besides, I doubt there would be anything that I would be able to do with it against them."

"What is that?" Sarah knelt in front of the shadowsteel sword and reached toward it.

"Careful," Rsiran cautioned. "I don't know if the metal will affect us. The last time I carried it, I wrapped it in lorcith."

"Like that?" Valn pointed to the metal sphere lying nearby.

Rsiran Slid to it and lifted the ball. There was something to it that he wanted to understand. Was it simply a solid sphere of shadowsteel, or was it like the device that Rhan had used against him?

"Like this," he said.

"We need to understand what this is," Sarah said. "If they are able to counter your ability with lorcith and heartstone, we have to understand how so we can know if there is any limitation to what they can do."

Rsiran thought about how the man had moved, how quickly he had spun as he knocked the knives from the air, leaving fragments scattered about the alley that Rsiran could barely detect. They were there, just on the edge of his awareness, but not as they should be. The contact with shadowsteel had changed them.

"From what I saw, they don't have many, if any, limitations."

Sarah stood and kicked the toe of her boot at the sword. "Still. I think Father can help us understand this better. The alchemists would have to know something, don't you think?"

Rsiran hoped they did. Otherwise, Venass might already have enough strength to defeat them.

CHAPTER 3

The inside of the Hall of Guilds glowed with a soft blue light. It seemed to come from everywhere: from the stone of the walls, to the wooden drawers set into the walls, and even the floor. Heartstone, or so it seemed, that suffused everything.

Lorcith was here, as well, but not in the same quantity as heartstone. And not pure heartstone. That had been what Rsiran thought when he'd first come to this place, but he detected no evidence of solid heartstone here, only traces embedded in everything.

"Are you sure we should bring that here?" Valn asked Sarah.

She carried the shadowsteel sword wrapped in her cloak, careful not to touch it, cradling it as if it were a child rather than something dangerous. "We need to study it so that we can understand how they managed to distort the connection Rsiran has to lorcith."

"It affected heartstone as well," Rsiran said. It troubled him more than he could share with Sarah and Valn. If Venass could impact his connection to lorcith and heartstone enough that he could no longer use it, it negated one of his advantages with them. He could still Slide—and Travel, which he didn't think they had replicated yet—but now, they could more easily counter him when attacked.

Worse, where did they manufacture all the shadowsteel? There had to be some kind of forge for them to make it, with smiths who did the work. But without any connection to the metal, he couldn't find it.

"Yes, heartstone, too," Sarah said. "You call this metal shadowsteel. Why?"

"That's what they called it."

They moved down the halls and stopped in a smaller room with a long wooden table. Sarah pushed the benches out of the way and set the wrapped sword on the table, slowly peeling her cloak away from it.

"Should you do that here?" Valn asked.

Sarah hesitated. "It's just a sword."

He sniffed. "Like that crazy sphere was just a ball?"

Rsiran pulled it from his pocket and held it out to Valn. "It's only a ball now."

Valn shook his head. "Are you going to figure out what's inside it?"

"Inside?" Sarah asked. "What makes you think there's anything inside it?"

"Because I don't think they were trying to play catch with Rsiran, and we saw what happened with the last weapon they used on him. Damn near killed him, if I recall correctly."

"You do," Rsiran said. The image of Rhan touching his two spheres together had come to mind when he'd seen the attacker send this sphere at him.

"And if it *nearly* killed Lareth, what would it do to the rest of us?"

"I'm not any more protected—"

Valn pointed to the table. "The rest of us would have died under such an attack, Lareth. We don't have the ability to *push* with lorcith like you do."

"That doesn't help with shadowsteel."

"Like I said, what would it do to the rest of us?" He glanced from Rsiran to Sarah. "And now you bring that sword in here. The Great Watcher only knows what they did to it. What if there's some sort of hidden power to it? Maybe you touch it and trigger something to explode."

Sarah eyed the sword and shook her head. "If it were going to explode, it would have done so when I wrapped it up. Besides, Venass and their Hjan assassins use them as swords. It's nothing more than a metal blade. A special metal blade, but a blade, nonetheless."

"I still don't like it."

"Anything we can do to help us understand what Venass might do next gives us an advantage," she said. "That's why we risked going to Eban, and Igalan, and even to Thyr, isn't it? To find out from Venass what they are planning?"

That was their intent, but what had they really learned? They had found a handful of Venass, and each time, they were forced to fight, leaving the scholars they discovered dead. They needed someone to question. Rsiran needed someone to ask whether his father still lived, and find out what his grandfather intended to do next.

"I've been going along on these scouting expeditions because I want to keep Venass from attacking our city again," Valn said. "We've barely managed to rebuild what they destroyed. If they come again… if they manage to attack and we don't have Rsiran's advantage… think of how much destruction they'll be able to bring."

"I have. That's why we need to understand this sword." Sarah hovered over it, staring down at the black blade that seemed to absorb the light around them. Whereas heartstone and lorcith practically glowed with light and energy of their own, shadowsteel appeared to have the opposite effect. Nothing came from the shadowsteel but emptiness.

Valn stopped at the edge of the table, making a point not to get too close to the sword, as if he was afraid to touch it. "If you're going to understand it, at least ask your father. The alchemists might know something about a metal like that."

"They do." Rsiran thought back to what Ephram had said when they were near the Elder Trees. "Ephram mentioned that the alchemists knew the secret to shadowsteel. He said they refused to create it."

Valn glanced over to Sarah. "Did you know this?"

"I was with Rsiran when he told him."

"Why didn't you share that with me?"

Sarah flung the end of the cloak over the sword, covering the blade again. "You're not of the Alchemist Guild. It didn't matter."

Valn's eyes reflected hurt. "Didn't matter? After everything that we've been through facing Venass? I would have thought that you recognized the need for the guilds to share information. If I'm going to be facing Venass, if the others of my guild are asked to face them, don't you think that we deserve to know what we're up against, even if that includes secrets of your father's guild?"

Her eyes widened slightly. "It's my guild as well."

"You're of the Thenar Guild," Valn reminded her.

He turned, and with a flicker of color, he Slid from the room.

Rsiran stood, debating whether he should follow Valn or stay to say something more to Sarah. He didn't know Valn as well, but they had grown closer since the Venass attack on the city, and he knew the man likely needed time away to cool off.

"He's right, you know," Rsiran said.

"I don't need you to start siding with him."

"I'll side with him if he speaks the truth. We need to know everything that we can about shadowsteel. All of the guilds should understand what we face."

"It's a secret of the Alchemist Guild."

"Why?"

Sarah stared at the bundle of her cloak around the sword. "I don't know. Father won't share that with me, which makes me realize that there is a reason. He wouldn't keep something from me unless it were dangerous for it to get out."

"As dangerous as having swords made of shadowsteel? As dangerous as strange exploding orbs of shadowsteel?" Rsiran asked. "It was this metal that they used to poison the Elder Trees. I think we *all* need to understand what it is so we can find a way to protect ourselves from the next attack."

Sarah didn't take her eyes off the table. "I'll talk to him."

He considered saying something more, but decided against it. He might be the smith guildlord now, but he was a newcomer compared to the others. Pushing himself into issues would only alienate him from the rest.

"Good. Do you still want to come with us the next time?"

Sarah did look up then. "You intend to go out again?"

"I haven't found my father. And we haven't heard anything about what my grandfather plans. I think we have to go out again."

"You will take Valn with you?"

"Valn can come if he chooses."

Sarah's gaze drifted toward the door, her eyes going distant, something like what Haern did when he attempted a Seeing. Did she use her ability to detect Valn? "And if something happens to him?"

"I don't want anything to happen to Valn any more than I want something to happen to you," Rsiran said. "That's why we need to understand what Venass intends with the shadowsteel."

"It's more than that."

Rsiran nodded. "The metal has strange properties much like lorcith and heartstone."

"Potential."

"Call it what you want, but that doesn't change the fact that it does. We need to understand it, determine if there is anything else that it might be able to do, so that we can be ready to stop the next attack."

"I said that I'll talk to him."

Rsiran watched Sarah for a moment. The corners of her deep green eyes wrinkled with her frown, her brow furrowing as she stared off distantly.

He had to trust that she would do what they needed. Sarah was guildlord for the Thenar Guild, a guild with her as its only member. Rsiran might be developing some aspects of the thenar skills—the fact that he could see flickers of color when others Slid near him made it likely—but he didn't possess the level of skills that Sarah did, specifically the way that she could influence Sliding.

He glanced down to the bundle of cloth. There was a part of him—and he didn't know if it came from his connection to lorcith and heartstone—that told him he should destroy the sword. Something about the metal grated on him. But they needed to understand it. Destroying the sword would prevent them from knowing what else Venass might attempt.

Leaving Sarah, he Slid.

Rsiran emerged on the street above. Since the attack, much of the rubble had been removed, leaving a massive wound within the city. The Elvraeth still seemed unconcerned about the attack, and had made no effort to assist in the cleanup. In the days following the attack, Rsiran and others who could Slide removed as much as possible. Rsiran moved the bodies first, sending them into the sea. Where stretches of magnificent homes once lined the street in this part of Upper Town, now there was nothing but destruction.

Some construction had resumed, but it was slow. The guilds coordinated the effort, but they didn't work well together. Had he not been guildlord, Rsiran would never have known how poorly the guilds cooperated. The miners refused to work with the Travel Guild. The alchemists tried to keep separate from all of the others, except for the Thenar Guild, and that was because Sarah had alchemist blood. Even some of the minor guilds, those not descended from the ancient clans and tied to the Elder Trees, had pitched in, offering to help, but there was only so much they could do when confronted with the resistance of the other guilds.

Rsiran stood next to a jagged wall of one of the fallen buildings. Moonlight filtered through thick clouds that carried the scent of a coming rain, but not enough light to help him see. Rsiran *pushed* on a pair of knives—the only two that he had remaining after the attack—and used their light to see around him.

The guilds had left the wall, supposedly thinking they might save it since it appeared sturdy, and build onto it rather than tearing it down, but no one had yet made an effort to rebuild. He didn't know why it troubled him to see nothing had changed since the attack, but it did.

"You look troubled."

Rsiran turned, startled. He hadn't expected anyone to find him here, especially not at night standing in the ruins from the attack. "Della?"

"You don't need those knives floating around me, do you?"

Rsiran *pulled* on the knives, drawing them back to him, but kept them hovering in the air. Without the knives, he couldn't see anything. "What are you doing out here?"

"I thought to ask the same of you. There I was, sitting at home with a nice cup of tea, when I Saw that I should come to Upper Town. I didn't know why, but I've learned not to question."

Rsiran sighed. There were times when he wished that Della *could* See him. Then he might know what he was supposed to do.

"I was in Thyr tonight."

"Not alone, I hope."

"Sarah and Valn were with me."

Della took a step toward him, batting a hand at his knives. "You left Jessa here?"

"We've been making trips outside the city for a while, trying to find out what Venass might be up to. Jessa came with me on a few of them, but I think she realizes that Valn is a better fighter than she is."

"And Sarah?"

"She can help if someone Slides."

"I'm glad to hear that you've not been attempting this on your own."

"We all have to deal with Venass."

Della surveyed the street. "You can almost imagine what it must have looked like before the city was here. In some ways, it is actually beautiful."

"The attack was anything but beautiful," Rsiran said.

"I didn't mean the attack, Rsiran."

"Venass used a new way to attack us this time." He described the sphere and the shadowsteel sword. "I worry that they might have discovered a way to counter my ability."

Della smiled and patted him on the shoulder. "They were always going to find a way to counter your ability, Rsiran. You have become powerful, but they have studied for years. Some would say centuries. In all that time, they have sought the secret to power, longing for more than what they possess. Does it really surprise you that they would find new and deadly ways to attack?"

"How can I stop them if they always manage to stay a step ahead of us?"

"You cannot do so alone."

"I didn't mean to imply that I wanted to."

"And yet you said 'I.' You are one man, but you are part of something more now. You are a guildlord, and that connects you in ways that you have never been connected."

"I don't always feel like part of the guild."

"That doesn't change that you are." She studied him, and his bracelets went cool for a moment as she tried to Read him. "That isn't the only thing that bothers you, is it?"

Rsiran swallowed. He hadn't told Sarah or Valn about what he'd discovered. They wouldn't understand what Josun had put him through, but Della would. "When we were in Thyr, I found a knife. There is something about the knife that tells me who last possessed it."

"Do you have that connection with all lorcith you forge?"

"I didn't think so. It's almost as if the lorcith tried sending me a message."

"There are times when you speak of it as something almost sentient."

"Jessa says the same thing. I don't know any other way to describe it."

"Perhaps there is no other way to describe it. Perhaps the Great Watcher has connected through lorcith to you, giving you some of his abilities." She sighed. "What did you find that troubles you so much, Rsiran?"

"Josun had the knife. He was the man I chased through Thyr, almost as if he knew that I was there and that I followed him."

Della remained silent for a moment. From the light of his knives, he saw her rub her chin and adjust the shawl around her neck. "Well, we knew that he was not dead. I am unable to See him, though, and do not know what it means that he has reappeared."

Rsiran Slid away from the wall, emerging in a clearing where he *pulled* his knives toward him. The ground had ash residue from the attack, leaving it blackened. This had been where he had faced his grandfather, and where he had nearly died. He had managed to *push* on the lorcith in the spheres he carried then, stopping Danis from harming him. What had Venass changed in those spheres that kept him from being able to do the same in Thyr?

"I should have gone after him as soon as I discovered he'd escaped the mines," Rsiran said. "I knew that he would come after us again. That he was in Thyr…"

Della approached him carefully, eyeing the knives he held suspended in the air. "You did what was necessary at the time."

"Necessary? Had I been more decisive, we wouldn't be facing the possibility that Josun Elvraeth accepted implants from Venass, thus cementing his alliance with them. I wouldn't have to fear that he might come after me, or work with my grandfather as they both come after me."

"Decisive? Do you really think that you could have killed him? That is what you mean by decisive, is it not?"

He'd kept Josun trapped in the mines above Ilphaesn, but Firell had rescued him in exchange for the return of his kidnapped daughter. Rsiran didn't blame Firell for what he'd done. He would have made a similar exchange had it been Jessa—or even Alyse. But it had been a mistake to not pursue Josun before now. The longer he went without finding him, the more likely Josun could simply disappear. Only, Rsiran knew Josun. He wouldn't simply disappear. Josun was overly confident, and didn't think that someone like Rsiran could beat him.

"I don't know what I could have done," he said. "All I know is that I should have sought him sooner. Now it seems he's coming after me."

"Are you so certain of that?"

Rsiran *pulled* on the knife he'd found, bringing it from his pocket. It was one he would not use against Venass, not until he had a chance to understand why he'd felt the connection to it that he had. Even now, he felt the connection to the knife, the way the metal practically told him what had taken place during the time since Rsiran forged it, including the way that Josun had used it.

Was there any way that he could track Josun through that connection?

Maybe if he took the time, he could discover a way. But where would he get that time? He already spent too much time away, Sliding away from Elaeavn, in some ways neglecting his role as guildlord. As a new guildlord, he couldn't afford to be gone from the city as often as he was.

"I don't know," Rsiran admitted. "I know that he was in Thyr. I know what he's done to us in the past. More than that... I don't know."

Della patted his arm. In the months since he'd learned that they were related, she had not treated him any differently, but then Della had always been welcoming to him. She had been the one who had ensured he got help when he needed it, and had helped convince him of the need to abandon his apprenticeship and accept the offering of friendship from Jessa and Brusus.

"Rsiran," she said, her voice a whisper, "I wish you would be careful. I have not had family for many years, and now that I know we are family, I would not like to lose you, too."

Rsiran breathed out heavily. "I'm being as careful as I can, but there are things that need to be done, and I don't know if anyone else can do them."

"There are others who can help. You may have to look beyond the borders of our city, but they are out there. For now, come with me. Let us sit by the fire and have a cup of tea. Worry about this tomorrow."

Rsiran *pulled* the knives back to him. As he prepared to Slide them to her home, he couldn't shake the worry that he felt, or the fact that with each passing day, there was more for him to fear.

CHAPTER 4

The door to his smithy was open and sunlight streamed in. Rsiran still found it strange to finally be able to leave the door open. For so long, he'd hidden his presence here, fearing not only the Elvraeth, but the Smith Guild discovering him. Either would have led to the same punishment. Now he worked openly, letting in the light from outside, not mindful of who might pass by, though few used the narrow alley outside his smithy. This part of Lower Town was dingy and run down, though Rsiran had in mind ways he could turn it around.

The lorcith-coated sphere of shadowsteel rested on the floor of the smithy. He hesitated placing it on the anvil or even too close to the lump lorcith he possessed, not wanting the shadowsteel to somehow taint his smithy. He had wondered if he should even bring the shadowsteel here to work on, but where else would he have gone that he could examine it? Now, as it rested on the floor, he realized he might have been better off simply disposing of it altogether.

"Are you just going to stare at it?" Jessa asked.

He glanced over to where she sat on their mattress, arms wrapped around her bare legs. Long brown hair hung half in her face, still mussed from sleeping. A mug of steaming black tea rested on the ground next to her.

"I don't know that it's safe to work with. The shadowsteel changed my connection to my lorcith and heartstone knives when we fought with the Hjan."

"And that's never happened before?"

He shook his head. Would there have been some way for him to reclaim that connection had he remained there? They were still knives that he had forged. That connection was stronger than any other he possessed.

Jessa stood and dusted her hands on her shirt. She slipped her arm around Rsiran's waist and gave him a brief hug. "What do you think you're going to be able to learn from that thing?"

"It targeted me. I don't know how they did it, but it seems to recognize me."

"Are you sure the Hjan didn't just control it the same way that you control lorcith and heartstone?"

Jessa often asked the very questions that were in his head. He knew she wasn't a Reader. It was simply evidence of how well she knew him.

Though he'd considered the same idea, the fact that the sphere continued to pursue him even when the Hjan were distracted told him it had a mind of its own, or a link to him somehow. But how was that possible?

When he didn't answer, she pointed to the forge. "Why don't you just throw it on the coals. Heat it up and see what comes out?"

"I don't want to ruin my forge."

She laughed. "Do you really think just heating it will cause problems?"

"I don't know anything about shadowsteel. Sarah is going to ask Ephram about it, but I don't think the alchemists alone will be able to determine what shadowsteel can do. They might know how to make it, and possibly even see the potential within it, but using it?"

"And you think that you can?"

"I think…" He paused and frowned at the sphere. The lorcith surrounding it still had a muted sense, but the longer watched it, the more aware he became that it continued to change. The lorcith thinned somehow.

As he watched, it began to bubble.

Rsiran grabbed a lump of lorcith and *pushed* on it, wrapping it around the sphere. As he did, it took the shape of the sphere, but he detected through his connection to lorcith that it would not hold. Whatever Venass had done with this shadowsteel wanted release, and if he did nothing, it would get free. Would it chase him again? Would there even be anything that he could do to contain it?

Maybe there wouldn't be any way for him to stop it short of destroying it. Only, where would he destroy it? Not in his smithy. He didn't want to place it on the coals here. What he needed was a place that he didn't care whether it ended up destroyed.

A smile came to his face as he thought of just the place.

"What?"

"Want to take a little trip?"

"I don't like the sound of that," Jessa said.

Rsiran grabbed the lorcith-coated sphere off the ground and held it away from him. He *pulled* all the knives that he had lying on his bench and pocketed some of them, slipping others into sheaths.

"Do you think that's really necessary?" Jessa asked.

"I don't know what will be necessary, but I've learned that you can't be over prepared when it comes to Venass—or the Forgotten."

"Forgotten? Is that where you intend to Slide us?"

With a nod, he took her arm and Slid.

They reached the Forgotten Palace. Why was it that he felt compelled—but not Compelled, he didn't think—to come back here as often as he did? Why did it seem like this place had answers to questions he had not yet learned to ask?

They emerged in the heartstone room. He could think of no other way to describe it. The soft blue glow of heartstone was everywhere, filling the space. Shelves that had held books, the entire collection once Evaelyn's, had been ransacked, either by the few remaining Forgotten or by Venass. What secrets had Evaelyn kept here? What might they have managed to learn from her if only they had a way of knowing what she kept here? Would there have been anything that might help him understand his family? Having learned that Evaelyn was related to him as well, surely there must be something here to help. Rsiran still found it ironic that, after all the years he'd spent wanting more of a family, when he finally discovered his newfound relatives, he wanted nothing to do with them.

No, that wasn't quite right. When he discovered his newfound relatives and learned of their evil intentions, it was clear he couldn't just turn away from them, he would have to kill them. First Evaelyn, and now Danis if he could ever find him. Now that he knew Josun still trailed him, even surviving Danis might not be enough.

Jessa glanced over to him. "It doesn't have to be done here, you know. There are other places where we could choose."

Rsiran shook his head. "Where else could we choose where I don't care if shadowsteel taints it? For all I know, this was where they made shadowsteel. It might be the key to stopping Venass. We have to find a way to keep them from making more."

"Where do you think they make it?"

He didn't know. "Thyr is most likely, but…" He frowned, looking to the back of the room. A doorway led into hidden rooms where he had discovered the place where the Forgotten and Venass experimented with lorcith, using paired metal in a way to increase their control. Hadn't he found the schematics? Not only that, but parts of it as well? Much like what Josun had wanted from him when he attempted to force him into making heartstone alloy, the schematics would be a way to make something, possibly shadowsteel.

"You look like you figured something out."

"I don't know if I did or not. What if they were trying to make it here?" And in the depths of Ilphaesn as well. That was another place where he'd found parts much like what he'd come across here. But, though there were what seemed to be parts of something bigger, he saw no evidence of a forge at either location.

But Venass had a forge somewhere. The question was where. They would have to destroy it if they intended to defeat Venass, but would that even be enough? If Venass knew the secret to creating it, wouldn't they just build another?

The shadowsteel worried him, especially as he continued to discover the ways Venass used it. If they added to its potential, and found more ways to use that against him, limiting what his connection to lorcith and heartstone allowed… he had to find the forge, as well as their supply of shadowsteel, and destroy them.

"We didn't find shadowsteel here," Jessa said.

He shook his head. "Not here, but we found what I think they used to build their forge."

He wanted to return to his smithy and study the schematics. Maybe he could find an answer there, especially now that he better understood how to read them.

Rsiran led the way out the back door of the heartstone room. The long hallway carried memories, like so much else in this place, of when he had needed to fight back those of the Hjan coming for his grandfather. No bodies remained, but Rsiran couldn't miss the stain of blood on the stones, or the splatter he caught on the walls.

Jessa pulled on him, dragging him through the hall.

They stopped in the room where they had discovered the paired lorcith. Tools lined a bench, still not claimed in spite of the fact that Venass and the Forgotten had come back through here. Maybe the tools weren't of any value, or maybe those who came for the bodies hadn't wanted to risk taking the time to recover anything other than the bodies.

Rsiran looked around for something that might help him to study the shadowsteel sphere. Near one wall, and vented through it, he found a supply for heat. A forge of sorts, if he could even call it that.

He searched the room until he came across coals that he could use and quickly lit them, stoking the fire until the coals glowed with a warm light.

Jessa sat back, watching him, saying nothing. She had grown accustomed to watching him work the forge, so even here in this strange place, she understood to wait.

When the coals glowed with a steady heat, burning brightly enough that he knew they were ready to heat the lorcith, he set the sphere atop it and took a step back.

Then he waited.

Slowly, the metal took on the heat. First the lorcith heated. Even muted, Rsiran could feel the way that the lorcith steadily grew warmer, the soft and distant song becoming clearer.

A warning.

Rsiran continued to focus on the metal, listening.

The lorcith grew warmer, taking on an orange glow. It flared suddenly in his mind.

The warning was clearer.

Something was happening to the shadowsteel that the lorcith would not be able to contain.

Rsiran grabbed Jessa and Slid to the other side of the wall.

As he did, a flash followed him.

Instinctively, he paused his Slide in the space between, that place in between Slides where he had discovered he could draw upon the strength of the Elder Trees.

From here, he watched as the flash passed through, as if unable to fully reach this place. Darkness streaked around him, exploding in a bubble of compressive power that thundered in his ears. Jessa gripped his hand tightly, as if unwilling to let go.

The explosion passed, and in this place, they were safe, untouched by whatever the shadowsteel would have done had they not paused in their Slide.

"What was that?" she asked.

"That was the sphere," he said.

"How did it follow you as you Slid?"

He wasn't sure that was what had happened. It seemed that way to him, but hearing it from Jessa, knowing that she would have seen something that he could not, made it clear that it had.

"Like I said, I think they somehow managed to link the shadowsteel to me." Rsiran didn't understand it, but that didn't matter. All that mattered was that Venass had definitely found a new and deadly way to track him. What would happen if there were other spheres that he hadn't seen? Would they follow him through his Sliding?

If they could, he might not be safe anywhere. Anyone who came with him might not be safe, either.

He Slid again and emerged back in the room where the sphere had been. Jessa gasped.

It took Rsiran a moment to catch what had happened here. The walls were coated with darkness. Not a pure darkness, but flecks of it, and he realized that when the sphere exploded, it had coated everything with shadowsteel.

"What would this do to you?" she asked him.

"I don't know. They have already used it to weaken my connection to lorcith and heartstone." If it coated him? Would something change in him?

What if they managed to prevent him from Sliding? Or somehow cut him off completely from his connection to the metals? He would be as defenseless as he'd been when the Forgotten used slithca on him.

Rsiran shivered and made his way to the forge. Nothing of the lorcith that had wrapped around the sphere remained. Whatever had happened with the explosion had incinerated it. Had he not had the warning… what would have happened to him?

What would have happened had he done this in *his* smithy?

"This was stupid," he said.

"I'm glad you see that now," she said.

He held out his hand for Jessa. As she took it, he couldn't help but think of what Della had said about how he needed to find help. But where would he find it? Who could withstand violence like this?

CHAPTER 5

Rsiran waited outside the Hall of Guilds, listening to the voices on the other side of the door. He could Travel and observe them more easily, but he had resisted the urge to Travel too often. Not only did doing so weaken him nearly as much as when he had first learned to Slide, but it also felt like something of a violation of trust to eavesdrop like that. He didn't want to lose the trust of Ephram, though he wasn't sure the man would even know if he listened in on their conversation.

The voices stopped and the door opened. Ephram stepped through and paused as he noted Rsiran. "I have been trying to reach you for the last few days," Ephram noted, touching his hand to his temple, scratching at his gray hair. Ephram was a tall man like most within Elaeavn, and willowy thin. His deep green eyes watched Rsiran with an unreadable expression.

"You've been looking for me? Is it about what Sarah—"

His quick shake of the head cut Rsiran off. "Not Sarah. This is about you and your responsibilities." Ephram watched as those who'd been meeting in the Hall departed, then motioned for Rsiran to enter and take a seat at the table. "You are the smith guildlord now," he said as he pulled out the bench and took a seat. "There are certain duties that you must abide by."

"I've been meeting with the master smiths."

"That's not what I mean. The guildlords used to get together to discuss the issues of the guilds. We have not done so as often these days. Now that you're guildlord… I had hoped your connection to the other guilds could change that."

"Why haven't they gotten along?"

Ephram took a deep breath. "The guilds… there are certain trust issues that you might have picked up on. The smiths resented the Miner Guild for restricting access to lorcith."

"They do not anymore."

Ephram shook his head. "They do not. That, I think, is because of you, Lareth. Your ability to detect the lorcith and teach the smiths how to listen for it has changed the way they approach it. The smiths now know the ample supply allows them to practice without fearing waste. They can truly master their skills with the ore, listening to it, learning how best to work each piece. There world has changed forever."

Rsiran hadn't considered that before. For some reason, the Miner Guild had restricted access to lorcith, limiting it in such a way that the smiths were barely able to use it. When they ignored the call of the lorcith, that hadn't been a problem, but now, the smiths listened. More and more of them had regained the ability to hear the call of the lorcith. And then there were those like Rsiran—and now Luca—who had never ignored the call of lorcith. There was no way to hide the lorcith from him when he could hear it so easily.

"What do you think I can do?" he asked.

Ephram took a deep breath. "The guilds need to be unified. Now that one of the Elder Trees is dead—"

"Not dead," Rsiran said.

Ephram frowned. "I thought you said that it did not glow as it had."

"It doesn't, but that is not the same as the tree dying."

Ephram waved his hand. "There might be leaves on the tree, but that doesn't mean that it lives. If the power of the tree is gone, it is no different from any of the other sjihn in the forest." He sighed. "And we must be vigilant. We must protect the crystals. That is the role of the guilds, the way that we serve."

"Serve the Elvraeth, you mean."

Ephram tilted his chin. "Serve the people of Elaeavn."

"The people of Elaeavn do not have access to the crystals, do they? It's only the Elvraeth who enjoy that honor."

"Rsiran—"

He held up his hand. "I agree that we must keep the crystals safe. If Venass managed to acquire one, I fear what they might do. But don't pretend that we do so for the good of all our people."

Ephram watched him a moment. "You will have to be careful with that tone of yours when you meet with them."

"I don't intend to meet with them."

"It is customary for the guildlords to meet with the Elvraeth council. In particular, the new guildlords meet with the council."

"Do they have to approve me?" The master smiths hadn't warned him about that. Rsiran wasn't sure that he would be able to act the way he needed to if he had to be approved by the Elvraeth. Everything that had happened to him his whole life had been tied to the Elvraeth in one way or another.

"They have no approval authority," Ephram said. "That does not change the fact that we must still treat them respectfully."

"Respectfully? The Elvraeth did nothing when Venass attacked."

"What would you have had them do?"

"Care about the fate of the city, for starters."

"They care, but in their own way."

Rsiran met Ephram's eyes, waiting for him to explain more, but he didn't. "Why do you defend them? You know what they have done as well as anyone. What have they done to deserve your loyalty?"

"Not loyalty, but there is tradition that must be respected."

"Tradition also said the Smith Guild should ignore the call of lorcith. Do you think we've been well served by tradition?"

A troubled expression crossed his face.

"Tradition has said that those who can Slide should remain hidden. The Elvraeth were responsible for declaring that talent a dark one. An entire guild, forbidden! Tradition has said that our people should not carry weapons and have no way of protecting ourselves. I know the constables are guild members, but how many suffered because of *that* tradition?"

Ephram leaned back, crossing his arms over his chest as he took a few breaths. "What would you have me do?"

"I would have us approach the Elvraeth from a position of strength, not weakness."

"The guilds have never come to the Elvraeth in a position of weakness."

"No? It seems that you defer too much to them."

"Only because you do not understand."

"Perhaps not," Rsiran said. "But I've seen the way that Venass continues to progress. They don't stick to tradition. They've found a way to target me, to connect shadowsteel to me, and in doing so, they would separate me from my abilities."

"That's not possible."

"I wouldn't have thought so, either, but I found something when we were in Thyr. Hasn't Sarah told you about it?"

"I've not seen Sarah, so no."

Rsiran frowned. She had intended to show the shadowsteel sword to Ephram, and see what answers he might have about the blade and the metal. Why wouldn't she have done that?

"What have you found?"

"Shadowsteel," he said.

"You already knew about shadowsteel."

Rsiran nodded. "We did, but this is different. They have done something with it, modified it in some way. Now when it touches lorcith or heartstone, my connection to the metals changes."

"Does this happen gradually or immediately?"

"Immediately."

Ephram touched a finger to his lips, as he seemed to contemplate. "That should not be possible."

"Why do you say that?"

"Your connection to the metals has intrigued me, and I've come up with only one way to explain why you have the ability to use lorcith and heartstone as you do. I think that it's tied to the potential of the metal, that you are somehow able to access it, and through your connection to it, you can draw on that potential. I have not heard of anyone with quite the same ability, but it is the only thing that makes sense."

"Then how would Venass manage to prevent me from using it?"

"They must somehow drain the potential trapped within the lorcith and heartstone. Shadowsteel has been known to have dark and dangerous properties, but never have we known it to sap the potential of other metals."

Was that what it had done? Could that be all there was to what Venass had devised? The answer made as much sense as any, though he had a hard time imagining the power stored in lorcith could be removed that easily. "Do I drain the potential from lorcith as I use it?"

"I don't know enough about what you do to know how to answer that," Ephram said. "It's possible that you do, and that over time, the metal would become less responsive to you, but it's just as possible that you have a way of connecting to that potential that does nothing to it, a neutral effect if you will."

"Is there any way to determine if that's what happens?" If he drained lorcith as he used it, he would have to think about what that meant. The lorcith had never resisted him when he attempted to use it, almost as if it understood that he had a need, but part of what made him successful with it was the fact that he listened to it, worked with it, rather than forcing it to comply with his needs.

"I suppose, with the right focus, we should be able to determine if that is possible. Does it matter? We know that lorcith is plentiful. What does it matter if you use up the potential stored in any given piece?"

"It matters," he said. There was no way to really explain to someone else *why* it mattered to him, only that it did. Had he not listened to lorcith from the beginning, he would never have learned what he was capable of doing. He would never have learned to forge and shape metal. He would never have learned to control it as he had. Much of what he had become, he owed to his connection to lorcith. He could not betray that connection by misusing it. Doing so felt wrong.

"I need you to tell me about shadowsteel."

"That is a secret of the Alchemist Guild," Ephram said.

"Am I not close enough to the guild? Do I not see the potential stored within metals?"

"That doesn't make you an alchemist."

Rsiran sighed, wishing he didn't have to argue this with Ephram. "With what we have to face, you need to share with me what you know.

We are dealing with Venass, and they do not hesitate to learn, to push themselves as they strain to understand what it is that we can do. They study and learn. They *share*. What happens when they discover a way to replicate all of our abilities? We won't have any way of protecting ourselves then."

Rsiran wasn't sure that they had any way of protecting themselves now. Not with what he'd seen from Venass, and the new ways that they used shadowsteel, but they could continue to learn, and if they could work together...

"As I said, that is a secret of the Alchemist Guild."

"If you want us to work together, you will have to work with me."

Ephram clapped him on the arm. "I *have* worked with you, Lareth. I have shared more than I have with anyone outside the guild. Be patient. There are times when tradition matters."

Ephram stood, pushing back the bench as he did. Rsiran sat there, wishing he could convince Ephram that there might be times when tradition mattered, but there were others when it did nothing more than slow their progress.

"I will summon you when the council desires to meet."

"I'll think about it."

"You will be there. You are one of the guildlords now. You have an obligation to your guild."

Rsiran watched him leave, frustration bubbling within him about what he would do next. They needed to stop Venass, but he needed to find a way to prevent them from creating and using shadowsteel. If he didn't... He didn't want to think about what would happen if he didn't.

CHAPTER 6

The knife streaked through the trees of the Aisl Forest toward him, but with no real force. Rsiran batted it away, slicing at it with his sword, not bothering to even Slide away. It was almost as if Haern didn't even want to try.

Elms and oaks rose around him as they sparred on the edge of the forest, not getting any deeper or closer to the sjihn trees. Haern hadn't wanted to get that deep into the forest, and Rsiran hadn't though it necessary.

But Haern's attack had been much weaker than Rsiran would have expected. In the past, Haern had pushed him, testing him, forcing him not to use his abilities as they sparred so that Rsiran could develop other skills. But now, even without using his abilities, he had no trouble with Haern, and he didn't think it was because he had improved that much.

Haern held back, but Rsiran didn't know why.

He Slid forward, catching Haern from behind, and swung the sword. Haern turned, but did so almost lazily, managing to catch Rsiran's sword, but in the moment before he would have struck him.

Rsiran jumped back, sliding his sword back into his sheath. "What is it, Haern?"

"What are you talking about?" he asked.

"You're not even trying."

"You've gotten skilled enough that I don't need to worry about you."

"You've seen what Venass is willing to do in the city, the way they are willing to attack. I think we need to continue to improve, to grow our abilities."

Haern's jaw clenched. "I know more than most what Venass is willing to do."

Rsiran watched him. Something bothered him today, though he wasn't sure what it was. "Tell me about Venass. What do you know that you haven't shared with us?"

"Rsiran—"

"Haern, they continue to attack. The last group that we encountered had a new weapon, one that they had trained on me. I'm not sure I know enough about how to stop them. So I need to know everything you know that might help us."

"I was never a part of the deeper conversations with Venass. I was almost one of the Hjan, but even then, I was a lower level."

"How did they bring you into the Hjan?"

Haern looked away, shaking his head. "That's not important."

Rsiran couldn't help but think that it might be important, but he wouldn't push Haern on it. "We need to know what they might do next. Where they might attack."

"You want to know what they intend to do with your father. And you want to know about where to find Danis."

Rsiran nodded. He wouldn't deny that, and certainly not to Haern. "Is there anything that you can See?"

"Not when it comes to you. And with Venass... it's as if they managed to blanket themselves in some way. There was a time when I could See them, but that was before..." He touched the plate in his face and let out a slow breath. "I don't know if there's anything that I can do that will be helpful."

Rsiran hadn't expected Haern to be able to See anything about Venass, but it was helpful have it confirmed. "I need to understand shadowsteel," he told Haern.

"You're asking the wrong person."

"Is there anything that you learned while you were there that could help?"

"I knew Venass had something that gave the Hjan different abilities than I had been given, but only the senior members of the Hjan were granted it."

That was something that he hadn't known. "What did it take to be a senior member of the Hjan?"

"Rsiran, you're asking questions that won't help you face the Hjan."

"Fine. Then let me ask who else might be out there who could help us face them? Della suggested that we find allies to help. If they were a league of assassins, then we should be able to find people who have suffered at their hands."

"There were many people who suffered under the Hjan," Haern said. "But few knew that it was the Hjan. That's the key to what they do. They hide in the shadows, working in ways that keep their identities secret. When they attack and you finally understand, it's too late." He shook his head. "What we're facing is nothing like my prior experience with the Hjan. This... this is open warfare. And that makes me nervous."

"Why?"

"Because it's nothing like what they typically do. The Hjan—and Venass—would prefer that you not know they are coming after you.

For them to face Elaeavn—and you—so openly, means either they feel they no longer have to hide in the shadows, or this isn't their primary target."

"What other target would they have?" Rsiran asked. "If not for the crystals, and the Elder Trees, what do you think they might be after?"

"As I said, that's what worries me. Venass has never been open about what they pursue, not like they have been about the crystals and now you. They have demonstrated much more strength than I knew them to possess. Had I only known sooner, I would have shared my concerns with you and the others, and we could have been a step ahead."

Rsiran Slid forward a few steps, *pulling* on his knives, sweeping them through the forest so that they lit the trees. "Then we need to figure out what else Venass might be after."

"That's just it. They have been after the same thing for as long as I've associated with them. It's always been about power, getting stronger."

"That's what the crystals are for them."

"Yes," Haern started, the troubled expression still on his face, "but this is not the same."

"Do you think they want to take over Elaeavn?"

Haern frowned. "Ruling has never been important to Venass, at least not from what I know. They have cared more for exerting their strength and not having limitations, but the actual ruling?" He shook his head. "They would leave that to someone else."

Haern fell silent.

"Are we done?" Rsiran asked.

"I'm sorry, Rsiran."

"You don't have to be sorry. But I can help with whatever bothers you."

Haern sighed. "I'm not sure that you can." He nodded to the trees. "I think I'll walk back, if you don't mind."

Rsiran nodded. "If that's what you want."

Haern started off without another word.

Rsiran watched him disappear. He'd have to find out from Jessa what bothered him. He hadn't been the same since Venass attacked the city. At first, Rsiran thought it had to do with him getting injured, but the more time that passed, the more likely it was that something else troubled him. Maybe that had been it at first, but there was more to it now.

He considered returning to his smithy. Luca waited for him, and Rsiran had been gone a great deal over the last few weeks, leaving the boy he'd promised to train unsupported. Members of the guild, including Seval, also wanted to reach him. The other masters wanted to meet with him regularly, but he'd been too busy with everything he'd been working on with Valn and Sarah, too busy chasing Venass to focus on guild business, but that would have to change. He'd committed to working with the guild, and needed to be available for them.

The shadowsteel troubled him, and he needed to know more about it. If there was any secret that Venass hid, that would be it, wouldn't it? He felt certain that the shadowsteel was the key to how they would gain the power they sought.

After considering for a moment, he Slid and emerged in the depths of the Ilphaesn mine.

He didn't come to the mine as often as he wished he could. Now that lorcith glowed within the walls, he had none of the fear that once consumed him when he'd been here. Now he felt welcomed, not only by the stone of the mountain, but by the lorcith within.

The air smelled of the bitterness of lorcith. Whereas he had once felt the scent a reminder of his disappointment to his father, he now found it pleasing and reassuring. Heartstone once had a sickly sweet odor, but now he found it equally reassuring. Some of that came from the fact that he smelled both during his Slides, as if the Sliding itself was somehow tied to his connection to the metal, but that couldn't be, especially since those of the Sliding Guild did not require the connection to lorcith—or heartstone—in order to effectively Slide.

Rsiran made his way through the tunnel, Sliding at times and at others, simply walking. As he did, he focused on the pull of lorcith around him. When he found a piece that called to him more strongly than others, he paused and *pulled* it from the walls. He no longer had need of pick or hammer to remove lorcith; that was probably the reason the Miner Guild disliked the fact that he came to the mines alone. They didn't prevent him access, and he wasn't sure they could if they wanted to, but he'd seen the irritation on their guildlord's face the first time they met.

None of the convict miners worked this deep in the mine. If he focused, he could hear the miners above him, and could sense the way they chipped away at the mountain, slowly working at the lorcith. Now more often than when he had served here, the miners found larger lumps of lorcith, the restrictions that some from the guild had once Compelled now removed.

He paused as he *pulled* at another piece of lorcith, this one larger than any of the others he'd *pulled* from the mine today. It seemed to have multiple songs for him, as if it would let him use it in different ways than most of the lorcith that he found. It came away from the wall with a high-pitched squeal of metal on stone, and he caught it before it could crash to the ground and put it in his pocket.

This wasn't the reason that he'd come here. And continuing to wander and search for lorcith didn't give him any more answers about what Venass might want from him. What he needed was to return to the chamber where he'd discovered the fragments that he thought were based on the schematics. They seemed tied to whatever Venass intended to make, whether it shadowsteel or something else.

Rsiran Slid and emerged in that chamber. He paused and listened, focusing on the metal around him, searching for what might be out of place. He found nothing in particular. Why would Venass have come here? What was here that they couldn't find elsewhere?

And was there anything that would tie it to the shadowsteel?

Rsiran found nothing. Scanning the area, he sought the same metal that he'd discovered before, but he'd taken that out of Ilphaesn and left it in his smithy.

Why did this have to be so hard? All he needed was to find out where Venass might create shadowsteel. If Ephram would only help, it might be easier.

He had another question that he might be able to get answered while here in the mine. Rsiran wasn't quite sure how to ask the lorcith if his using it drained the metal of its potential, but of all places, this was the most likely one in which he would find an answer.

But not here. Where Venass had set up and forced Luca to mine seemed like the wrong place for him to search for answers, as if the metal here might have been changed by their presence. There was another place he could go, one where he knew lorcith had responded primarily to him. He Slid and emerged in the open space of the chamber at the center of the mines.

He risked the miners finding him, but it was early enough in the day that they likely were deeper in the mine. Not long ago, he had discovered massive amounts of lorcith here and had taken it to his smithy for safekeeping. He still didn't know if the Miner Guild had pulled that lorcith from the mine, or if it had been someone else. Rsiran didn't want to ask the guild—that risked their anger when he attempted to build a rapport with them—but his curiosity remained.

The walls glowed with a steady white light from the potential of the lorcith, pushing back the darkness that he'd known when sentenced to serve here. A single lantern hung from a hook that had been pounded into the wall, giving a strange orange glow that contrasted with the potential from the lorcith, but only to him. He Slid away from the light where he didn't have to risk the miners coming up from below, and where he could practically bathe in the potential from the lorcith. He listened to the song, focusing on it as it hummed around him.

How did he ask lorcith if he sapped its potential by using it?

Could he do anything like he did when he forged it?

Emptying his mind, he thought of the lorcith, even envisioning his forge, and sent the question, doing it without words but as an imagined question to lorcith.

Rsiran stood, waiting for a response.

Surprisingly, the lorcith in his pocket that he'd collected deeper in the mine answered. Maybe that shouldn't be surprising to him. He had *pulled* this piece from the wall because he was more attuned to it. It made sense that it would answer him first.

The song within the metal hummed within him. As it did, he became aware of the song changing, of it shifting, growing muted, but then becoming louder once more.

What does that mean?

The metal flared again, this time vividly within his mind.

Rsiran had a vision come to him, and he didn't doubt that it came from the lorcith itself rather than from anything that he did. The vision showed the Elder Trees, but not the Elder Trees as he knew them when he stood within the forest. This was the Elder Trees as he knew them when he Slid to the place between, when he waited, where he had healed Della, using the power of the Elder Trees that he could only see in that place.

What did the lorcith mean in showing him that?

Did the power of the lorcith come from the Elder Trees? For that matter, did his?

All his life, he had believed that his people had abilities given to them by the Great Watcher, but Rsiran had no abilities of the Great Watcher. His all came from the ancient clans, and were tied to the guilds of today. In some ways, he wondered why his eyes were even green, though they were faint compared to most, more of a gray green. As he learned about the ties to the Elder Trees, he wondered why he should be so tightly bound to them. What made him different? Della claimed that Seers of long ago saw that someone with the Blood of the Watcher and the Blood of the Elders would unify the connection, but she described it as something that would help the people of Elaeavn, and Rsiran didn't think that his abilities were able to help Elaeavn.

The vision returned, stronger than the last time. Strangely enough, in the vision from the lorcith, all five trees glowed brightly with power.

Noise from down the mineshaft caught his attention, and he let out a deep breath as he Slid back to Elaeavn. As he did, he couldn't shake the vision of the Elder Trees, and he couldn't shake the sense that he needed to do more to help them.

CHAPTER 7

Rsiran Slid, unable to remain in Elaeavn. With every moment that he remained in the city, he felt more pressure to be doing something else, even if it was nothing more than roaming outside of the city.

Standing now within the trees of the Aisl Forest, darkness felt oppressive, and almost a living thing. An occasional howl deeper in the forest caught his attention, and he shivered, trying not to pay too much attention to it.

Thoughts raced through his mind. How would they defeat Venass when Venass seemed determined to continue to improve the types of weapons they used against him? And they were targeted at *him*, not at anyone else in the city, making him even more uncomfortable with doing nothing more than continuing to forge knives that he was no longer confident would be effective against Venass. Somehow, *he* had to continue to improve, but how would he?

The next Slide took him past Ilphaesn. He sensed it behind him, a massive weight of lorcith that he could practically feel pushing against him. Another Slide carried him farther north. Not east. East would have taken him toward the Thyrass River, and to Thyr. He feared getting close to Thyr and the heart of Venass.

Asador was another matter entirely. He didn't fear Asador, though he had nearly died there more than once. The next Slide took him within the city. Night kept the streets dark, fitting his mood. He emerged with the next Slide inside the smithy where he'd discovered his sword when Josun had stolen it.

The smithy remained dark, and the air held a musty odor. No one had worked here in some time. Why had Josun brought the sword here? Rsiran needed some way of discovering what he intended, but other than the knife that Josun had left for him in Eban, he had nothing. A bin of metal looked untouched, a layer of dust atop the iron and steel making it clear that no one had been here in ages. The lorcith was gone, though.

He suspected that this was one of the places the Forgotten had forced the abducted smiths to work, but there were other places, as well, deeper underground where they had recovered some of the smiths.

Rsiran Slid again, this time, emerging back in the street. Here, they had faced the Forgotten, friends of his nearly killed. Many had died that day. Without Valn, Jessa would have died, and the Forgotten would not have been slowed.

Why had he come here?

This had been where he had found his father. There was a reason that Venass wanted the master smith. Maybe they had him working with shadowsteel, devising the weapons that they now used. Perhaps he was even responsible for creating the implants they used.

Would his father know who they targeted, or would he have simply done what they asked, hoping that Venass would leave Alyse alone? It was possible they had even told his father how Venass targeted Rsiran. Given that his father had no use for Rsiran and had done his best to remove him from the family, that might have been enough to get him working on their behalf.

He shook the thought away, thinking through what he needed. Della's advice rang true in his mind, like most of what she told him. Venass had to have enemies other than Elaeavn. But how would he find them? Until all of this started happening, he had never even left the city, and knew relatively little about the outside world. What he needed was someone who *did*. Haern wouldn't help, but what of Brusus?

The next Slide took him to the edge of the water. Asador, much like Elaeavn, sat on the shores of the sea. Unlike Elaeavn, the shoreline here was flat and sandy rather than the rocky shore of his home. He could just make out the dark shapes of ships moored out in the bay, outlined by the weak light from the new moon. Men and women moved along the docks, an unusual sight compared to Elaeavn where everything would be quiet at this time of night. Taverns lined the streets along the docks, at least a dozen of them, all bawdy and full of loud music. Were he more of a local, such places would be a way to get information, but Rsiran was an outsider in Asador.

But weren't most people outsiders in this city?

He patted his pockets, ensuring he had his knives. Doing so was nothing more than reflex. The lorcith and heartstone within the knives drew on his awareness, so he always knew when he had them with him. Drawing his hood up over his head, he chose to wander the street.

As he did, he let his focus drift, looking for lorcith or heartstone or anything that might tug on his senses. Nothing really did. There were some of the metals here, but they were decorative for the most part. He found a few items that he'd made, even one knife, but nothing that would be out of the ordinary. Given that Brusus and Firell had made such an effort to ship his knives out of Elaeavn, maintaining the secrecy of their efforts, as well as trying to get as much money for them as possible, there *should* be things that he'd made in the city, much like he hadn't been terribly surprised to discover something of his in Cort.

Rsiran nearly Slid away, when a particular item caught his attention.

Not another knife. He wasn't prepared to face Josun Elvraeth tonight. But something unexpected, and an item that he hadn't made, but one that he had held before, and had held him.

Could he be here?

Rsiran stopped at the door to the tavern and pushed it open.

Loud music assaulted him, that of a steady rhythmic drumming and a stringed instrument that he had never seen before. A singer attempted to scream his voice above the drumming, but failed. Rsiran rubbed at his ears, fearing for the safety of his hearing, but he'd never been a Listener, so what would losing a little matter?

The tavern was full, packed with people standing at tables and mingling between them. Most had the familiar look of fishermen, the same look that he'd seen from men along the docks of Elaeavn. These were hard men, some with piercing through their ears or nose and even a few through their lips. One man had what seemed to be a fishhook through his brow.

Rsiran made an effort not to stare as he scanned the room.

Women made their way through the tavern, as well, but fewer in number. Most of the women appeared as hard as the men, many dressed in loose-fitting or practically non-existent clothing, and several with the same types of piercings as the men. They were fishers, as well, he suspected, but not the kind that came through Elaeavn. Other women had painted faces and wore tight-fitting dresses, and leaned in to whisper softly in men's—and sometimes women's—ears before leading them toward the back of the tavern.

He had almost given up on finding Firell when he saw him sitting at a table in the corner of the tavern, a drink clutched in his hand, another man sitting across from him. Firell tossed dice on the table, and the frown that came to his face made it clear that he wasn't pleased with what he'd rolled. The Elvraeth chains that Rsiran detected were wrapped around his neck, hidden by the heavy cloak that he wore.

Rsiran pushed his way through the crowd, making his way to Firell. As he approached, Firell glanced up, his eyes going wide for a moment before he nodded to the man across from him. The man stood and faced Rsiran. His hand lunged toward him, catching him off guard.

Rsiran grabbed it and twisted the man's arm behind him, forcing him into a vulnerable position that Haern had shown him. "That's how you'll greet me, Firell?" he asked.

The man banged a hand on the table, his head craned around trying to see Firell, but Firell only watched Rsiran. "Why did you come here?" he asked.

"Not for you, if that's what you're afraid of." He nodded to the man. "If I let him go, will he leave me alone, or do I have to put a knife into him?"

Firell watched Rsiran for another moment. "There was a time when I'd have thought that an idle threat from you."

"Try me," Rsiran said.

"I did. I think you've answered that quite clearly. Let him go. Jonas will leave us alone."

Jonas nodded, and Rsiran released his arm. He backed away from Rsiran carefully, and Rsiran took his place but repositioned himself against the side wall, giving him a chance to watch Firell and not worry about someone approaching him from behind.

"Why did you come here if not for me, Rsiran?"

"Venass."

"Don't you think that's a dangerous game to chase Venass? They're known to be deadly, especially their assassins."

"Haern was one of their assassins. I think I understand them better than you."

A woman at a nearby table jostled forward, glancing briefly at Rsiran before making her way out of the tavern, weaving heavily from too much ale.

"Ah, well as a man who has lived his entire life within Elaeavn, I think that you don't *quite* understand Venass nearly as well as some of us who have faced them outside the protection of the city."

Rsiran scooped the dice off the table. "Protection? There wasn't much protection when Venass attacked the city."

Firell leaned toward him. "Venass attacked? You're sure it was Venass?"

"I'm sure, why?"

Firell glanced at Rsiran's roll. A pair of ones. Watcher's eyes. "Only that Venass would not act openly. That's not there method. They prefer the shadows and hiding."

Rsiran glanced around the tavern, noting how Firell sat obscured in the shadows here. "Sort of like you, then?"

Firell shrugged. "I'm a smuggler, Rsiran. What else would you expect from me? You wouldn't expect me to operate openly now, would you?"

He sighed. "You were supposed to be a friend."

"You know why I did what I did."

"I know. How is Lena?"

Firell shot Rsiran a heated look. "Careful mentioning names around here. They can be dangerous if overheard by the wrong person."

"Fine. But how is she?"

"She's… well. She's with family. Safe for now."

Rsiran nodded. "I'm glad to hear that. Truly."

Firell watched him and snorted. "You actually are. After everything that happened, you aren't angry?"

"I'm angry enough, but I understand what you did, and why you did it."

Firell took the dice and shook them, dropping them on the table without taking his eyes off Rsiran. "You haven't said why you're here, Rsiran."

"I have. I'm trying to find a way to stop Venass."

Firell chuckled. "Many have tried to stop them over the years, but there is no stopping, especially when they send their assassins after you. Why do you even care? If they're after the Elvraeth, what does it matter to you?"

Firell had been gone from the city for too long for Rsiran to feel comfortable sharing with him what he knew of the crystals, but there was something that Firell could know about, and that wouldn't matter if he knew.

"My grandfather leads them. I learned of him when they attacked the city. And they still hold my father. I would like to get him back."

Firell whistled softly. "That… that is unexpected. Thought you didn't care anything about your family."

"They hurt me," he admitted, "but that doesn't make them any less family, does it? I've got to do what I can to find why they've taken my father, and I'm going to be the one to stop my grandfather, family ties notwithstanding."

Firell picked up the dice without ever looking to see what he'd rolled. Rsiran realized that the mug of ale next to him remained untouched. "These are dangerous times, Rsiran. You'll need to be careful. Not sure that you can keep safe with what's coming."

"I'm not the same person that you knew, Firell."

"I see that. That boy wouldn't have nearly torn Jonas's arm off. You got stronger."

"That's not all I got."

Firell tipped his head as he considered Rsiran. "No? What else you got?"

"It doesn't matter."

Firell leaned forward. "I think if you're facing Venass, then it matters very much. Something like that will get you killed, and I know that you got someone you care about back in Elaeavn. Unless she's here with you." He glanced around the tavern. "I hope you weren't stupid enough to bring her with you here. This isn't really a place for a nice girl like Jessa."

"She's not here."

"You came alone? That's almost as bad."

"Do you think I'm in danger by coming alone?" Rsiran asked.

Firell shrugged. "No more than me." He leaned back against the wall and shook the dice in his hand. Rsiran waited for him to drop them onto the table, but he didn't.

"Do you know what happened with Josun?" he asked.

Firell paused. A troubled look passed across his face, lingering fleetingly before disappearing. "I haven't seen him since he released Lena."

"That wasn't the question."

"That's all the answer that you're going to get."

"You know something about him. I need to know or I'll—"

"Or you'll what?" He flicked a knife from his pocket and set it on the table, point aimed at Rsiran. A steel blade, and well made. "You'll attack me? I don't threaten so easily these days, Rsiran."

He grunted. "I didn't think you threatened so easily before. And that's not what I was trying to do. I only wanted to tell you that I need to know what happened to him. I know that he lives."

"Of course you do. That was the price to release my daughter."

Rsiran had an awareness of the chains around Firell's neck. It would be an easy thing to constrict them, and force Firell from the tavern, but that wasn't why he'd come here. Firell wasn't his enemy, regardless of what he'd done to him… or what he had failed to do for them. He had betrayed them, and wasn't any sort of friend that he had claimed to be, but Rsiran couldn't blame him for what he had done.

"I know that he was in Thyr. I came across a knife of mine there."

Firell smiled and laughed softly. "A knife? That's how you know that he was there? Damn, Rsiran, there are plenty of your knives scattered around. What do you think Brusus was doing with them when you were pumping them out?"

"Some were bribes. Others you shipped. I can tell you exactly how many are along the dock here if you would like."

His eyes widened slightly and he leaned in. His breath smelled slightly of ale, but not as strongly as Rsiran expected. "You can do that? You know how many there are?"

Rsiran shrugged. "I have a connection to the knives. To everything that I make these days. There are more than my knives here. Would you like me to *pull* them to you to demonstrate?" Rsiran leaned toward Firell. "Maybe you'd like me to *pull* on the chain you've got wrapped around your neck." He did, but only slightly. Firell pushed away. "I didn't come here to antagonize you. I thought that maybe you'd have a few answers, and I think you know more than you're letting on."

Firell grabbed at the collar of his cloak, trying to move the chain, but Rsiran held onto it, keeping it from moving. "Enough. You've made your point."

Rsiran eased his connection to the chain. "What do you know about Josun?"

Firell shook his head. "You do *not* want to go after him."

He didn't, not really, but then Firell didn't need to know that. "Try me."

"He was dangerous before, and that was when all he wanted was to join the Forgotten. Now… now he's something else. Worse."

"He's gone to Venass," Rsiran said.

Firell nodded. "From what I can tell. I don't follow him, mind you, and I swear I haven't seen him since he released Lena. But I keep my ears open for word on him. Better that way, with what he done to me. Last I heard, he had gone to the tower. Only one reason a man like him goes to the tower."

Rsiran sighed. The Hjan.

Hearing that Josun might have become one of the Hjan made it more real, for some reason. Finding the knife in Thyr had worried him, as did what the knife had shared with him.

But was Josun any worse than Danis?

In some ways, he was. Josun hated Rsiran, and for good reason. Without Rsiran, he would have reached what he wanted. He would have managed to reach the Forgotten, but Rsiran had stopped him, and exposed him. And then he had trapped him, leaving him stranded in Ilphaesn until Firell had rescued him and exchanged him for the safe return of his daughter.

Danis might be powerful, but he acted out of a desire for power. Josun… he would work out of a desire to hurt Rsiran.

That would be dangerous, not only to him, but to those he cared about.

"I see that you already knew that," Firell said.

"I suspected."

"How did you survive an attack on Elaeavn?"

"Because I'm not the same person you knew. They tried to kill me, but they failed. They tried again, and they failed again. Now… now it's my turn. I will make sure that Venass doesn't continue to hurt people. That's my purpose."

Firell started to smile, but it faded. "Damn," he whispered. "I'd say be careful, but don't think that matters."

"Can you do something for me?" Rsiran asked.

Firell frowned. "What do you want?"

"If you hear of Josun, or of a man named Danis, send word to me."

"And how am I supposed to do that?"

"I don't know. You're the smuggler aren't you?"

CHAPTER 8

Rsiran Slid from the tavern without standing from the table, leaving Firell and emerging outside where the sounds from the taverns drifted out into the street, creating a festival-type atmosphere, one of almost celebration. Gulls cawed overhead, and the sounds of the waves crashing against the shore gave him a reassuring sense, one that was more soothing than it should be.

He moved to the shadows and waited. Firell had seemed to know something, and more than he had let on. Rsiran waited outside the tavern, wondering if he could follow Firell and discover anything. But Firell would see him here, so he Slid to the top of one of the buildings where it would be less likely for Firell to look up and see him.

He didn't need to wait long. Jonas came out first, glancing along the street, and then Firell followed, his eyes narrowed as he searched the shadows. Neither man had bothered looking up.

Rsiran Slid after them, moving from building to building. Firell paused often, glancing around, almost as if he feared that he might be followed. He still didn't look up, or seem to notice that Rsiran followed him from above. He thought it strange that Firell would move away from the shore where he would have his ship, but this way was easier for Rsiran to follow. When the street darkened to the point where he couldn't see anything, he *pushed* a knife ahead of him to light the way. Firell might see the knife—that was a risk he would have to take—but he wouldn't see the light off the blade.

The men moved deeper into the city. The buildings were spaced farther apart here, and he was afraid that he might lose him because he had to wait between Slides. But they continued to walk along the darkened streets, Jonas appearing to lead them, rather than Firell.

The men stopped outside a long, low row of buildings. Rsiran Slid to the rooftop and emerged as they entered. He paused, detecting the chain Firell wore, and realized that he wouldn't have lost him as he tracked him through the city, not now that he knew what to listen for. Firell was inside, and had stopped moving.

He wanted to hear them. Were he a Listener, he wouldn't have any difficulty. Not for the first time, he wished he had some of the skills of the Great Watcher, abilities like the Elvraeth, but then, he wouldn't trade what he could do for any of them. Traveling risked weakening him, and he didn't have anyone able to watch him, so he would have to determine what happened inside some other way.

Sliding to the ground outside, he searched through windows until he found a room where Firell and Jonas were. A dim lamp glowed inside and he could just make out the door to a darkened room on the other side. Rsiran debated whether he should return to Elaeavn or see what else Firell might be up to. Curiosity won out.

He Slid into the room, readying his knives in case one of the men noticed him. He would not be caught unaware by Firell again. The last time, the Forgotten had used slithca on him, and he was not willing to repeat that.

Voices drifted to him through an open doorway. Rsiran Slid, emerging near the door. The light of his knives allowed him to see that he was in an older home. Shelves lined the wall where he stood. A table and chairs were in the middle of the room. Opposite where he'd entered, a cold hearth occupied most of the wall. Dust filled his nostrils.

"Dangerous for us to stay here now," Firell was saying.

"You know the assignment."

"I know it. That doesn't change the fact that I see how dangerous it is. After Lareth came…"

"That was always a risk."

Was it Jonas talking to Firell or someone else? It seemed the other person seemed superior to Firell, rather than the other way around.

"You saw how easily he handled you."

Jonas then.

"I allowed him to handle me. We can watch him now."

What did that mean?

"Do you really think it so easy?"

"Not easy. Fortuitous. Had he not come to you, we would have spent countless hours searching for him. Now we don't have the need."

"I think you misjudge his ability," Firell said. "From what I have heard—"

"Heard. Not seen. There is nothing you need to fear, unless you don't want to see her again."

"Enough."

Rsiran cocked his head as he listened. Had something happened to Firell's daughter again? Once, he could understand, but a second time… Either Firell wasn't able to protect her, or there was something more at play than Rsiran understood.

"Now we wait," Jonas was saying. "It should not be long."

What did Jonas expect to happen? Was someone coming to the house?

Was it Josun?

The idea terrified him—and excited him.

He counted the knives he carried. He might not fully know how to counter shadowsteel yet, but he would find some way to do so. Venass wasn't the only one with the ability to learn. Rsiran *could* learn; facing Venass, he would have to.

A door opened and heavy feet thudded in, leaving the ground practically shaking. Not Josun. He would have Slid into the room, having no need to walk.

"What be the problem? You do be sendin' word about somethin'."

Rsiran almost let out a soft gasp. The voice… it could be none other than Shael. The last time he'd seen the man, he'd been dying, the broken end of a blade crushing into his skull. How could he be here? And why would Firell still be working with him?

"Had a visitor tonight," Firell said.

"That be why you stayin' down by the docks. We need you to be havin' a visitor."

"Not who you thought. This was unexpected."

"There be many unexpected visitors in Asador. You need to be more specific. Damn, but you shouldna sent for me unless there was something I needed. Can' have it be known we working together again."

"Lareth."

Feet thudded across the floorboards. "What do you be sayin'?"

Firell sniffed. "That was my visitor. Lareth. Came to the tavern tonight. I think it was these," he said, and rattled the metal chains around his neck. "I think he controls it now."

"He done be controlling it the las' time we saw him."

"He's changed, Shael. We'll need to be careful around him."

"Changed? Lareth be nothin' but a boy protected by your city."

"That *boy* managed to twist Jonas around before he could even move. That *boy* claims he's faced Venass and lived."

Shael laughed. The sound was rich and easy, and there was a time when it had been a welcoming sound. Rsiran resisted the urge to Slide to the other side of the wall and attack. After what Shael had done, and the way he'd used him, Rsiran wasn't sure that he *could* leave Shael alive.

"Facing Venass don' mean the same as facing the Hjan."

"He knows Josun Elvraeth lives. Claims he saw him in Thyr."

"Thyr? Well, damn. Guess we better be pullin' up anchor and gettin' out of port, then. Oh… tha's right. Josun Elvraeth do be havin' the same ability to jump from place to place as Lareth. When we fin' that bastard…"

Had Rsiran read this wrong? They were *after* Josun?

But why? What reason would be convincing enough for Firell to risk his daughter? And why work with Shael after what he'd done to him? Shael had proven that he wasn't anyone's friend. He was more concerned about the coin he could earn than in maintaining friendships.

And then there was the ability Shael possessed, that strange ability that resisted Sliding. The second time, he thought he caught him off guard. If there was something about what Shael could do, Rsiran needed to understand it.

"Lareth could help," Firell said softly.

"You do be thinkin' that he come help you after what was done to him? Thought you said he be changed?"

"He was changed, but we could ask. After what we've been through, it can't hurt to have help."

"Help don' be comin' from Elaeavn, and certainly not from a man we done attacked. If it were me, I think I be guttin' the men responsible jus' fer what they did. You be lucky, Firell. If he changed as much as you claim, he could have jus' done the same to you." Shael laughed again. "Thinkin' 'bout Lareth like that… that do be funny."

"He escaped you."

"He escaped me once. Won't happen again."

"You intend to try to capture him?"

"Not capture, but think of what we could trade him for. Chip like that would be valuable, regardless of what he done."

Jonas laughed, a nervous sound. "You told me the chains didn't hold him."

"I do be sayin' that. Not sure that changed."

Rsiran had enough of them talking about him. He didn't fear capture from them, and now that he knew that they weren't working *with* Josun, he didn't have any reason to remain hidden.

He *pulled* himself in a Slide.

When he emerged, he *pushed* a dozen knives away from him, ringing Shael, Firell, and Jonas. He readied to Slide again, but there wasn't anyone else there.

"You be leadin' him here?" Shael snapped at Firell.

"I followed him," Rsiran said. "And now that I know the way the chains sound, I can find you wherever they are, so don't think that it would challenge me to reach them." He nodded to Shael. "You think you can use me? Who are you working for this time? It didn't sound like Venass, but then, the last time I saw you, I thought you were dead. You look pretty good for a man whose skull should have been caved in."

Shael raised his hand to his forehead, touching a deep indentation. Rsiran felt no remorse for the injury that should have killed him. In his mind, he'd already mourned what he'd done to Shael. The man *should* be dead. After betraying them twice, Rsiran expected nothing different now.

"I be harder to kill than I look."

"I see that."

"What you be doin' here, Rsiran? Where that girl of yours? You know I always liked her."

Jonas had started to move. Not just move, but colors started to swirl around him.

Sliding.

Rsiran *pushed* on the knives nearest Jonas. Two of them pierced his skin, drawing a small line of blood. "Don't think you can be Sliding away just yet. Trust that I'll know if you try again."

Jonas stared at him. "You shouldn't be able to see that."

"There are a lot of things I shouldn't be able to do," Rsiran said.

"Like those knives," Shael said. "That be smith blood, isn't it? But you do be a traveler, too."

Rsiran didn't think that Shael meant it in the same way that he knew about Traveling. "I can Slide."

Shael grunted.

"Why are you in Asador?" he asked Shael.

"Smugglers, Rsiran. Don' you know that we do be businessmen?"

"I seem to recall the last time Firell did business with you, he lost his daughter." He glanced at Firell. "I assume this time, you don't think anything will happen to her?"

"There are protections in place."

"And you have some way to prevent Shael from betraying you like he did the last time?"

"This do be nothin' like the last time," Shael said.

"No. Now the Forgotten are mostly destroyed."

"You thinkin' so?"

Rsiran shrugged. "Their palace is empty. Their leader dead. Most of the others within their chain of command are dead. I think that's pretty well destroyed."

Shael and Firell glanced at each other. Jonas tried to Slide again—a faint trail of color that disappeared as soon as Rsiran *pushed* on his knives.

And Rsiran began to understand Jonas. There was a reason that he tried to Slide away from Rsiran, and why Firell seemed so inclined to fear him, letting the other man lead when they left the tavern.

"You're one of the Forgotten, aren't you? I thought you might be Venass, but I don't detect any lorcith or heartstone on you. And for you to Slide so openly… I've only seen that with the Forgotten." It was different in Elaeavn now, but none of these men knew that.

"They be done?" Shael asked Rsiran.

"Evaelyn is dead. Inna gone. A few others. I didn't bother getting their names."

Shael actually laughed again, ignoring the knives hovering in front of him. "You be really believing that you stopped the Forgotten?"

Rsiran watched Shael. The large man had a strange tension to him, one that he couldn't put a finger on. He feared the Forgotten, and he clearly feared what they might do to him if he didn't do what they asked. Shael was a strong and powerful man. What could the Forgotten possibly have over him that terrified him so?

"As I said, I've been to the Forgotten Palace. I was there when Evaelyn died. I was there when Inna died. There were others—many others—who died that day."

"You be sure of this?"

Rsiran nodded. "As sure as I can be. I was the one who killed them."

Jonas watched Rsiran with a different light in his eyes. Even Shael and Firell watched him differently.

"Evaelyn be gone?" Shael asked.

Rsiran nodded. "Her brother isn't. That's who I chase now."

"Who be her brother?" he asked.

"Her brother is a man named Danis. He rules Venass, though I don't know how long he has ruled there. Venass and the Forgotten eventually worked together."

"They intended to reach you," Firell said.

Rsiran nodded. After his time in the Forgotten Palace, there was no question that they had been after him, including having gone as far as designing a special prison cell, seemingly to contain him. With the Forgotten now destroyed, he didn't have nearly as much to fear—only Venass now, though they were worse—but he still wondered what they might have intended for him. And now that he had Jonas here, he wondered he might be able to supply some answers.

"Why do they want me?" he asked of Jonas.

"They don't want you," Jonas said.

Rsiran grunted. "I've been back to the Forgotten Palace. The place is empty now. And I've stood within Evaelyn's room—the one lined with heartstone, thinking that she could use the power of that metal in some way to prevent Venass from reaching her." Rsiran hadn't known why she had enveloped herself in heartstone before, but that answer made as much sense as any. She knew what her brother was capable of doing, and she knew that he would be dangerous. She had opposed him for as long as she could, trying to keep the Forgotten and Venass separate, but after a while, it became clear that they wouldn't succeed. Venass had the knowledge that the Forgotten lacked, and that had been the reason Evaelyn had gone to them. But Venass had used them. The same way they have and would continue to use others who might be coerced by what Venass told them.

"So, you actually did it?" Jonas asked. "Evaelyn... She is gone?"

"She's gone. She tried to side with Venass. I couldn't let her do that."

Shael and Firell watched Jonas, as if trying to decide what to do with him. Rsiran had the sense that they had allowed him to lead because of the threat of the Forgotten. With that threat gone, what leverage did Jonas really have over them? He was only a man with the ability to Slide.

"What of the others?" Jonas asked. He didn't try to fight against the knives that floated around him. He didn't even try to move anywhere, maybe having given up on trying to get away.

"As I've said, the others are gone. The guild has helped those they have been able to find as much as they can, but there are those outside the guild, those who had no interest in aligning with the guild…"

Jonas stared at the knives floating in front of him. "If they are gone, then there is no choice but to side with Venass." He glanced at Shael who only frowned.

"Venass will do nothing but try to destroy you and those you care about."

"The Elvraeth have seen to it that we have no other options."

"You can return to Elaeavn."

Jonas shook his head. "Return to what? The penalty for returning is clear. If they discover that we've returned—"

"You can Slide. You've never attempted to return?"

He shook his head. "Sliding is dangerous. Venass can pull us out of our Slides, and there are different concerns when it comes to the Elvraeth, but no less worrisome. At least with Venass, we have the chance to live."

"I've seen the chance that Venass offers. That's no sort of life."

"Life?" Shael asked. "What kind of life do he be havin' the way it is? Venass might no' be any better than the others, but they don' have a plan to kill them for existing."

Rsiran felt troubled. The Forgotten had been his enemy, but then, had it been all of the Forgotten or only those who had sided with

Venass? Was there any way that he could work with the scattered Forgotten?

He *pulled* the knives back to him and stuffed them into his pocket. "Don't come after me," he said, "and stay away from Venass. If I find you working with them, I won't have any mercy."

"You leavin' us be, after all that we done?"

"Venass is my enemy. Don't join them." With that, he Slid back to Elaeavn.

CHAPTER 9

The inside of the Barth carried less of the vibrant and lively air that he'd found in the tavern where he'd discovered Firell. A lutist played near the hearth, the mournful sound a slow and quiet layer atop the soft murmuring of voices within the tavern. Nothing like he'd found in Asador. There, all the voices seemed to jumble over each other, piling on until he could hear nothing but noise. There was a certain protection to it, in the anonymity and the fact that they couldn't be easily overheard. Not in the Wretched Barth. The tavern might be busier than it had been when Lianna ran it, but it still wasn't like what he'd found in Asador.

Brusus made his way through the tavern, stopping and speaking to people at each table, smiling and laughing with them, so much more at peace than he had been before he took it over. Alyse popped out of the kitchen briefly, only to rush back in for another order. Savory smells drifted out through the kitchen door and then faded.

Haern sat with Jessa at their usual table. This late in the night, it wasn't hard for them to claim it. But with the increased business, it had become more difficult to keep others from getting to it first. Brusus usually managed to keep those poachers away with a steely glare.

"You've been gone a while," Haern noted.

He told them of visiting Asador, and of finding Firell, carefully wording the news about having come across Shael so that it wouldn't anger Jessa. She watched him, an unreadable expression on her face. He hadn't been in any real danger with Shael—not this time.

"I think we could use them to help us with Venass," Rsiran said.

"Do you think that Shael and Firell will suddenly see the light and offer to help?" Jessa said. "Think about what they were willing to do the last time. They sacrificed our friendship, and for what? How much was it worth to them?"

"Firell had other reasons than wanting to hurt us. You know that his daughter—"

"His daughter then, but why now? What would keep him working with Shael if he had already been hurt by him?" Jessa leaned forward and rapped her hand on the table. "I don't think they're the right help. Not for what you need to do."

"What needs to be done?" Brusus asked, stopping at their table and lowering his voice. "Hopefully not anything that puts you back in Thyr. I heard about what you did there."

"I didn't do anything in Thyr."

"No? The way I hear it, you could have gotten yourself killed. Some new weapon that Venass has taken to using. He tell you about this?" Brusus asked Jessa.

"He told me."

"At least you're not hiding it from her. That's good." Brusus pulled a stool over and sat as Rsiran repeated to him who he had discovered in Asador. At the mention of Shael, his eyes became drawn. With mention of Firell, and the fact that they were working together again, Brusus became visibly agitated. "You can't think to use them, Rsiran. I know that you want help facing Venass."

"I think we need help."

"I don't deny that, but after what Shael and Firell did… and using them… that's a dangerous thing, man. Especially with that grandfather of yours so close to the city."

Jessa looked over at Brusus, shooting him a glare that could burn through steel.

"Where is my grandfather?" Rsiran asked.

Brusus raised his hands and stood, taking a step away from the table. "Ah, maybe that was a mistake to say anything."

"No. Where is he? What have you heard?"

"Only that he's been seen in Eban. And Cort before that."

Rsiran frowned. Both were cities he'd been to, but had found no other evidence of Venass. They came across a few of them, but never in enough numbers to create problems. That had made it relatively easy for him to go with Valn and with Sarah as they tried to clear out the others of Venass.

Or had they?

He glanced at Jessa. She had been awfully willing to allow him to go with Valn and Sarah, more so than he would have expected from her. Did she know that he wouldn't find anything?

She met his gaze unflinching. "Did you know this?" he asked.

"You've been running around the countryside with Valn and Sarah. I think it's clear what you intend."

"I need to stop Venass," he said.

"You? Only you?"

Rsiran shook his head. "You know what I mean. We're trying to do something more. That means that we have to find what Venass might be intending, and we have to go after them wherever they might be hiding."

"You're after Danis because of what he did to your family," Jessa said.

"Yes."

She stared at him but didn't say anything more.

Rsiran turned to Brusus. "Where is he?"

"Rsiran—"

"Don't. Where is my grandfather? I find him, and we can end this."

"Can you?" Jessa asked softly. "If you find him, are you sure you can truly end all of this? You're the one who told me about Josun, and the fact that he's after you again. Now you find Shael and Firell and… and it's like we're back where we started."

"We're nowhere close to where we started. This time, we know their plan. We're in a position of strength."

"Strength? How do you suppose?" Jessa asked.

"Because we don't have to hide. I'm the guildlord now—"

"You haven't been with the guild long enough to have that title mean anything," Jessa said.

"I may not, but I work with the guilds. And I'm going to keep working with them."

"And then what?" Brusus asked. "What do you intend to do next? Now that you're legitimate, you don't have to hide. You're the guildlord, and we know that means you rule over the Smith Guild, but that don't mean you control all the guilds. Damn, Rsiran, you still haven't even met with the council. What happens when you do?"

"You know about that?" he asked Brusus.

"I heard Ephram talking to Della one night. He thought he was being secretive about it, but it's clear they want you to meet with them. I get the sense that it's important that you do. Do they make the final decision about whether you remain guildlord?"

Rsiran didn't think so. The meeting was more a formality than anything else, but it made him nervous. He'd spent months trying to hide his presence from the guilds and from the Elvraeth, and now he was expected to go to them, and show them who he was and maybe even what he could do.

"They're not going to care for you," Haern said softly.

Rsiran shrugged. "Does it matter? I don't care for them, either. Think of what they did to Brusus. Were it not for the Elvraeth council, he would have been able to grow up in the palace, and wouldn't have to hide himself from anyone, wouldn't have to fear that they would learn about what he could do."

"I've come to terms with it," Brusus said. "You should, too."

"Then there's how little they did when the city was under attack. They couldn't even be bothered to come out of the palace when Venass was in the city, actively destroying buildings and trying to take down the guilds. It's almost like they don't care about what happens outside of the palace."

"They don't," Brusus said. "They never did, but that doesn't matter, either. It can't matter."

"So you think I should just meet with the council and pretend that nothing has happened? That I should let them move on as though there was never an attack on the city?"

"You're the guildlord, you have to decide what you do with the council," Brusus said. "I think you have to be careful about how you do it. There are ways that you can approach them that are safer than others."

Rsiran couldn't believe what Brusus was doing and telling him. It seemed like he was trying to get him to fear the Elvraeth. After everything they had all been through, Brusus should be the one who wanted to see that the Elvraeth understood exactly what they had to do, and what still needed done. Brusus should be the one who wanted to get revenge for what he had been put through. Had he changed so much?

"I think we should talk about something else," Rsiran said. "Like where you heard I could find my grandfather."

Brusus looked over at Jessa and then Haern. "There's nothing that you can do to find him, Rsiran."

"I have to find them. Venass is hunting me, Brusus. They aren't going to stop, not until one of us is done."

"But there are too many of them."

"I'll do what I have to do," Rsiran said. He stood, frustration forcing him to his feet. "And that means finding my grandfather and Josun so that I can keep us—all of us—safe."

Jessa reached for him as he stood, trying to latch onto his arm before he Slid, but he disappeared before she could.

CHAPTER 10

Rsiran *pushed* two knives away from him in his smithy, leaving them hovering in the air. He held them like that for a moment, and then spun them in place, tipping one end around as he practiced control. With lorcith, such control would be easy, but these were heartstone knives.

Bluish light glowed from the metal, bright even in the daylight—the metal's potential. At least, that was what the alchemists believed. He wasn't sure he agreed. It wasn't potential so much as it was something about the metal itself.

It was bad enough that Ephram and the guilds still treated the Elvraeth like something to fear, but now with his friends doing it as well? He needed to get away, to have a chance to clear his mind. That was why he'd come to his smithy.

A scuffling of steps behind him, and he spun, *pulling* the knives back to him and slipping them into his pocket. Luca stood watching, his eyes wide with an interested hunger, lingering on the pocket where

Rsiran had put them away. The boy hadn't gained much weight in the time he'd spent with Rsiran, but he had managed to lose most of the wild-eyed insanity in his eyes. There were times when it returned, when it seemed that in spite of everything Luca had gained, he still hadn't managed to forget, or even distance his mind from what had happened to him in Ilphaesn.

"Will I be able to learn that?" he asked.

Rsiran patted the knives in his pocket. "I don't know. There haven't been smiths willing to listen to lorcith in generations. So only the Great Watcher knows what will happen."

"And the Seers."

Rsiran nodded carefully. "And the Seers." There had been a time when he'd thought that the only Seers he would encounter would be the Elvraeth, and in Elaeavn. Learning how Venass used the metal to augment the ability of their Seers, making them more capable than any found within Elaeavn, reminded him how little he really knew.

"Have you finished what I asked of you?" It was something he'd asked of him days before that gave Luca a chance to work unimpeded.

Luca turned to the forge, where the coals glowed brightly, the pleasant heat raising a healthy sweat along their skin. "I did what you asked, but I'm not sure that it turned out like it should."

"Show me."

Luca lifted a piece of metal off the anvil that Rsiran hadn't seen when he returned. Immediately, Rsiran could feel what he'd been trying to create with it, recognizing the way the metal must have called to him. It formed a bowl, the lorcith layered in a way that left it with a pattern to the metal. Rudimentary, but an important stage in learning how to become a smith.

"That's really good," Rsiran told him. He took the bowl and ran his fingers along the edge, *pushing* the still-soft metal as he did. It smoothed some of the harder lines and gave the bowl more of the shape it wanted.

"It's nothing like what you make." He motioned toward the bench where Rsiran's latest forgings rested. There were dozens, each forged with a combination of his hammer and his ability to *push* on the metal. In that, he had become something other than a traditional blacksmith. Now, his creations were found throughout the city, and often displayed openly. That was something he would never have thought possible, but then, he would never have thought it possible that he'd be welcomed to the Smith Guild, either.

"I've held a hammer for much longer than you. You've been at this for all of a few months. I think what you've accomplished is impressive." He handed the bowl back. "Besides, when I learned, I wasn't allowed to use lorcith."

Luca's eyes widened. "How did you manage to learn if you weren't allowed to listen to the song?"

He smiled. "You learn the basics. How to heat the metal. Where to use the hammer. When to return it to heat and when to quench it. There are smiths who never learn to listen to the song who can make amazing forgings."

"I don't know that I would want to learn without listening to it. The song… It changes as I hammer. There's something so… so *right* about it."

"It changes because you're working with it. Much like there were smiths who worked without hearing the song, think of those who can hear the song, but choose to ignore it. They waste entire lives missing a part of themselves."

"Even they can eventually learn."

Rsiran had heard Seval enter, but more than that, he'd detected the combination of knives and the bracelet that he wore. He couldn't *push* on metal the same way that Rsiran could, but he'd been a master smith for so many years that it didn't matter. He could almost do more with lorcith than Rsiran, and he could definitely do more with the other metals than Rsiran.

Seval took the bowl from Luca. "Interesting work," he commented. "I see how the patterns here merge. And the metal… the way that it's layered…" He looked up and met Luca's eyes. "Are you sure that you've only been at this for a few months?"

Luca grinned. The compliment from Seval seemed to matter more than any compliment from Rsiran. "I'm sure."

"You've got a great instructor. Make sure you listen to him when he teaches. I know that I do."

Luca looked from Seval to Rsiran and nodded vigorously. "I will."

Seval clapped Rsiran on the shoulder and steered him away from the forge. "You didn't come to inspect my apprentice's work," Rsiran said.

"No, but I probably should have. He's already at the level of someone with a year behind him. I think you're going to prove the guild's faith in you even more than I could have hoped. You were the right choice for guildlord."

Rsiran hadn't known how far along Luca had come. He had no experience with other apprentices, and he'd had the advantage of having grown up with it, sitting by his father from his earliest days. Some apprentices didn't pursue the career of a smith until they were much older, often in their early teens. Luca couldn't be much older than that—and possibly younger—but he'd been troubled when Rsiran first started working with him. Years of living alone in the mines would do that. Pulling Luca from the mines had been the kindest thing he could have done, but it had been hard on the boy. The way he looked around, or held his head down when no one watched, told Rsiran that more than anything.

"If not to check on him, then why the visit?" Rsiran asked.

"Thought I might show you something. It's about time, I think." When Rsiran frowned, Seval only grinned wider at him. "You'll want to see this, Rsiran."

Rsiran glanced over at Luca. He had already chosen another lump of lorcith and held it out from him, tipping his head to the side as he studied it. Rsiran knew that he'd be listening to the metal, focusing on the song, and trying to determine what the metal was willing to become for him. He still marveled at how they were able to use lorcith so openly now, and that the supply of it was no longer constrained as it had been. There had been a time when even a small amount of lorcith was considered precious. Now it was valuable, but more for what it could be, and the way that he might sculpt it, than for its scarcity.

Seval led him outside where they stood in the narrow street leading to the smithy Rsiran had renovated, with the help of his friends—and Shael. Back then, he'd had to hide the presence of his illegal forge from the rest of the guild. But no more. Rsiran wondered how long ago the smithy—and its owner—had been a part of the guild. For a brief moment, he though about where that smith may have gone. Why he left. But he quickly turned his attention back to Seval.

"I could Slide us wherever you want," Rsiran suggested.

Seval's eyes widened briefly, a sign of his persistent discomfort with Sliding. Though Rsiran now knew that the guilds had never truly abandoned Sliding, there were many who were uncomfortable with it. He hadn't realized Seval felt that way when they first met, and when Rsiran had Slid him to Ilphaesn.

"We can walk," he said.

Seval guided them through the streets, quickly reaching Trembel Street, a wide pathway that ran from Upper Town to Lower Town. It was late in the day, and though sun shone overhead, a chill remained in the air. As they stepped away from the protection of the stout buildings hugging the sides of the city, wind gusted, carrying with it the stench of the shore. Rsiran had grown accustomed to the odors during the time that he'd now lived in Lower Town, but wasn't sure that he would ever really be used to them.

"Where are we going?" he asked Seval.

The larger man only glanced back, an amused smile on his face as they turned up the street, heading toward Upper Town. "You're of the guild now."

Rsiran touched his finger to the mark he wore around his neck. Not just of the guild, but the guildlord. There were still times when he couldn't believe it possible that he'd not only been restored to the guild, but risen to its head.

"And I appreciate that you have given me such responsibility. I will continue to do what is needed to prove myself."

Seval paused and gave him a funny look. "Prove yourself? You've done nothing but prove yourself from the moment we finally convinced you to come back to the guild." That wasn't *quite* how Rsiran remembered it, but he wouldn't argue about those details. "It's about time the Smith Guild had a louder voice in the Hall of Guilds. I think even Ephram listens when you speak." Seval smiled and patted Rsiran on the shoulder. "Your student improves at such a pace. I think you've shown yourself to be the right man for what we need, Rsiran."

They turned onto another street, one exceedingly familiar to him. This was the street he'd grown up on, where his father's smithy had been, and the place from which he'd been exiled and sent to the mines. Not forgotten, at least not in the same way as some, but sending him to the Ilphaesn mines had been exile enough, especially considering the fact that his father had apparently not intended for him to return.

"What is this, Seval?" Rsiran asked.

Seval stood in the middle of the street, his hands clutched over the belly that hid what had once been a muscular frame. He pointed down the street. "You see that shop?" he asked. When Rsiran nodded, he went on, "That is Boldan's shop. And there," he said, pointing to another smithy down the street, "is Kevan's shop."

"I know all of this, Seval. You seem to forget the fact that I grew up here."

"Forget? How could I? You're a Lareth, and *that* is the Lareth smithy." He motioned to his father's smithy, the paint on the sign faded, and the window dirtier than it should be. The smithy had been closed for months, reclaimed by the guild and left empty. "The rest of the guild would like you to return to your family smithy."

It took Rsiran a moment to register what he was saying. There had been a time when he'd wanted nothing more than to take over his father's shop. Even after he'd been banished to Ilphaesn, there had been a part of him that had thought he might be able to return, that he might one day be allowed to inherit his family's smithy. But time had given him a different perspective, and he had made his own way. Now… now there was something *right* about the fact that he had his own shop, and that it was not near the fringe of Upper Town, but closer to Lower Town, the place he considered home.

"I have my smithy," he told Seval.

"You have *a* smith, but that is the Lareth smithy." Seval stopped in front of the faded sign, with Rsiran's surname written in a flowing script. "Since Neran disappeared, the guild has held his smithy, kept it closed, but safe. But now—"

"He'll return, Seval, and the smithy should still be his."

Seval smiled sadly. "After all this time, and all that you've done to search, you think that he'll still return? If Venass intended to release him, they would have done so by now. That they haven't…" He shook his head. "I'm sorry, Rsiran, but I think Neran is gone. Which means this smithy—your family's smithy—should pass to you." He clapped Rsiran on the arm and nodded at the dusty window. "At least consider it. For the guild. This way, you'd be connected to the guild as the guildlord should be."

"I can always Slide," he said.

"You can. But others cannot, and when they need to reach you…"

"That's the real issue, then," Rsiran said.

"There is an advantage to the tunnels, Rsiran. Now that we're all talking again, now that the guilds seem open to truly work together, something they only gave lip service to in the past, we need to keep the guildlords connected. That's how we will defend ourselves from the next attack."

Rsiran had sat in on one meeting of the guildlords since assuming the title, and that had been an awkward one. He was not like the other guildlords, men who had served their trade, working their way up to master in their guild before eventually getting voted into the position of guildlord. But the meeting he'd attended made it clear that there was ongoing concern about the safety of the guilds, and the safety of the city. That had been the role of the guilds he'd been most surprised by.

"I can see that you're not convinced," Seval said.

"It's not only that," he said. "The smithy—*my* smithy—is the first place that ever felt like home. If I return here, it won't be the same." How could he ever express to Seval discomfort he felt about his family's smithy? It might have been in his family, but there was no longer a desire on his part to reclaim it. Better that another ran the smithy than him.

"Just… just think on it. That's all I ask. All that any of the master smiths ask."

It seemed like such a simple request, and with everything they faced, one that seemed almost unnecessary. The threat of Venass remained, with their connection to shadowsteel, now more dangerous than before. Other Forgotten were scattered, some who might search for a return to power. Shael and Firell again plotting. And one of the Elder Trees was gone, an issue more pressing than the rest.

More than anything, all Rsiran wanted was a chance to understand the depths of the threat shadowsteel posed. After the last Venass attack, that was the answer he needed to understand the most urgently. But how could he if he was trying to appease the guild or the other guildlords or even the Elvraeth council?

"I will," Rsiran promised.

The smile on Seval's wide face made the deception harder.

CHAPTER 11

Rsiran stood alone in his smithy, the coal cooling and the line of newly forged heartstone and lorcith knives lying on his bench. Rsiran had used most of the lorcith that he'd collected when last in Ilphaesn to make the knives, almost as if the lorcith recognized that he was not yet done fighting.

Unlike when he normally worked the forge, his mind continued to race, filled with fears and worries. He had to know about Venass, and more about what they did with shadowsteel.

So far, he had failed to learn anything that would help him locate where they made it. What he'd discovered in the Forgotten Palace hadn't been enough to help him understand what Venass might plan with it, or even how they made it.

There was one place he thought he could go for answers, but until now, he had avoided it.

Rsiran sat on the pallet he and Jessa used as a bed, and crossed his legs. Did he dare risk Traveling to find out what Venass might be hiding? He didn't *think* they could trap him when Traveling, but what if they had discovered some way to do so?

He had to confirm they had some sort of shadowsteel forge and where it was, even if only to confront Ephram with the information so he would share more about it.

Rsiran glanced at the door. Though he often left it open these days, the locks were in place. Jessa would be able to sneak in—the locks on his smithy had never prevented her access—but no one else should be able to reach him.

He closed his eyes and focused on what he remembered of Venass.

Months had passed since he had been there, but that memory remained etched deep in his mind. He remembered the way the inside of the tower appeared, much as he remembered the way it smelled.

Taking a breath, he Traveled.

Rsiran stepped free of his body and appeared inside of Venass.

A slight pressure worked against him as he did, likely from whatever protections existed around the tower to prevent someone from Sliding into it. When he'd gone the first time, he had been *pulled* in a Slide. He liked to think that he was skilled enough now that they wouldn't be able to do the same to him, but he didn't really know, and wouldn't dare risk it. At least with Traveling, there was no real threat to his person.

He appeared inside the massive entry hall. Faint light came from everywhere, and it took a moment to realize that it was lorcith in the walls. He had detected it in massive amounts when he had been here before, and that lorcith had almost managed to prevent him from Sliding, but it was during that visit that he had discovered he could *pull* himself into a Slide.

Rsiran floated, moving from room to room on the main level. He saw no sign of any Venass. Before, he had thought them scholars.

Likely they *were* scholars of a sort, only what they studied was a way to wield power and destruction.

He drifted down and found the room where he'd managed to reach Jessa. The tile still seemed cold and lifeless, and the hearth looked as if it had never carried the warmth of a fire. Nothing about the room seemed as if it was lived in.

Moving on, Rsiran drifted. He came upon a row of massive doors of lorcith. On the other side of these doors were cells. This was where he'd been held. Traveling in this way, he went in and then back out of each cell, searching for his father or anyone else that Venass might hold, but found each of the rooms empty.

From there, he went back up, looking through the tower. Strange that he should find no one here, but equally strange that he found nothing that would help him understand what Venass might have been working on. When he had been here before, there had been evidence of the cylinders, as well as the scholars, but where had they gone?

The tower appeared empty.

He approached stairs that wound along the outer wall, leading to a landing. A hall opened up and he searched, finding no sign of anyone. Not his father or smiths who might be responsible for shadowsteel, not any of the Hjan, and no scholars. There was nothing here.

Where were they?

Unless… Could they present some sort of mirage to him? Did Venass plan for the possibility that he might Travel to the tower, and shield themselves from him?

They might shield the people, but could they shield the entire tower?

Doubtful.

Continuing upward, he found more rooms, all of them seemingly empty. He worked his way up and up, and there was nothing.

The farther he went, the less likely it seemed he would find anything, almost as if Venass had abandoned the tower.

Then he reached what had to be the top. He drifted through another door, and this time, he felt a strange sensation, something almost like a warmth washed over him. When Traveling, he shouldn't be aware of any physical sensations. That he could made him worry about what Venass might have for him here.

Atop the tower, he came across three slender black bars that seemed to pull on the light, bending it in strange ways. Rsiran moved toward them, but was careful not to touch them, not certain that he could, but also not wanting to risk it, especially if it was shadowsteel.

He hesitated, feeling the strange tingling warmth, and realized that there was something more that he'd missed. The shadowsteel started to move, spinning around him.

The movement answered the question of whether anyone remained in the tower.

Did Venass know he was here?

He didn't dare risk staying, but when he tried to return to his body, he was held in place.

Rsiran tried again, his heart racing, and still couldn't.

With the next try, he *pulled*, dragging himself back. He moved slowly, easing away, reminding him of when he had first Slid through heartstone.

Then he was back in his body.

He sat up, exhausted. And terrified.

Venass had a way of holding him when he Traveled, but somehow he had still managed to escape. Worse, he found no evidence of his father, and no sign of how they made shadowsteel. They made it seem like the tower was abandoned, but he didn't think it really was. Likely, if he attempted to return, they would find a way to trap him.

Doubting there was any shadowsteel forge in Venass, where would he search next? And how would he stop Venass if they continued to find new ways to attack? He needed help, and he didn't know where to go for it. Worse, Firell and Shael proved that the Forgotten hadn't completely disappeared as a threat. The guilds couldn't overcome the entirety of the Venass threat, but what more could he do? Each time they'd attacked, he had come away realizing there was even more he didn't understand.

Rsiran tried resting, but sleep didn't come easily for him that night.

CHAPTER 12

The inside of the Wretched Barth glowed brightly with lanterns and the fire in the hearth at the back. The lighting was much brighter than when Lianna had run the Barth, but Rsiran suspected much of that had to do with Brusus wanting to push away the memories of what had happened here. Men had died in the tavern, men that Rsiran and Haern had killed.

Brusus moved between tables, stopping long enough to speak to the patrons before moving on to the next table. He glanced up at the sound of the door opening and nodded briefly to Rsiran as he continued making his way through the tavern.

Jessa sat at their usual table, sending dice skittering across the surface before scooping them up and shaking them again. Haern sat next to her, two knives spinning in his hands, the scar along his face twitching as his gaze continued to survey the tavern. After everything, Haern wasn't able to relax. Neither was Rsiran, especially after the mistake he'd almost made. He still hadn't fully recovered, and tried to hide it as best he could.

He wasn't the only one bothered by something he didn't want to speak about. Haern still hadn't shared what had bothered him when they'd last sparred.

Rsiran dropped onto the stool and grabbed the dice from Jessa, shaking them before dropping them on the table. A pair of threes. Beggars. Fitting that he'd throw them.

Jessa leaned in and gave him a quick kiss before grabbing the dice. "Where have you been? Luca said you left with Seval."

"He took me to my father's smithy," Rsiran said. "Said the guild wants me to be closer to the other smiths." He didn't share that he had Traveled to Venass. That would only anger her. Now that he knew Venass could trap him—or likely would be able to soon—he didn't dare Travel, did he?

Another ability of his countered, most likely by the power of shadowsteel. Soon he would have no way to defeat them.

Haern nodded. "Makes sense. Keep you closer so they can keep an eye on you now that you're sanctioned."

"You're going to take Father's smithy?"

With his back to the kitchen, he hadn't noticed Alyse coming up behind him. She carried a tray laden with plates for them. A sheen of sweat covered her face, and she wore a finely woven dress today, one of much higher quality than she'd worn since moving to Lower Town. In some ways, Alyse always seemed to belong anywhere but in Lower Town.

"The guild wants me to take over the family smithy," Rsiran said.

Alyse set plates in front of each of them, followed by mugs of steaming ale. "You've been recognized and sanctioned. It's time you have a proper smithy."

"I have a proper smithy," Rsiran said.

Alyse's nose crinkled. "Brusus has told me all about your smithy, Rsiran," she said, her gaze drifting to where Brusus approached. The corners of her mouth pulled into a hint of a smile. "And the smithy should be yours. It's the Lareth smithy."

Rsiran forced a smile and nodded. His sister couldn't understand what he'd been through. She had been through her share of issues since leaving their childhood home when their father lost his business, but she still felt a sense of connection to what she'd lost. In that way, Rsiran had moved on more than his sister.

"It is," he agreed.

"So when will you be making the move?" Alyse asked.

Brusus glanced to Rsiran and seemed to see the anguish on his face. "Alyse, there's a man near the back who would like to compliment the cook. I tried to take the credit…"

She took a sharp breath. "You wouldn't!"

Brusus met her eyes, and a warm smile spread across her face. "They know that I can mix up a tasty stew with the best of them. And the bread I bake—"

"Is not fit to be served," Alyse finished. She grabbed Brusus and pulled him to the back of the tavern. Brusus gave Rsiran a pointed expression over his shoulder, one that promised they would be speaking more later.

"You didn't agree, did you?" Jessa asked.

"There's a reason for me to do so," he started.

"Such as serving as guildlord," Haern said. When Rsiran frowned at him, Haern only shrugged. "You've not really tried to hide it, and with all the master smiths coming to see you, there was really only one explanation. Makes sense that they'd choose you. And that they'd want you closer."

Rsiran studied Haern for a moment. "There's nothing that you've Seen?"

"That would tell me that you shouldn't do this?" Haern shook his head. "Nothing there, Rsiran. Wish I could help you, but I think you're on your own. Besides, I think it's helpful to have you closer to the rest of the guilds as we try to find Venass. The attack on the forest was only a first step. Now that they've taken it… we've got to be ready. They're weakened, but that makes them more dangerous."

"That's what you said before."

"And I meant it," Haern said. "With your position, you need to get access to the council."

"They want me to meet with them. I'm not willing to go as quietly as the rest of the guilds."

"I suspect the council knows that."

Jessa frowned. "How would they?"

"Think about what we know of the guilds. They serve the city and protect the crystals. And the council knows that they do. Likely, they know what Rsiran has done, as much as he wants to deflect the credit. You get access to the council, and you can find out what the Elvraeth are willing to do."

Rsiran was still perplexed by the Elvraeth's lack of action, both during and after the last attack. He had assumed they would want to do something, but now wasn't sure if they'd even noticed. The Elvraeth rarely left the Floating Palace, sending servants down into the city. They might not know or even care about anything that happened outside the walls of their palace.

The door to the tavern opened and a single person entered.

Haern leapt to his feet, his knives stuffed into his pockets and his face turning a bright shade of red.

"What is it, Haern?" Jessa asked.

A woman entered, but as she turned, Rsiran noted that she had no green to her eyes. Rather, they were a flat grey, and hard. She surveyed the tavern before turning to face Haern, as if she had expected to find him there the entire time.

"Haern?" Jessa said again.

"I didn't think she still lived," he said softly.

"Who is it?"

"A woman from my past," he answered as the woman approached.

She had a fluid way of moving, and Rsiran caught the glimmer of steel beneath the thick black cloak she wore. She stopped at the table, a step or so away from Haern. Rsiran noted the scent of a bitter spice from her, something that reminded him of scents in Della's home.

"The rumors are true," she said. "You still live."

"I could say the same to you," Haern replied.

The woman had a wolfish smile, one that showed a flash of teeth and then was gone. "Is that what they say?"

"The Hjan said the accords were no more. I assumed—"

"You assumed that I can't withstand the Hjan? Haern, I think you underestimate me."

"I doubt anyone has ever underestimated you, Carth."

"No? Yet you allow me to freely enter your tavern and get close enough to—"

She reached for her sword. Rsiran didn't wait for her to finish, unwilling to allow anything to happen to Haern.

He Slid, grabbing Haern and jerking him away, before dancing back a few steps and emerging. The woman spun to him, as if expecting to find him where he emerged. She studied Rsiran, her eyes narrowed in a dangerous way. "You have friends."

"I'm not in the Hjan anymore, Carth," Haern said. His voice shook. Rsiran had never heard him afraid before, and it rattled him.

"Not anymore, but you still must pay for what you've done."

"I've paid for my crimes," he said. "More than you can know."

She darted forward, moving with speed that reminded Rsiran of Venass assassins. Streamers of something that he almost imagined were shadows moved with her before fading as he Slid Haern with him to the side. When he emerged, the woman was there, ready to attack.

She was fast, and anticipated his Sliding. Could she somehow See him?

He had to consider the possibility that she could.

If so, then he had to try a different tact.

Jessa watched him, eyes narrowed. "Don't," he saw her whisper.

He flashed a reassuring grin, but doubted she saw it the same way.

Releasing Haern, he Slid to the woman. As before, she seemed to have anticipated it, but all he needed was to grab onto her. She stabbed at him with her sword, and he grabbed her arm, yanking her with him in a Slide.

He emerged far outside the city, standing on a wide grassy plain.

She seemed unfazed that she'd somehow left a tavern and suddenly appeared far outside the city, and swung her sword in a quick arc. Rsiran Slid back a dozen steps, far enough away that she couldn't reach him easily.

"What do you want with Haern?"

"He owes penance for what he's done. I've come to collect."

"You'll have to come through me first."

She cocked her head to the side. For a moment, Rsiran thought he saw a smile play across her lips, as if she had expected his presence, but then it faded. "Do you think that you're the first man I've faced with such an ability? I thought that Haern had abandoned the Hjan, and you don't strike me as quite the same as them, but you have many of the same abilities."

"I have nothing to do with Venass," he spat.

"Nothing. I think that you have more in common than you let on." She started forward, and he Slid back another dozen steps, emerging with a pair of knives hovering in front of him. "Interesting ability. Another the Hjan possess."

"Leave Haern alone or—"

"Or you'll what? Do you think you can kill Carth of C'than when none other ever has?"

Rsiran shook his head. She'd thrown her name out there as if to impress him.

Not impress, he decided. Intimidate. There was more to this woman than he knew, and the way she managed to avoid his attack told him there was reason to fear her.

"I don't know who you are. And I don't care. But I *do* care about my friends. And Haern is my friend."

The woman slipped her sword back into her sheath. "You can't protect him everywhere. Even now, my network closes in around him. He will have the punishment he deserves."

Rsiran thought she might say something more, but she didn't.

Rather than risking another attack, he Slid back to the city and back into the Barth.

CHAPTER 13

"Who is Carth of C'than?" Rsiran asked, once more sitting at the table in the Barth. The food on his plate had gone cold, and he picked at it, but after the attack, he wasn't really hungry anymore. Across the room, Brusus looked up as if he'd heard the name, and started over.

Jessa kept her hand on his leg, as if she intended to keep him from Sliding away again. With her other hand, she ate with more gusto, finishing everything on her plate before starting on his.

"Carth?" Brusus said when he stopped at their table. "Carth was here?"

"Lower your damn voice, Brusus," Haern said. "Don't need others to hear that name."

"Why? Who is she, and why does she seem completely unconcerned about the fact that I can Slide and control metal?"

"Probably because she's been facing the Hjan for years," Brusus said. "There's not much that scares Carth, mostly because she's more capable than pretty much anyone I've ever met. Until I met you," he said with a nod to Rsiran. "We get you trained well enough, and you'll be able to keep a step ahead of her."

"Is that why you've been pushing me?" Rsiran asked Haern. "Did you know that she was coming after you?"

"The man she's after is dead. He has been ever since Jessa's father helped me escape."

"Then why does she seem so intent on attacking you?"

Haern sighed. "Because of who I once was." He shook his head. "Thought I could get away from it. I thought that by coming here, and hiding with someone like Brusus, I might be able to escape what I'd done in my past. Never expected her to make an appearance here. The city should keep her out."

"Why should the city keep her out?" Rsiran asked. If there was some way to prevent access to the city, knowing would be helpful.

"It's not so much that the city would keep her out, but that she would remain away," Haern said. "She has never wanted anything to do with the people of Elaeavn, and even less with the Elvraeth." He paused, looking toward the door, and his eyes took on the distant expression he had when he attempted a Seeing. "What did you do with her? She's not dead, but I can't See her, either."

"Do you think that you should be able to See her?" Brusus asked. "I know that you still have some of the ability you developed when you were with Venass, but this is Carth we're talking about, Haern."

Haern flicked a pair of knives from his pockets and twirled them in his hands. "I know who we're talking about. Better than anyone here, that's for sure. She's one of the reasons Venass wanted those with the ability to See."

"I don't understand," Jessa said, "I've heard of her before, but never in the same way that you describe. She's known as something of a protector."

Haern sniffed as he nodded. "I'm not sure that protector describes her well," Haern said. "She's... she's more of a spymaster. She has a network everywhere, probably even in Elaeavn. It's the reason Venass wanted her as badly as they did. They wanted access to her network."

Rsiran tensed at the mention of a network. It was too close to the way that Carth had described it, threatening to bring her network down on Haern. "I need to know what she's capable of, Haern, if we intend to keep you safe."

Haern swallowed and looked from Brusus to Jessa and then finally to Rsiran. "If Carth is after me, there's nothing we can do that will keep me safe. Not only is she a spymaster, but she's the huntress. When she knows where you are... There's nothing that will stop her. She's persistent and deadly."

"But she's after the Hjan," Rsiran said.

Haern nodded slowly.

"And they're a part of Venass. Can't we find a way to work with her?" If this Carth really was as powerful as Haern described, then didn't they *need* to work with her? If they could find a way, then they might be able to finally get in front of Venass, and discover a way to defeat them for good.

"You don't know what you're suggesting," Haern said. "Carth... She's not someone who can be trusted. She will have her own agenda. She's smart, and she plans better than anyone I've ever encountered, so coming here probably fit into her agenda..." He looked up and shook his head. "Ah, damn," he whispered.

"What? Brusus said.

"If her spies are active here, they would have known about me, much as I try to hide it." He looked toward Rsiran. "She didn't come here only for me."

"Why would she have come?" Rsiran asked.

"Probably wants to know why Venass is afraid of you," Haern said.

"I think she's going to find that I'm harder to use than I would have been a few months ago," Rsiran said.

"I don't think Carth would use you the same way the Forgotten or Venass have tried to use you. She's not interested in power in the traditional sense."

Brusus coughed. "From what I've heard of Carth—and I *have* heard of her—I believe that she's interested in her own sort of power. It may not be the crystals, but it's definitely something."

Haern sat back in his chair and tipped his mug of ale back, finishing it in one long gulp. When he set it down, he rubbed his eyes, staring blankly. Not a Seeing. More a tiredness… and almost a look of fear.

"We'll get you through this, Haern," he assured him.

"Not sure you can, Rsiran. I know you'll want to, and that you'll do anything you can, but this… this might be a bit more than even you're able to help with, especially given everything else you got going on."

"You're more important than anything else that's going on," Rsiran said.

"More than getting rid of Venass?" Haern stood and shook his head. "Nah, I think I'll deal with this and keep the rest of you out of it. You stay focused on Venass. I'll figure this out."

He made his way to the door, and Rsiran considered Sliding after him, but what would he say? "You have some way of keeping track of him?" he whispered to Jessa.

"This is Haern," she said.

Rsiran grabbed a lorcith coin and slipped it into her hand. "Can you get this on him?"

She eyed the door where Haern had disappeared and raced out with a quick nod.

Rsiran turned to Brusus. "What's the story with this Carth?" he asked.

Brusus blinked, the flash of bright green in his eyes fading back to a more muted color. "There's a story I never thought I'd be asked to tell."

"I'm sorry that I don't know."

Brusus shook his head. "That's not it at all. Just… This woman is nothing like anyone you've ever met. Rumors swirl around her like shadows. Some say she can simply appear, like when I made my first trip to Eban. Others say she's stronger than any man. Still others claim that she's able to read minds."

"Like the Elvraeth," Rsiran noted.

"Like the Elvraeth, only *more* in some ways. Not like the Elvraeth in others. Some talk about her having powers that are nothing like ours, a kind of magic."

Rsiran knew the things he could do might be considered magic by others. Especially his ability with lorcith and heartstone. And when he'd faced Carth, he had been aware that she seemed to know where he would Slide, almost as if she could See him. But no one could See him. His ability with Sliding protected him. When his ability to Slide didn't protect him, then his ability with lorcith protected him.

But not anymore. Venass had managed to counter every one of his abilities, and he knew it involved shadowsteel, the same way the dark metal was somehow involved in destroying the Elder Trees. He needed to get to Ephram and persuade the man to tell him what the alchemists knew about it.

Jessa came back in and nodded to him. Rsiran reached for the connection to lorcith and found where Haern moved along the streets of Elaeavn. He held onto that connection. If he could maintain it, he'd be able to track Haern wherever he went. At least that way, he might be able to keep him safe.

"You two look like you're up to something," Brusus said.

Jessa glanced over to Rsiran and he shrugged. "Jessa slipped a piece of lorcith onto him so I could track him."

Brusus laughed. "You think Haern won't know that you did that?"

"Have you?"

Brusus frowned. "I carry your knives with me. I've got no reason to try and hide from you." He started pulling things out of his pockets and setting them on the table. Brusus carried more with him than Rsiran would have expected. There was a pair of knives, but also a few vials of some thick liquid, a small coin purse, and scraps of paper.

Rsiran laughed. "I don't really need to use the knives you carry," he said. When Brusus made a face, he laughed again. "You've got two bracelets that I forged, Brusus. That's enough for me to follow even when I'm not in the city."

"So does Haern."

"But Haern removes his from time to time, doesn't he?" Rsiran noted.

"You know how he likes his privacy."

Rsiran nodded. There had been a time when he had questioned Haern's friendship and loyalty, but that had been a long time ago. Haern was secretive, but he'd done nothing but try to help them all. And Jessa trusted him, especially after what he'd done for her father.

"I know he does. But I'd still like to be able to help him, whether he likes it or not."

Brusus glanced to the back of the tavern where Alyse engaged in a lively conversation with a couple near the fire. The corners of his eyes softened as they did when he looked at Rsiran's sister. "You ever think of fate?" Brusus asked.

"Haern says the future isn't fixed," Jessa said. "His visions can be changed."

Brusus nodded. "Oh, most of them can. Some are so strong or Seen by so many different Seers that they're practically certain to happen. Fate. A path the Great Watcher sets us on that he means to have happen, regardless of how we get there." Brusus sighed and pulled his gaze off of Alyse. "I think… I think I was always going to discover you, either that night when I bumped into you or another. You needed me to, and we needed you as well."

"Damn, Brusus, love makes you sentimental," Jessa teased.

He shrugged. "Not sentimental, only… I wonder if there are things that we *can't* change. Parts of our future that the Seers know are fixed, regardless of how we might fight against it."

Rsiran had often wondered what would have become of him had he *not* met Brusus that night. Would he ever have escaped Ilphaesn? For that matter, would he ever have been sent to Ilphaesn in the first place? It was possible that meeting Brusus had set into motion everything that had happened to him. Or none of it. Maybe all of those events would have happened, regardless of meeting Brusus. Maybe the path he'd taken had actually been harder, or longer. Had he gone another way, he might have come across the guild sooner, and maybe been receptive to working with them. But then, would he ever have developed the abilities that he now had? Not only with lorcith and heartstone, but with Sliding and his ability to Travel?

It was possible the Great Watcher had intended him to travel the path that he had. To suffer so he could come through it stronger. And he had gained so much, even if he had suffered as well.

Brusus shook his head and flashed a grin. "Ah, maybe you're right, Jessa. That girl… She's changed me, too." He stared for a moment, the hint of a smile fading as he did. "Still wonder why we had to lose Lianna to get to this point. She never wanted to be a part of any sort of deeper plotting. All she wanted was to run her tavern and serve good food and ale."

"You still honor her," Rsiran said.

Brusus nodded. "I know I do. And your sister… She understands why I do it. Never met a woman like her. She's strong and levelheaded. Keeps me going where I need to be," he finished with a smile.

Jessa watched Brusus and shook her head as he left their table. "I never thought I'd say it, but I don't think Brusus can help us anymore."

"He's happy."

"So am I," Jessa said, "but I get that there is more I need to be doing. More you need to be doing. We get through all of this, and we all get to relax. *That's* what I want. And now with Haern distracted… I worry about what help we have left."

Rsiran touched her hand as they sat at the table, the same question troubling him, and without any clear answers.

CHAPTER 14

Rsiran stood at the forge in his smithy, holding the heavy hammer as he pounded on the massive lump of lorcith he'd taken from Ilphaesn, one that had called to him in a certain way. He hadn't used a piece this large in some time, and the metal had taken a while to take the heat. Now it glowed a bright orange as it rested on his anvil. Each strike flattened it somewhat.

As he hammered, he listened to the song of the lorcith, letting its steady call come to him. The song now had a subtlety to it that hadn't been there before. He struck the lorcith, pulling the potential from it each time. When the song shifted, he lifted the lump and turned it over, striking it from a different angle.

His mind worked through what he had learned about Carth, and what his reaction should be. There was a powerful woman with some unknown intent in the city, and she was after Haern. From what Haern had said, she might even be after Rsiran, wanting to know how he resisted Venass. If Rsiran could find a way, they might be able to work together. That would be the best outcome, and one that offered them both the chance to succeed. Her presence meant that Haern was distracted, and given what they faced, Rsiran couldn't have him distracted. He needed Haern, whether the man believed it or not.

He hammered again, pounding steadily.

He was guildlord now. Responsibility had been laid upon him, and he had to live up to expectations that he still didn't fully understand. Some of them were surprisingly hard, like what the guild wanted of him. Not only to move to his father's smithy, but the level of accountability that would be involved there. Staying in this smithy, with the bars of heartstone he had placed to prevent others from Sliding inside, provided necessary safety, but it also protected him in some ways from the accountability of the guild. Though he no longer feared discovery and losing the smithy, the distance from the other smithies offered a layer of security for him.

The song shifted again, and he turned the lorcith, striking it again and again. He let the lorcith guide him, this time not trying to push any desire of his onto the metal, just letting it help him discover what the metal wanted to be. At the same time, he suspected that the song responded to the anxiety he felt, the desire for protection, and finding a way to help his friends.

Well, not only his friends now. As guildlord, he had a responsibility for more than Jessa, Brusus, Haern, and Alyse. Now he had the safety and security of the guild to keep in mind. With that came a responsibility to the city, and with one of the Elder Tree damaged, to the crystals themselves. It was one that he couldn't take lightly.

And eventually, he would have to meet with the Elvraeth council. Rsiran dreaded that, but as guildlord, it was his responsibility. Like so many other things that he now had to do, he wished there was an easier way for him to do it.

The song shifted again and he turned the metal.

He still needed the heavy hammer, and worked to flatten the lorcith. What was the metal asking of him?

Rsiran continued to let it guide him, hammering steadily, rhythmically, alone in his smithy for the first time in a while. Luca was a skilled apprentice, but there were times when Rsiran wanted nothing more than a chance to free his mind the way that hammering at the forge could do.

A separation. Strange that the lorcith would want him to separate it into two pieces, but it did, and he followed the suggestion. The smaller of the two pieces he set back onto the coals, letting it remain hot and soft. The larger, he continued to flatten, now flipping it over as he did. The shape emerged in his mind, and he understood what the lorcith guided him to do, if not the reason why.

Now that he knew, he managed to create the shield more quickly, fully falling into the work. There was a steadiness required, and the heavy hammer had to move all along the surface as it flattened. When that no longer was as effective as he wanted, he began to *push* on the metal, using that ability to form the shape, creating a soft curve in the shield. A pattern emerged, a combination of *pushing* and hammering that dimpled the metal in something that drew out the potential and the power stored within.

With the shield completed, he turned to the other piece, recognizing what it was to be, and that he needed to mix heartstone into this as he formed another sword. Strange that the lorcith would *want* him to create a sword, but his other heartstone sword was damaged now.

Reaching for his supply of heartstone, he layered it over the lorcith, not blending it into an alloy. That wasn't what the lorcith wanted of him. This was a combination of both metals, letting them both retain their stored potential. An interesting creation, and one that was not like the sword he already carried.

When he finished with the sword, he added a few pieces of heartstone to the shield as well, but nothing that would decrease the strength of the lorcith.

Then it, too, was done.

Rsiran stood back and wiped the sweat from his face. A sword and shield, but both forged from the same lump of metal, paired in that way, but not like the paired lorcith that Venass had used on him.

"Those are exquisite creations."

Rsiran turned to see Della sitting on a stool near the back of his smithy. Her shawl had thick stripes of color that contrasted with her pale gray hair. A long gray dress settled almost to the ground.

He flicked his gaze to the door of the smithy. Jessa had been here with him when he started, and had locked the smithy when she left. Unless Della could Slide—and regardless of her protestations that she could not, he wouldn't put it past her—that made her a skilled sneak to manage to enter his smithy.

"I just needed to clear my head." He set the sword and shield over near his bench with the other creations that he had made over the last few weeks.

"Men with responsibility often need to clear their heads as they consider what they'll do next. Have you come to any decisions?"

Rsiran sighed. "None that provide me with any insight." Rsiran ran his thumb along the edge of the sword, *pushing* as he placed a sharper edge to it. With his abilities, he no longer needed a grinding wheel to sharpen the sword, and could feel just how fine an edge he managed to place. "As much as I want to chase Venass, and with Danis still free, I don't think we can risk rushing in, not with what I've learned of shadowsteel."

"Yet you fear delay as well."

He sighed. "Delay only gives Venass the chance to better organize and plan." More than that, delay gave Venass the chance to test whether losing the damaged tree would allow them to take one of the Great Crystals. "Delay gives them a chance to overcome anything I might be able to do. I'm losing those who could help. First Brusus and now Haern…"

Della smiled sadly at him as she limped over to the coals. Ever since they'd healed the tree, her limp had remained. Before, she had only had the limp after performing a particularly challenging healing, but Rsiran didn't think she'd been healing anyone lately.

She pulled a small ceramic pot from a hidden pocket and set in on the coals. Immediately, the scent of her mint tea began to reach his nostrils, already soothing him before he even took a drink. "There are certain things that I See that give me pause," she said, pouring the tea into cups that she'd brought with her. Rsiran smiled at the fact that she had.

"Did you have one today?"

"I would not have come to you if I hadn't."

Rsiran wondered which of the issues he dealt with Della would have had a vision about. Had it been the guild? The guildlords? Venass? Maybe even Haern, especially now that he had disappeared into the city, only the coin Jessa managed to sneak onto him letting Rsiran track him.

"Sometimes when I have a Seeing, it is one that I intentionally seek. With you, most of those are dark, Sliding or your ability with metals preventing me from seeing anything. Every so often, I can manage flashes of color, and those flashes tell me more than any other vision."

Rsiran turned away from the sword. He would need to fashion a different sheath for it; the blade was wider than the other heartstone sword had been, and this time, he wanted to have the sheath better made than the last. With the guild resources, he even thought he might be able to carry it more openly.

"What flashes have you had this time?"

She smiled and offered him one of the cups of tea. Rsiran took it and lifted it to his nose, inhaling deeply.

"These colors are more prominent when I focus on those near you. Some are brighter than others, and others are darker. In that way, I have slowly come to realize that I *can* See certain things even when they involve you."

Rsiran frowned. "I appreciate the insight into your ability, but why are you telling me this?"

"Because it's important for you to understand. The flashes changed today. For a moment, there was a flurry of color. I don't know quite what it means, or who might be involved, but everything shifted, no longer flashing around you. This would only happen if there was another power interfering, but everything I've learned about you tells me that it would have to be *very* powerful. There are not many with that kind of natural power."

Rsiran took a drink. The tea flowed down his throat, warm but not quite hot, as if Della somehow had control over the temperature of the water. "A woman came to town today, one who Haern fears from when he was still with Venass."

"A woman?"

"Her name was Carth," Rsiran said.

Della took a sip of her tea and set the cup on his bench. "Haern served a dangerous role, Rsiran. It is possible that if his time as Hjan has caught up to him, that you will need to do more to protect him."

"I did what I could. I Slid this woman away from Elaeavn, but Haern suspects that she can still reach him. From what I experienced with her, he might be right. And I don't know if I can even defeat her if it comes to it. He thinks to leave us so that we won't have to worry about him."

"Yet you do."

"Haern is one of the few who really knows what we face with Venass. I can't sit back and not do anything to help."

"You mustn't try. Power like what came to Elaeavn today is pure. Natural. It is nothing like Venass. If she possesses this kind of power, you need to understand it."

Rsiran set his cup next to Della's. "What kind of power does she have?"

"There are many ways to power in this world, Rsiran. You have seen only a few. Those of Elaeavn have abilities of the Great Watcher, and you have now experienced the pull of the Elder Trees. There are others, equally ancient."

"Are they bad?"

"Power is neither good nor bad. It is how it is used that defines it. Danis chooses to use his power in a dangerous way, and for dark purposes. He wants power to oppress. Others would use their power to protect, and ensure freedom. That is what you have shown you strive to do. You must understand this woman and decide which side she falls on before you do anything about her. Perhaps she could be the ally you seek."

He'd considered that, but Haern doubted that Carth would help. "And if she harms Haern?" That was what he feared. A part of him hoped that he might be able to side with Carth, especially if she opposed Venass as well, but if she went after Haern, he would have to protect his friend.

"Haern has changed, Rsiran. Those who know him well know that he has. Perhaps you can help her see that."

He set the sword down, placing it near the shield. As he did, a surge of power came with a flash of light and a vague pressure against him. They were paired, but not like the paired lumps of lorcith that he'd *pulled* from Ilphaesn. The pairing within these came from the metal's willingness to separate into parts.

"I fear for Haern, just as I fear for the guild, and for what Danis might try next." He'd been too slow returning to Danis, and now his grandfather had escaped. Rsiran had barely managed to stop him once. If he faced him a second time… he wasn't certain he would survive.

"You have reason to fear those things," Della said. "Your world has changed much in the last few months."

Rsiran looked around his smithy, chuckling. "It has."

"Not only your world has changed, but others as well. There are some who would prefer that things return to how they had been, and others who have chosen to ignore what comes."

"You lived in the palace once." Della nodded. "Why have the Elvraeth ignored the attack as though it never happened?"

"I do not know the will of the council as I once did, Rsiran, but they have always been hesitant to look beyond the walls of the palace, preferring to hold onto the power they possess."

"But they don't really even possess that power, do they? They think the crystals belong to the Elvraeth, but without the guilds, they would have lost access to them long ago."

"And without the Elvraeth, there would be none able to access them. Don't assume that the Elvraeth remember that it's a delicate balance. Many of the Elvraeth resent the role of the guilds in restricting access to the crystals. The few who understand don't have a loud enough collective voice to convince the others."

Rsiran leaned on his bench, staring at the forgings he'd made. Delicate works of lorcith, now sculpted in ways that he once would have believed impossible to create without Sight rested on his bench. He had made them, *pushing* on the metal in such a way that he could bring out even more detail than he ever could have imagined. In doing so, he unlocked something in the potential of the metal that gave it even more power.

He lifted one particular sculpture of a sjihn tree. The first that he'd made had been done while in Seval's smithy, as a way to prove his competence with forging. He'd given that one to Brusus as a memorial to Lianna. This one was almost a copy, but reflected something of the image he carried in his mind of the Elder Trees. Rsiran could *feel* the power resonating through the sculpture, something akin to what he imagined when he stood in the place between Slides when he'd been able to mostly restore Della.

"We have to get the Elvraeth engaged in this," he said.

"Interesting that you've chosen to use the word *we*."

Setting the sculpture down on the bench, he turned back to Della. "I guess now that I'm guildlord, it has to be me, doesn't it?"

"The guilds respect you. As something of an outsider, you might not see it, but I can. Others within the guilds as well. The only other person the rest of the guilds respect in a similar fashion is Ephram, and that has mostly to do with the fact that he is of the Alchemist Guild. You have a chance to lead, to bring the guilds together—truly together in a way that they haven't been in many years—if you're willing to take on that responsibility. A different sort of alliance than the one you were thinking about with the woman, but no less useful. Remember that when you meet with the council."

"The council doesn't want the guilds united."

Della smiled slightly. "No. Which is why they must be."

She made her way to the door, slipping open the locks before pausing in the doorway. She cast her gaze around the smithy before settling her eyes on him. Her eyes widened slightly, rolling upward as they did when she attempted a Seeing. It passed quickly and she shivered, stepping back out of the smithy without saying another word, closing the door behind her so that all the locks latched at once.

Rsiran shook himself and took a deep breath. What had she Seen? Did it affect him and those he cared about? And why had there been a brief expression of terror on Della's face?

CHAPTER 15

The palace wall stretched high over his head, seemingly made of a single sheet of stone. Up close, Rsiran could see small pits in the stone, and moss and thin threads of dry vines ran along the surface. The air had less of the briny scent of the sea this high in the city, carrying less of the stink of fish than in Lower Town, and more of the fresh earthy aroma from the forest, as if the Elvraeth sought to remember the past and the time when their people had lived in the trees.

His hand went to his sword, and he gripped the hilt, a flush creeping up his neck with he realization that he wore it so openly now. Ephram nodded to him with a knowing smile. "You're of the guild now, Lareth."

"Still feels strange. All the time that I spent hiding who I was… what I could do…"

"A shame that you did. As much as I wish you'd come to us sooner, had you not experienced the journey that helped you discover and hone your abilities, we'd not have you with us now, helping the guilds, helping Elaeavn."

Rsiran wasn't certain *what* would have happened had he come to the guilds sooner. Had he stayed with his father in his apprenticeship, he would have progressed through journeyman, and then eventually to a full smith, maybe even master smith where he would have been eligible to join the guild. Doing so would have required that he ignore the part of him that allowed him to do all that he had. It was likely he never would have managed to learn the full extent of his abilities. The guild thought his abilities unique, but they weren't unique at all, only through the challenges that he'd faced had he managed to learn what he was capable of doing. If others of the guilds opened themselves up to more exploration, would they develop additional abilities?

"It's more than the sword," Rsiran said. Carrying the sword openly was odd enough; only the constables carried swords in Elaeavn, though he now knew that the constables came from the guilds, which gave him the right to carry one. "It's coming to the palace like this."

"Through the door?" Ephram asked with a smile.

"There is that."

"You have kept the newest guildlord from the council as long as possible. Tradition requires us to present new guildlords to the council. In that way, the council of the guilds meets the Elvraeth council."

Ephram rested a hand on Rsiran's shoulder. His deep green eyes caught the early morning sunlight, making Rsiran all the more aware of how limited *his* other abilities were. He might carry the Blood of the Watcher, but he had none of the abilities given to his people by the Great Watcher. Everything that Rsiran could do came through the connection to the Elder Trees and the guilds.

"In many ways, we are their equals," Ephram said.

He'd told Rsiran the same when first suggesting the need to visit the council, but Rsiran knew Ephram didn't fully believe it. He might speak openly about being equals, but there remained a deference to the Elvraeth, especially when faced with the imminence of going into the palace. Not sneaking in as he had in the past, but invited. Expected.

"Perhaps not to the rest of the Elvraeth," Ephram went on, "and certainly not to the city, but the council knows the truth of how we must work together. You cannot be scared in front of them. Many on the council have served for years, and two of them are incredibly powerful Seers."

"They won't See anything about me," Rsiran said, though it was more to himself than to Ephram.

"They won't. Just as they cannot See much from any of the guildlords. It's almost as if the Elder Trees protect us in that way. They are experienced, though, and use what they *can* See in ways that you and I are not capable of understanding, much like you can use lorcith and heartstone in ways that even *I* do not understand." He patted Rsiran on the shoulder and dropped his hand. "Do you think yourself able to do what I asked?"

Rsiran took a deep breath, thinking of what Ephram wanted. The council wanted another docile guildlord, which Rsiran wasn't certain he could be. "Where are the others?"

"The other guildlords will meet us in the council chamber. Were it not your first visit, you wouldn't have need of me to guide you."

Ephram made his way toward the wide doors leading into the palace. Once there, he paused a moment and the doors swung open. In all of Rsiran's time in the city, he had rarely seen the doors to the palace open, and never for more than a moment when servants would come and go. The Elvraeth led a totally sheltered existence, avoiding interacting with the people of the city. When he was younger, that had lent them an air of mystery, but now that he knew what he did about the Elvraeth, and had seen the petty ways they acted, he no longer saw them in the same light. It might be easier for him to face the council now than it would have been had he come up through the guilds, blinded by their misguided reverence.

Rsiran had been to the palace twice before, and both times he'd snuck in, Sliding. When he'd come for Josun the first time, he had barely understood the extent of his abilities, not even knowing how he could *push* on lorcith. The second time, he had been better prepared, but still hadn't known what all he would be capable of doing just these few months later.

"What is it?" Ephram asked when Rsiran hung back.

He shook his head, getting rid of the memories. "I could Travel to the meeting," he said, though it was mostly to himself. At least by Traveling, he wouldn't have to wonder what to expect.

"They might know if you did," Ephram said.

"How?" If he knew how Venass expected him, he could discover some way to counter it.

"I don't know. That's a secret of the Elvraeth. I'm not certain whether you would be able to Travel there or not. The council would have protections in place to prevent it."

Protections like they had to prevent Sliding? The council thought they could deter him from Sliding using the heartstone laced into the palace, but that hadn't managed to stop him, especially once he developed a mastery over heartstone.

"Please, Lareth. This won't be what you think. And Sarah will be there as support."

The idea that she would be there did comfort him somewhat, even if she hadn't delivered on the promise to discover what the alchemists knew about shadowsteel.

The halls of the palace were empty. White marble tiles gleamed under the bright light coming through the open door, and reflected the light of the dozens of blue Elvraeth lanterns recessed into the walls. The walls matched the flooring, only there were streaks of dark mixed into the marble. These glowed a faint blue, as well, but likely only to Rsiran. Heartstone. Infused into the marble as a way to prevent Sliding into the palace.

He'd once thought that Sliding had been one of the abilities given to their people by the Great Watcher before he learned that it was one he gained through his connection to the ancient clans. In that respect, he probably shouldn't be able to Slide and hear the lorcith. They were separate abilities. But then, he shouldn't be able to detect others Sliding, either.

"Where is everyone?" Rsiran asked in a hushed voice.

"This is the main hall. There are few of the Elvraeth who use this hall. They prefer more privacy than this. They have their rooms in the upper levels."

"I know."

Ephram studied him a moment. "Of course. You have been here before. Is that why you have such concern?"

"A part of it," he admitted.

Ephram led him down the hall, stopping in front of a pair of ornately carved double doors. "The council is on the other side. You will let me enter, and then they will call you in. It is customary for the newest guildlord to join last."

"I'm not sure that anything I've done is really customary," Rsiran said. "And what I would have the guilds do—"

"That doesn't change the fact that the Elvraeth would prefer to maintain certain elements of custom. I think that in this, we should be able to accommodate them, don't you?" Ephram seemed almost to plead with him, but didn't wait for his answer before he pushed on the doors to enter.

Rsiran debated following him in, but ultimately waited. As he did, he focused on the sense of lorcith and heartstone. Within the doors and walls, and all around him in the palace, there was evidence of lorcith and heartstone, bound together in the alloy. Particularly here, where the walls and even the door surged with the strength of both metals, as if the council thought to exclude those who might Slide into their chambers.

Ephram had asked that he not Travel, but Rsiran didn't care for surprises, especially not when it came to the Elvraeth. They might not be the same as Josun Elvraeth, but this was the council that had exiled people of their own families, women like Brusus's mother. What would happen if they decided he shouldn't be guildlord? Would they banish him as well? Or would they choose a different punishment? He'd already proven that Elvraeth chains couldn't hold him. And he could Slide past the heartstone.

Regardless of what Ephram said, he needed to know what he might encounter.

Looking up and down the hall, he saw no one nearby. What he intended to do carried risk—especially here. If someone came upon him while he was incapacitated, he could be harmed.

Perhaps it *was* better for him to do as Ephram suggested and wait.

But Rsiran didn't want to simply stand off to the side and wait for what might come. He wanted to know what was on the other side of the door, and he didn't want to be caught unprepared. Now that he was no longer terrified of them, he was determined to know what it was that they might want from him.

He stepped into the darkness near the door where the bright light of the heartstone lanterns wouldn't quite reach. Closing his eyes, he Traveled.

CHAPTER 16

The sensation was strange each time Rsiran Traveled. He felt a kind of separation as his mind lifted from his body. With it came the sense of movement, but none of the colors that he experienced when Sliding, and none of the smells of lorcith or heartstone that he'd grown accustomed to, either.

Rsiran pressed through the door and paused. Ephram believed they would know if he Traveled, and Thom had certainly known, but that didn't mean that these Elvraeth would be able to detect him quite as well. He held himself back, hovering along the wall, holding close to both the lorcith and the heartstone, thinking that might actually help keep him from being detected.

He saw Ephram first. He stood at the end of a long table, with Sarah on one side, and two others on his other. Sarah wore a long white robe that draped to the ground, and kept her hands slipped into the sleeves. Her long, blonde hair hung below her shoulders. When she glanced over to Ephram, Rsiran noted the way her deep green eyes flicked toward the back of the room. Had she noticed him somehow?

Unlikely that she did. She might be able to detect Sliding, but Rsiran had managed to hide his ability from her when he learned to Slide by *pulling* himself along rather than stepping into the Slide. As far as he knew, she didn't have any way of detecting him Traveling, but then, he didn't know enough about Traveling to know whether that was true.

He looked around the table at the other guildlords. He recognized Gersh, a stocky and short miner, who had streaks of black along his face from where metal had lodged into his skin during a mining accident long ago. A slender woman, and short compared to most within Elaeavn, stood next to Gersh. Tia was guildlord of the Travel Guild, and had an intensity about her that Rsiran found intimidating. He had been shocked to learn that Sliders had a guild of their own, but even more surprised that they had a guildlord. Tia was deserving of that title, though he'd only met her a few times since becoming guildlord.

Five Elvraeth sat on the other side of the table. All wore heavy cloaks of fine wool, embroidered with the Elvraeth crest in navy-colored thread. One of them, a man with deep wrinkles at the corners of his green eyes and what appeared to be letters embroidered along his sleeves, flicked his gaze to the door.

"The Smith Guild was fragmented," Rsiran heard the man say. Wrinkled hands rested atop the armrests of his chair as he somehow managed to look down his nose at the guildlords. "How is it they have chosen a new guildlord."

"A better question, Naelm, is how we have only come to hear of it now?" The woman's words reverberated in the air, almost musical. Clothed in a robe similar to Naelm's, she leaned forward, her aged face worked with worry, the green in her eyes bright. Her pale hair streamed down her back and seemed almost to glow in the light cast by the heartstone lanterns.

"That is a guild matter, Sasha Elvraeth, as you well know." Tia crossed her arms and thrust her jaw forward.

Naelm Elvraeth leaned back. Rsiran had heard his name mentioned before, and knew from Brusus that he led the council. One of the most powerful Elvraeth, he was the one Rsiran would have to watch.

"A guild matter, but do the guilds no longer value the council's insight?" Naelm asked. He had a deep and rich voice, and it carried when he spoke, almost bouncing off the walls.

"I think in this matter, the council's opinion would not have mattered," Ephram said.

A younger man sitting to Naelm's left sat upright at that comment. "You forget our role in the rule of the city, guildlord."

Ephram tilted his head to the side. "Do I? Or is it you, Yongar, who has forgotten what role that you play?"

Rsiran almost ended the Travel, so surprised was he that Ephram actually seemed to rebuke the Elvraeth.

"Interesting choice of words, don't you think?" Naelm asked.

"Which one?" Ephram said.

"Forgotten."

"Interesting in that you are responsible for them, or that you have ignored the danger they posed until now?" Sarah asked.

The comment was brash for her, especially when directed at the Elvraeth. Sarah was the youngest of the guildlords—or had been, before Rsiran. And though he'd only been present during a few of their gatherings, she'd always chosen to be relatively quiet around the others. Except for her father. With Ephram, she had been willing to stand up for herself, but then, she had alchemist blood, too. If only she would use it to determine what the guild knew about shadowsteel.

"Careful, guildlord. Your position is tenuous at best," Sasha said.

"Do not presume to know the will of the guilds," Ephram said.

"Do you speak for all of them now?" Naelm asked. "Has so much changed that the guilds have unified?"

The other two Elvraeth remained silent. One of the men, a very elderly man with rheumy eyes that barely looked up at the others, rested with his head on his fist. Every so often, his head would bob, as if he struggled to stay awake. Why would the council keep a man so old among them when he could barely stay awake for their meetings? The other Elvraeth was a beautiful younger woman with black hair and blazing green eyes. She rested her hands on the table and drummed her fingers as she did.

"The guilds have always been unified," Ephram protested.

"The guilds have *never* been unified," Naelm said. "That is why we have the predicament that we have. Had you managed to coordinate your efforts, there would never have been need for those without your bloodlines to reach the crystals, would there?"

"That no longer matters." The old man barely moved his head when he spoke, but somehow managed to send his gaze across to each person in the room. Rsiran even managed to feel the weight of it and almost returned to his body. He had listened to enough to know that the guilds were not intimidated by the Elvraeth as he had expected.

Everyone turned to the old man.

"The smith guildlord has held one of the crystals."

"You don't know that, Luthan," Naelm said. "We haven't been able to See—"

Luthan turned his cloudy gaze on Naelm. "I still See well enough. I might not be able to See *him*, but I can see what has changed. As can you, if you would only shift your focus."

"He's here," the younger Elvraeth said.

Ephram nodded. "As we agreed, I have brought him to the council. He is not like the rest of the smiths. He was not brought up through the guild in the same way that most have been, so you will find him—"

"That is not it," the woman said. She turned and focused on where Rsiran hovered near the wall. "He is here. Now."

Ephram's face blanched.

Rsiran quickly returned to his body, and rather than waiting for the council to summon him into their chamber, he Slid beyond the door—noting a hint of resistance that he barely struggled to overcome—and emerged next to Sarah.

She pressed her lips together and almost frowned, but he saw the glimmer of a smile in the corners of her eyes.

"I am here," Rsiran said.

Now that he was in the room, he noted that the sculptures along the back wall were lorcith made, and done with exquisite skill. Had they been from a time when the smiths still listened to lorcith? Would he ever reach *that* level of skill?

"Lareth," Ephram whispered, the agitation plain in his tone. In spite of his firm stance with the Elvraeth, he still remained fearful of them. "I warned you to wait."

The Elvraeth all started talking at once. Only Luthan did not.

Rather, he stood.

He had a stooped back, but even bent over as he was, it was clear that Luthan had been incredibly tall, even for someone from Elaeavn. He weaved his way around the table, leaning on the back of each chair for support as he did. His eyes seemed to look past Rsiran, as if he attempted a Seeing continuously.

"You are him," Luthan said.

Rsiran nodded. "I am Rsiran Lareth." His voice was stronger than he would have expected, and it felt good to be able to speak so openly about himself, and not fear his ability. If nothing else, he would no longer fear what he could do, and who he had become.

"The smith's son, but also much more," Luthan said. He reached toward Rsiran with a withered hand and grabbed Rsiran's arm.

Not knowing what to do, Rsiran stood transfixed. He didn't fear the man Reading him, not with the heartstone bracelets that he wore, but he didn't know what else this man might attempt. He *was* Elvraeth, and Rsiran did not trust any of them.

"You have the Blood of the Watcher," Luthan said. The rest of the Elvraeth had fallen silent, and each stared more at Luthan than at Rsiran.

"My grandfather is Danis Elvraeth," Rsiran said.

Naelm looked at the others. "Was that name stricken from the Elvraeth?" he asked.

The dark-haired woman nodded slowly. "I believe he was Forgotten."

Rsiran turned to him with Luthan still clutching his arm. "You might have exiled him, but I can assure you that he is *not* Forgotten."

"You side with the exiles?" Naelm said.

A surge of anger clouded Rsiran's face, and he shook his head. "Danis Elvraeth attempted to destroy my family, nearly killed me, and has attacked the city."

Naelm frowned. "That is no answer."

"No?" Rsiran asked. "It is all the answer that you will get." He shook his wrist away from Luthan's grasp and stepped away from him. "The Forgotten have attacked this city. Venass has attacked this city. And the Elvraeth do nothing, much like you have done nothing for many years, when it's been well within your power to help."

"You would allow him to speak to the council this way?" Sasha directed the question at Ephram, but his face remained neutral.

"He doesn't allow me to do anything," Rsiran said. "I have done more to protect this city from threats that this council has been ignoring than any of you. I have held one of the great crystals twice. I know how powerful they are. And I am the reason they remain protected."

Tia actually smiled. It was the first time Rsiran had ever seen her smile. Gersh clenched his jaw. Rsiran hadn't expected him to do anything different. The miners were nearly as dependent upon the Elvraeth to maintain their wealth as the Smith Guild. The other guilds did not depend on the council for protection. As far as most within the city knew, there was no such thing as a Thenar Guild or a Travel Guild.

Yongar looked at the other Elvraeth, his neck growing increasingly red. "The crystals can only be held once. If this... boy... claims that he has held them twice, then what else has he lied about? The smiths should be advised that he makes claims like this—"

Luthan watched Rsiran, his eyes still seeming to see through him. "I cannot See whether what he says is true."

As the woman watched Rsiran, he realized that her eyes went distant in the same way that Della's and Haern's did when they attempted a Seeing. All of the Elvraeth had the ability to See, only some were more skilled than others. Luthan likely was a powerful Seer, and he had suspected Naelm was as well, but what if this woman had the ability?

"He Travels," she said.

"I think we all saw how he Slid into the room," Yongar said. His gaze drifted to Tia, and it was clear from his expression how he viewed Sliding.

"Not Sliding, though he should not have managed to Slide into the chambers as easily as he did, but Travel. A lost Talent."

Luthan blinked. "Is that how you reached the crystals? If so, that is dangerous, indeed. We thought they were protected from such an ability."

"Not Traveling," Rsiran said. "At least, not the first time. The first time, I Slid to them."

Naelm jerked his head to Ephram. "Your protections are so weak that he could *Slide* to the crystals?"

"I think you will find that when it comes to Mr. Lareth, any protection is bound to be weak. He is… unique… in ways that I'm still not certain of."

"This is why the guild chose him," Luthan said.

Ephram shook his head. "They chose him because he is the most competent of the smiths."

Yongar laughed. "Competent? The boy can barely be twenty! How could he be more skilled than smiths who have worked with metals for twice as long as he's lived?"

"Because he has not forgotten how to listen to the potential of the lorcith," Ephram said.

"There's that word again," Naelm said.

Ephram cocked his head. "Forgotten? Lareth does have a point, regardless of the angry way that he made it. He *has* been the reason the crystals remain protected. After the last attack, it is even more critical that we have someone with his ability to offer protections. I presume the council would like to keep access to the crystals?"

"What kind of question is that?" Yongar asked.

"The same kind of question you're asking the guildlord," Tia responded.

No one spoke for a moment, and then Ephram nodded. "As is custom, we have brought the newest guildlord before the council. I think we have accomplished all that we can today."

He turned to Rsiran and motioned hurriedly to the door. The other guildlords all followed as Ephram made his way across the tile.

Luthan grabbed Rsiran's wrist before he had a chance to follow. He leaned in and spoke in a whisper. "The guilds need to come together or everything fails."

Rsiran stiffened. "The guilds are together."

"More than they have been in some time," Luthan said, "but that is still not the same. I See that you can unify them. Perhaps you can do more, but I cannot See you clearly enough for that."

Luthan released Rsiran's arm. "Careful. There are those who would prefer that the guilds not be unified. There are those who would prefer the old ways fail, and the guilds lose control over the crystals."

He leaned on the table and began to weave his way back around to his seat. Rsiran watched him for a moment, and then Slid outside the palace, emerging into the morning sunlight. After his time in the palace, even the sun didn't feel as warm as it should.

CHAPTER 17

"You said *what* to the council?" Brusus asked.

Rsiran flushed. Retelling what had happened left him feeling more foolish than ever. As frustrated as he might have been with the council, maybe he *should* have been more careful. Luca sat silent, and Jessa shook the pair of dice in her hand, sending them across the table over and over. Rsiran stood behind her, resting a hand on her shoulder.

All around them, the Barth bustled with activity. A couple of servers rushed in and out of the kitchen, carrying steaming trays of food and drink. A lutist played near the back corner, the bright sounds of his instrument mixing with the steady strumming from the bandolist. A singer added her voice, but wasn't able to drown out the cacophony of sound from dozens of conversations around the Barth.

"I probably shouldn't have spoken so freely," he said.

"You're the…" Brusus leaned forward and lowered his voice. "You're the guildlord. At least the council knows what that means, even if most of the Elvraeth do not."

"That doesn't change the fact that I should have been more cautious," Rsiran said. Ephram claimed he wasn't upset with him, but had said nothing when he left the palace. Sarah had smiled, and even Tia had offered something of a nod. Gersh had been the hardest to read. The Miner Guild had returned to Ilphaesn, and lorcith flowed once more, but Rsiran knew they didn't care for the fact that he could *pull* lorcith from the walls of the mines without the approval of the guild.

"You speak for each of the guilds now," Brusus said.

"Not all of the guilds."

"No? You can Slide. You detect the lorcith better than the miners and the alchemists. You're descended from the smiths. And you've as much as admitted that you've begun to develop the ability to detect Sliding. You're practically *from* each of the guilds."

"Like the Elvraeth," Luca said softly.

Brusus turned to the boy and frowned a moment. He rubbed at his pale green eyes. Every so often, they flashed a darker green, as if Brusus lost control of Pushing, before fading once more. "Like the Elvraeth. I hadn't thought of that before." He looked at Rsiran. "The boy's right, Rsiran. You have abilities from each of the guilds. That makes you like the guild version of the Elvraeth."

"And none from the Great Watcher," Rsiran said.

Brusus considered him as if seeing him for the first time. "No. Strange, I think. You should at least have *something*, even if it's nothing more useful than Sight."

"Hey!" Jessa said.

"Well, maybe she's not the best example," Brusus said. "Damn girl can see in the darkest of nights. But you should have something. Everyone born in the city has something. Besides that, you're supposedly descended from one of the Elvraeth. Even if your abilities were diluted, most descendants of the Elvraeth have aspects of multiple abilities."

Rsiran saw his sister moving in the back of the tavern carrying a tray laden with food. Alyse could Read and was Sighted. He'd always thought it amazing that she was gifted with two abilities while he had only Sliding, but it turned out that even his ability wasn't what he thought. Now it turned out that he hadn't been given *any* of the Great Watcher's abilities. Instead, he'd been granted the ability from the Blood of the Elders, and in such a way that even the guilds didn't understand what he did.

"It's fine, Brusus." Jessa watched Rsiran, and he noted the way the corners of her eyes twitched, the same way they did when she worried about him. The flower tucked into the lorcith charm she wore had large purple petals that fell outside the cage of the charm. Every so often, she leaned into the flower and sniffed. "Rsiran can do more than most of us. He doesn't need the powers of the Great Watcher."

"He has a mixing," Luca said.

Luca held the lorcith sculpture of Ilphaesn that he'd made him. For Luca, the sculpture gave him a sense of reassurance, and helped him to still hear the song that he heard in Ilphaesn. Without it, he had an edge to him, and the wildness returned to his eyes.

"What do you mean by a mixing?" Brusus asked.

Luca shrugged and set the lorcith Ilphaesn onto the table. Light flickered off the sides, giving it the appearance of the sun setting on the mountain. "I can't say exactly, but Master Lareth has something like a mixing of abilities, doesn't he? He can hear the song, but he can sing back to it as well."

"What's he talking about?" Brusus asked Rsiran.

Rsiran motioned to the Ilphaesn sculpture. "He's talking about the ability to hear lorcith. When I work with it, sometimes I speak to the metal."

Brusus shook his head. "I know that already. You've made a point of sharing that more times than I've needed to hear it, when all I *really* needed was for you to give me something I could sell. And now that you're reputable again, you shouldn't have any problem making me things I can sell. But now it doesn't make a difference." He made a face, something between a glare and a half-smile as he looked around the tavern. "What's he doing calling you Master Lareth?" Brusus asked, the grin spreading across his face.

"You're an idiot," Jessa said as she tossed the dice across the table. They came up a one and a two. She scooped them up quickly. Rolling a Bladen Curse was unlucky. She rolled the dice again and sent them skittering across the table. One of them fell off the edge. The other came up two again. Jessa's jaw clenched, and she swept her long hair back from her neck. "Where's Haern?"

Brusus shrugged. "Haven't seen him in a few days."

"Not since that woman came here?" she asked. "And given what she wanted, you don't think that's a problem?"

"He's still in Elaeavn," Rsiran reminded her. She'd asked him about Haern at least five times already today. Each time, he could focus on the location of the coin that she'd slipped onto him, and each time, it had still been within the city. The last time, Rsiran had even Traveled to him, and found him sitting quietly in a small home on the outskirts of Lower Town, sharpening knives. That had bothered him, and he hadn't shared with Jessa that it appeared Haern was making preparations.

"*You* know that, but Brusus didn't. You'd think that he'd care about what happened to his friend."

"I care. Haern and I have an understanding. I don't interfere in his business, and he doesn't interfere in mine."

"That was fine when your business was smuggling and thieving, but now, your business is this tavern," Jessa said. She slammed the dice into a cup on the table, and Luca jumped.

"What does that mean?" Brusus asked.

"Only that Haern still hasn't found his way, not completely. First you make an honest man of yourself, then Rsiran gets recognized by the guild, and even Della turns out to have chosen to be outside the palace. Where does that leave Haern?"

"What about you?" Brusus asked. He crossed his arms over his chest, the smile fading from his face. "I seem to remember that you were a skilled sneak at one time. Now, you're all domesticated to the point where you're fretting about Haern?"

Jessa jumped to her feet. "You know what he did for me!"

"I know what he did for you. Just as I know that he wants more for you than to just sit by and watch Rsiran while he gets the recognition he deserves." He glanced at Rsiran. "Don't get me wrong. I love it that I don't fear the constables anymore and that we're friends with the guildlord, but Jessa here makes claims about Haern and seems to forget that she's lost something of herself in all of this."

She slumped in her chair and looked up at Rsiran. He wanted to reach for her, but doing so might only make it worse. "I didn't lose anything. That's what you don't understand, Brusus. I've gained something I thought I wouldn't have. Something I didn't think I deserved to have." Her voice caught on the last part, and she swallowed. "And now my friend wants to give me a hard time about wanting stability?"

"Ah, damn, girl. I didn't want to make you feel bad." Brusus came around the table and slipped an arm around her shoulders. "We want you to be happy. The Great Watcher knows that's what you deserve after all you been through."

She pushed him away. "You think I don't know that I don't have the same to offer as others?" She spoke softly enough that Rsiran didn't think she intended him to hear, but the words still pierced him. He wouldn't have managed half of what he had accomplished without Jessa. "You think I don't know that he doesn't need me anymore? Now that he can use the knives like... like some sort of lantern, he doesn't need me."

"He still needs you," Brusus said. "Probably more now than before. Can't let him get a big head and go running off on us, thinking that he needs to be the perfect guildlord."

"I can hear you," Rsiran said.

"You better hear me," Brusus told him. "Otherwise, I would have wasted my words." He patted Jessa on the arm. "Even though he needs you, doesn't mean you have to be there for him. You have to find what drives you. That's what Haern wants for you, and what he thinks your parents would have wanted, too. Now I think I've done enough for the night," Brusus said, and turned to where Alyse made her way to the kitchen.

"What does he hide?" Luca asked when Brusus was gone.

"What do you mean?" Rsiran asked.

"His eyes. He's not as weak as he seems."

Rsiran smiled. How long had it taken him to realize how strong Brusus really was? It had taken his friend nearly dying in order for him to learn, and Luca had managed to detect it through simple observation. "There's much about Brusus that's not as it would seem," he said.

Jessa stood and pushed Rsiran's hand off her shoulder. "And there's just as much that's exactly as it seems."

"Jessa—"

"I'm fine," she said.

"You don't seem like you're fine."

She started toward the door, tipping her head toward the flower charm she wore. "Well, I am."

She turned and left the Barth. Rsiran watched her leave, debating whether he should chase after her, but suspecting she needed time to herself.

"You're not going after her, Master Lareth?"

Rsiran took a deep breath and turned back to Luca. "Just Rsiran," he said.

Luca took the Ilphaesn sculpture and cradled it in his arms. He tipped his head to the side as he did, listening to the song from the lorcith. What did Luca hear when he listened to the sculpture? When Rsiran focused, he could hear the steady sound—what Luca called the song—but nothing with any real intensity, and certainly not like he would have found in Ilphaesn. But it helped Luca in a way that nothing else really had.

"Meet me at the smithy tomorrow morning," Rsiran said, pushing back from the table. "We'll continue to work on some finer forgings."

Luca flashed a smile and nodded. "Is there anything you're working on that I can help with?"

Rsiran almost told him that he didn't really need help with anything, but that wouldn't help Luca learn what he needed. The boy was now Rsiran's apprentice, and he was determined to treat him better than he had been treated during his apprenticeship. Letting him work with and learn from lorcith was only the first step in the process, but it was a necessary one.

"Brusus has been pushing me for a few things for the Barth. I think we'll work on those together."

He left Luca to finish his meal and made his way outside the tavern. Once there, the cool air sent a shiver down his spine. He focused on the lorcith and heartstone Jessa wore and found her wandering along the shores. Shifting his focus, he listened for Haern, and found him in the same place he had before.

Why would Haern not have moved?

That troubled him, as did the strange argument with Jessa. He could work on one of the two more easily.

Pulling himself into a Slide, he emerged in the small room where he had found Haern when he'd Traveled. When Traveling, there were none of the scents—the staleness of warm ale, the stink of sweat, a hint of dried jerky. Even his vision was different when Traveling, leaving him with a hint of bluish white light all around, as if the Traveling were infused with his ability with lorcith and heartstone. The windowless room had no light other than that which came from the bracelets Rsiran wore, and the sword he'd pulled from his sheath, but it was enough to see the room was empty.

Rsiran focused on the sense of lorcith that Jessa had snuck into Haern's pocket, and found it on a table, resting on its edge, with nothing else around it.

Haern had known what they'd done. And now was gone.

CHAPTER 18

W*AVES CRASHED ALONG THE SHORE* in a steady rhythm that had become comfortable to him in the time he'd lived in Lower Town. Moonlight filtered through the clouds, barely enough to light his way. Though Rsiran no longer feared the darkness as he once had, he still *pushed* a knife before him to light his way. Without that, he *would* have been more uncomfortable. A gull cawed overhead, but he couldn't see it from where he stood on the rocks.

Jessa moved in the distance, a dark shadow against the rest of the night. The lorcith in her necklace and that within her bracelets pulled on him, but he made a point of not getting too close, not wanting to anger her. If she needed her space, he would give it to her, but at the same time, she would want to know that Haern had disappeared.

She paused at the end of the rock and turned toward him, the metal on the chain she wore lighting her face, giving a faint glow in the distance that he might be the only one able to detect. She didn't move, but he knew she saw him.

When he Slid to her, emerging a step away, she leaned toward him and wrapped him in a hug. "It took you long enough."

The comment stole from him what he needed to share with her. "I thought you wanted time to yourself. After what Brusus said—"

"I wanted time, but you should know that you have to be a part of it. Besides, Brusus spoke the truth. What do I have, now that I'm not a sneak?"

"You're still a sneak."

"Really? When have I needed to use that particular skill since I met you?"

Rsiran could think of several ways that she had managed to use it, but that wasn't what she was really asking him. "Is that what you want?"

She let out a frustrated sigh. "I don't know. I want to have that sense of purpose, that thrill that I had that comes from getting someplace that you're not supposed to be. It was never about taking something, not for me at least. It's always been about the challenge."

"You can still challenge yourself."

"Really? When you can take us wherever we need to go? No lock stops you, Rsiran. In that way, my ability as a sneak is useless." She sighed again. "So I need to find something else, only I don't know what it is. You've got your smithy, and now the guild, and all these things going well. I'm happy for you—for us—but…"

"But what?" he asked.

Jessa turned away and skipped a rock out over the cresting waves. When she spoke, her voice came out thin and strained. "I… I can't be the doting wife if that's what you want."

He laughed before cutting himself off when Jessa glared at him. "Who said that's what I want?"

The glare changed over to hurt. "It's not?"

"The doting, not the part about the wife."

She punched his shoulder and then let him pull her toward him again. "When I returned to Elaeavn—when Haern brought me back—I thought I knew what would become of me. That I would work with Brusus and Haern on different jobs as a sneak. But everything has changed."

Rsiran laughed, and she punched his shoulder again. "You're just now realizing that?"

"When have we had the time to think about anything? Between Josun using you, and then the Forgotten and Venass chasing after you, we've been running. Now… now you can have a measure of peace. You can lead the guild and whatever happens outside the city becomes less of a real threat." She shrugged. "I finally have the time to think about what's going to happen to me. What will I become now that everything has settled?"

"But it's not settled, not for me. Danis is still out there. Venass is the same threat that they were before. When we stop them, then we can think about those things."

"Eventually, we'll defeat them. You have to know that."

Rsiran wasn't as certain as Jessa about that. The past few times he'd faced Venass, he had barely escaped. There was a reason he hesitated racing after them again. Until he understood how to avoid a shadow-steel attack, he wasn't sure it was safe for him.

"I hope so," he said.

She sniffed. "You've defeated them. They might attack again, but they know what you can do, the abilities that you have and the fact that you were able to stop him. They won't risk attacking again soon."

"I don't think that's as true as we would like," he said. "Venass… They *will* find some way to stop me. If it's something like that shadow-steel sphere or something else"—he thought of the way he was nearly trapped while Traveling—"the longer we wait, the more likely it is that they'll be able to overwhelm whatever my abilities can do. Then what? We need help and without Haern—"

"What about Haern?"

"He's gone."

"Gone? Can't you follow the coin I slipped into his pocket?"

"I can." Rsiran pulled the coin from his pocket and held it out to her. "If he had it with him. Doesn't have his bracelets, either."

"Damn him," she said. "How long ago did he disappear?"

"I don't know."

"You've been keeping tabs on him, though, haven't you?" she asked. "You've been watching him?"

"When I Traveled to Haern the last time, he was still in the room."

"When was that?"

"This morning."

"Take me there," she said. Jessa pushed away from him and jumped the rocks closer to shore. Rsiran Slid after her before Sliding her into Haern's small home.

Once again, the smells struck him first. They were stale, the scents of a place that had been heavily lived in. Jessa held her nose, scanning the room as she did.

"Not here," she said.

"That's what I said."

"But you also said he was here this morning. That gives him nearly a full day."

"With Haern, he could get pretty far in a single day," Rsiran said.

"Not as far as you."

"No, but if Haern doesn't want to be found, then we're not likely to find him."

She leaned over the wooden table. In the light coming off the knife he held suspended in the air, he could see a faded stain and a stack of pages resting on it. A pair of dice was set atop the pages. Jessa lifted the top few pages and began rifling through them before setting them back down. She moved on to the trunk at the end of the bed and flipped it open. Inside were neatly folded clothes, a couple of steel knives, and the strange black shirt that he'd seen him wearing in the past.

Jessa lifted that out and held it up. "He wouldn't have left this."

The fabric of the shirt seemed to push away the light from the knives, making it look impossibly black. "What is it?"

"This is from when he was still an assassin. There's something about the fabric. Without Sight, you probably can't make out the ways that it practically draws in shadows."

"I don't need Sight to see that," he told her.

She handed the shirt to him. "Feel it. If this came from Venass, is there anything that we can learn from it?"

Rsiran turned the shirt over, searching for signs of anything that might help him know how Venass might have made it. "It's not lorcith or heartstone," he said.

"And that's the extent of your abilities?"

"When it comes to this? Pretty much. I'm not a seamstress or a tailor."

"No, but you've got experience with strange qualities of things. I thought maybe one of your other abilities might be able to help you figure out what this is made from."

"What other abilities? I don't have your Sight, or any of Brusus's abilities—"

She pulled the shirt from his hands, shaking her head. "No. You have much more than any of us. It's time you stop thinking of what you can't do and focus on what you can. You're more skilled than any of us. Well, maybe not Brusus if he ever lets himself use all of his abilities."

"Or Della."

She nodded. "Della, too."

"And all the Elvraeth."

She punched him. "The Elvraeth wish they knew what you could do. Now. Is there anything from this that you can pick up?"

"Like I said, it's not heartstone or lorcith."

"And with your alchemist connection, is that all that you can detect?"

He started to object, before catching himself. What if there was something more that he could determine from the shirt? There was no denying the fact that he did seem to have aspects of each of the talents of the guilds, including the ability of the alchemists to know the potential within metals. The shirt wasn't one of the metals that he knew, but it did have a metallic sort of sheen to it. What if he could use his ability to determine something about the shirt?

And if he could? How would that help them?

He watched Jessa, and the hope she had in her eyes. Maybe it would do nothing. No—likely, it would do nothing. But Jessa wanted him to try, so he would.

Rsiran shook the shirt out, and then started to push away the sense of lorcith and heartstone. They pulled on him, as if trying to draw him back, demanding his attention. Once, it had been easier to push away the awareness of the metals, but he'd become so attuned to them, they were practically a part of him. Sending the awareness of them away was like sending a part of himself away.

Slowly, they became little more than a distant sense in his mind. He didn't think that he could totally remove his sense of them, not anymore. He turned his attention to the shirt. If it was woven completely, he doubted that he would pick up on anything, but what kind of fabric had the ability to draw shadows and practically bend light? That was more like what some of the metals could do.

Running his hand across the smooth fabric, he felt pressure against the tips of his fingers.

He had never felt anything like it before. It was almost like the fabric resisted him.

"I… I can't," he answered.

She sighed. "It was worth a shot. That shirt is from before. When he worked with Venass. I thought maybe they used shadowsteel in it or something."

"And you wanted me to feel it?"

She shrugged. "It's not like it's the same as those spheres."

"I think shadowsteel is something newer for Venass," he said. "And if we can understand how they're making so much of it, we might find a way to stop them. It'd be helpful to have Haern with us for that, though."

"Probably, but there's nothing else here that might give us a clue," she said.

"No. So what now?"

Jessa looked around. "I need to know if Carth found Haern."

Rsiran started to tell her that they needed to focus on Venass, or even on the guilds, searching for a way to unify them to oppose the Elvraeth. They had no time to look for Haern. But the set to her jaw and the determined look to her eyes were all too familiar, though he'd not seen them in a while. How could he deny her?

"I'll help," he said. "But there's something I need to know about first."

She waited for him to explain, and then began nodding.

CHAPTER 19

The bar of shadowsteel encased in the remnants of his sword throbbed against Rsiran's senses. Mostly, it came from the way the heartstone and the lorcith wrapped around it, fusing with the shadowsteel to make it harmless, but there was something about the dark metal itself that pained him.

What would happen were he struck by shadowsteel? With his connection to lorcith and to heartstone, would he be protected in any way, or would the strange, dark metal damage him?

Maybe that was why Venass had worked with it. If shadowsteel had managed to poison the Elder Trees, what would happen to him, a person somehow connected to the Elder Trees and the power they possessed?

He Slid with the shadowsteel, out of his smithy and to the Hall of Guilds.

It was late, well after midnight, but Jessa wasn't going to rest while she worried about Haern, so he couldn't, either. Losing Haern only reminded him that time was short and he needed answers.

The Hall of Guilds was empty, though he hadn't expected anything different. Blue and white light glowed everywhere, stronger than the first time he'd come, though that had been a time when he had snuck into the guild house, searching for answers that he would have found had he been willing to remain even a little while longer.

Rsiran made his way into the wide, open chamber to the rows of drawers he'd found during that first visit. He closed his eyes, focusing as he had then. Was there anything in here that would guide him to what he needed? Even if there was, what he really needed was to find Ephram—

"It's late."

Rsiran turned to see Sarah standing in the doorway. She wore a low-cut white dress that swished across the floor as she walked toward him. "Is your father around?"

"You came for Father at this time of the night?"

Rsiran nodded.

She smiled. "You really are a strange man, Rsiran Lareth." She shook her head. "No. Father is not here. After what happened with the council, I'm not sure how excited he would be to see you, anyway."

"I could have been more careful."

"Careful is what keeps us where we are. I think you said what needed to be said, but the Elvraeth… They can be difficult sometimes, especially when you're as young as you are. They are more accustomed to guildlords fearing their position. When you came in, fearless as you were…"

"I wasn't fearless."

"No? It seemed that way to me. Even if you weren't, the things you can do are more than they can understand. That bothers them. I suspect it bothers others in the guild, too."

"Including you?"

Sarah shrugged. "Maybe it did when I first met you, but not any longer. I don't think you're our enemy."

He laughed before realizing that she was serious. "I'm not your enemy."

"That's what I said. But you have unique abilities. You are tied more tightly to the Elder Trees than any of the guild before you."

"I'm not the only one. You have more than one talent."

"Because I came from the merging of two lines," she said. "You are smith born, but you have shown talents of others. You can see the potential of metals. That is of the alchemists. You claim that you have begun to see when others Slide around you. That is Thenar Guild. And you have shown a predilection for pulling lorcith from Ilphaesn. Even if you aren't a miner, that is the purview of their guild. And you Travel. All of the guilds in one person."

"My apprentice claimed it was like I was an Elvraeth of the guilds."

Sarah's eyes widened a moment and then she nodded. "That would be as good a way to describe it as any."

"I thought I was supposed to be a crossing of the Blood of the Watcher and the Blood of the Elders, but I have no abilities from the Great Watcher."

"None? I thought you had some element of Sight."

He shook his head.

"Strange. There has not been a person in Elaeavn without any of the great abilities."

"Thanks."

"That wasn't said to offend, Rsiran. I find it interesting is all. You have unique abilities, but you're not dependent upon those gifted to our people when they held the Great Crystals."

"Only, I have held the Great Crystals. Twice. And I never received any of those types of abilities."

"Maybe you weren't meant to. Maybe the crystals unlocked your connection to the Elders."

Rsiran looked around the room, noting the way the walls glowed. When he had first come here, he had seen the same, but hadn't known what it was. Now that he understood his connection to heartstone and to lorcith and how he could see the potential, he understood it better but not why he would have seen it that first time, before he had ever held the crystal that had somehow unlocked in him the ability to see it.

"What are you doing here at this time?" he asked Sarah.

"I'm a guildlord," she answered.

"That's not much of a reason."

"This has been my home as much as anyplace," she said. "Since my father ascended to his position, I've basically lived here, especially since I'm the only one of the Thenar Guild."

He couldn't imagine a life where all he knew was the guild house and nothing more. In that way, it would have been more like what the Elvraeth experience walling themselves in the palace, and he couldn't imagine living like that, either. "You aren't the only one of your guild."

"Right. Now there's you."

"And Della," he added.

Her face clouded briefly. "Yes. I didn't know about her before. Strange that she should have the ability to detect Sliding. It's an ability of the Elders, and she is Elvraeth born."

Rsiran had wondered about that, too, but then Della had her strange ability with Healing as well, one that she hadn't possessed until she held one of the crystals. In that way, the crystal had unlocked something in her much as it had within him when he had held it. "There's much about Della that I don't understand."

"But you're related."

Rsiran shrugged. Della might be the first in his family who actually wanted anything to do with him, but even she had hidden much from him. Some of that was simply because she hadn't known of their connection. Were it not for his ability to Slide, she would have been able to See him and might have discovered their connection sooner. But some things she had hidden from him because she didn't think he was ready. It was possible that he wasn't, but it still stung that she hadn't attempted to share with him what might have helped him better understand what he was supposed to do. She'd even hidden the connection to the guilds from him, when they might have been able to help him earlier.

"Related isn't the same as family," he said.

"That must be important to you. I've seen how you did everything for your sister."

"Alyse... Alyse didn't choose what she did, I don't think." Rsiran still didn't know if she had been Compelled or if she had treated him the way that she had because she hadn't cared. Now it didn't matter. *He* had been the one to save her. Had he not, she would either have ended up with Venass or dead. Rsiran couldn't stomach either option happening to her, regardless of what she might have done to him. "Family isn't important to you?"

"My father is the Alchemist Guild guildlord. That we're both guildlords allows us to serve together in a way. There's a connection between us that we wouldn't have otherwise."

"And your mother? Sisters or brothers?"

"No siblings. And my mother died when I was young. I never knew her."

"She was of the Thenar Guild?"

Sarah nodded. "There haven't been many lately. The records of the guild are sparse, those of the Thenar Guild even more sparse, but what I can find tells me that we have never had many with our particular talent. Lately, it has not been useful."

"But now it is," he said.

"Knowing where others are Sliding doesn't really have that many benefits. I can help with tracking, and it allowed me to know when you appeared, and the stronger members of the guild could influence Sliding, but for most with the ability… it's sort of like the guild equivalent to Sight."

"But everyone has Sight."

"Maybe. Even then, it's not all that useful."

Rsiran watched her and shook his head. "It is when you don't have it."

"I haven't seen you struggle without Sight. In fact, I think that Sight would only have delayed your ability to learn what you can from your abilities."

"You think the Great Watcher intended for me to have no abilities so I could learn to use these ancient connections better?"

Sarah shrugged. "I can't say that I know the will of the Great Watcher. And I probably never will, not without holding one of the crystals, and since I'm not descended from the Elvraeth, I never will." She said it with more spite than Rsiran would have expected from her. "Anyway, what do we really know about the Great Watcher?"

Rsiran knew that he had experienced a connection to the Great Watcher when he'd held one of the Great Crystals. The first time, he'd felt as if he had floated above the world, but had sensed a presence with him. The second time, when he'd merged with the crystal while Traveling, there had come a sense of emptiness, a release from the pain he'd experienced when injured by Venass, and when he'd awoken, he'd possessed a greater control over the metals. What would happen if he went a third time?

Would he even be allowed?

"I'll tell Father you came for him," Sarah said.

"Or you could find out what I need to know about shadowsteel. Like you promised."

A flush came to her cheeks. "I'm trying—"

"And?"

"It's something of the Alchemist Guild. A secret of sorts. I… I can't find anything, but I intend to keep searching. I'm sorry, Rsiran. And if I see my father…"

"Please," he said.

She left him alone in the Hall of Guilds, and an idea triggered for him: What if he attempted to reach the crystals again?

There might not be anything that he could even learn, but what if he could? What more would he be able to do were he to hold one again?

But… what consequences might he face if he did?

Reaching the crystals the first time had been thought impossible, but he had managed to sneak into the room by Sliding there. The second time, he had gone in mind only, and Traveling. How else would he reach them?

Without really knowing what he was doing, Rsiran found himself tracing the steps that Ephram had led him on the first time that he'd come. He wound through darkened halls, the steady light of heartstone glowing deep within the walls. It prevented Sliding for most, but not for him. Layers of lorcith were there, as well, but less for protection. It took him a moment to realize that these weren't layers at all, just as the walls weren't really walls at all, but rather tunnels.

This was all a part of Ilphaesn.

The realization almost made him stumble.

Was this what Venass had wanted, and the reason that they had been burrowing deeper and deeper into Ilphaesn? Could his grandfather have learned that the chamber connecting to the crystals was somehow also connected to Ilphaesn?

He could almost imagine the way that the tunnel connected. It was possible that only those with Elvraeth blood would ever be able to reach the crystals, anyway, but what if there was a way for Venass to bypass those protections? Knowing the way they replicated the abilities of the Great Watcher, he wouldn't put it past them.

The tunnel stopped at a doorway. Rsiran *pushed* on the lorcith in the door to open it, letting it swing into the room.

Faint light filtered toward him, the steady blue glow from the crystals. Rsiran had been in this room once, had stood at this doorway once, and had Traveled into the room once. Now he intended to walk into the room.

Pressure at the doorway seemed determined to prevent him from entering, but he forced his way through. Not a Slide, or even something requiring his ability to *push*, this took his smith strength, that which he'd built from hours working at the forge, hammering over and over again.

He eased through the doorway.

On the other side, the air took on a still quality, with none of the hint of lorcith and heartstone that he'd detected in the hall. Had it been like that the last time he'd come here? He'd been so focused on the crystals and discovering as much about them as he could, that he hadn't really paid any attention to the feel of the air against his skin, the electrical quality that it possessed as it tingled against him, or the dank heaviness to it.

Rsiran made his way toward the crystals.

As he did, he felt something off before he recognized what it might be. The power in the room had shifted, now somehow unbalanced. He stared around the room, searching for the answer until it became obvious.

One of the crystals was missing.

CHAPTER 20

"Impossible," Ephram said from the doorway.

Rsiran stood just beyond the doorway, inside the chamber. He was the only one who could reach this side of the doorway, something that he found surprising. The rest of the guildlords stood on the other side, each peering inside, trying to determine which of the crystals had gone missing.

"Not impossible. One of the Elder Trees was destroyed," Tia said. "The protection is gone."

"We have kept this chamber under guard," Ephram said.

"I walked here and didn't see anyone," Rsiran told him.

"No one? Sarah was to watch—"

Rsiran looked to Sarah. Her face flushed. "I have watched, Father. There was no one other than Rsiran. As one of the guildlords, there was no reason he would be denied access this chamber."

"The farthest crystal is missing. Which tree does it correspond to?" he asked.

"That doesn't matter," Ephram said. "We have long suspected that the crystals somehow move, that there is no connection to the Elder Trees other than for protection."

Rsiran studied the remaining crystals. They glowed steadily, much like they had the first time he had come to this place. That time, one of them had pulsed, practically drawing him to lift it, so he had. Now they all glowed with the same intensity.

Would the missing crystal still have the same light, or would it have faded when taken from this chamber and away from the power of the Elder Trees?

That was a question he wasn't sure how to ask. Did the crystals have power of their own, or did they draw it from the Elder Trees? Since learning of the power of the Elder Trees, power that had healed not only him, but also Della, he had begun to wonder if they were more connected than most realized. What if the crystals drew upon and stored the power of the Elder Trees, concentrating it in some way? But if that were the case, then damaging the Elder Tree would have destroyed the crystal, and he suspected that he would have heard about that from the other guildlords before now.

"We will have to tell the council," Gersh said.

Ephram blanched. "I suppose we won't be able to keep it from them for long."

"How would someone have reached the crystal?" Rsiran asked.

"Other than you?" Ephram asked. "No one has ever proven capable of Sliding to this chamber. Even after the Elder Tree was damaged, we haven't managed to Slide anyone here."

"You tried this?" Gersh asked.

"We had to know whether it was possible," Tia said. "No one was successful."

"What other ways? Could they have come through the mine?" Rsiran asked.

Gersh frowned. "There is no access through Ilphaesn."

"None? I can detect the mine, and feel the way the lorcith presses on me in the tunnel. I might not have understood it the first time I came through, but it is the same as in Ilphaesn. The tunnels can connect. Whether or not they do is a different matter."

Gersh crossed his thick arms over his chest. "They do not connect."

No? As he watched Gersh, Rsiran decided he would have to check later. If there was a possibility that someone snuck into the crystal chamber through the mine, Rsiran needed to know.

That left another possibility, and one that required they go to the council. He hadn't wanted to present himself before them again so soon, but what choice did he really have?

"There's a ceremony where the Elvraeth can access the crystals, isn't there?" he asked.

Ephram's eyes narrowed. "There is. It's called the Saenr. Not all are granted access. Most Elvraeth never step beyond the door."

That must have been what Della had gone through. "Has there been one recently?"

Ephram looked to the other guildlords, and they each shook their heads.

"None?" Rsiran asked.

"We don't know. That's not something they share with us," Ephram answered.

"But you protect the crystals! Why wouldn't they share with you if they're bringing someone here?"

"Because they are the Elvraeth," Tia said. "That was the agreement made long ago. We would protect the crystals because we could not reach them, and they would be given free access to them."

He looked around the chamber. Would he even be able to find out if someone had been here? Probably not. If anyone had been here, he—or she—would have left no mark.

"What do you see?" Tia asked from the doorway.

"Nothing."

Rsiran moved to the middle of the circle of crystals. He didn't attempt to touch one—and wasn't certain whether he would even be able to reach one without it calling to him as it had the other times—instead, closing his eyes.

The power from the crystals pressed upon him, still with that strange sense of unbalance that he'd noticed when he first entered. Was it the same in the Elder Trees?

Sliding would take him to the heart of the Aisl, but there might be a better way for him to reach the Elder Trees, and for him to know what effect the missing crystal had.

Rsiran Traveled.

The separation from his body left him with a sense of nothingness, reminding him of what he'd experienced when he first Traveled here. Rising above the ground, he could see the four remaining crystals. None of them pulsed as they had before, and all still glowed steadily, as they had when he remained in his body.

Rsiran rose higher, drifting through a space between the crystal chamber and where he knew the heart of the Aisl Forest to be, letting the Traveling take him there. As he did, he stood among the massive sjihn trees, their enormous trunks rising high into the sky, blocking out all light during the day.

Power surged from four of the Elder Trees, illuminating them with a brilliant white light. There was power in that light. Rsiran had used that power before, and suspected that he could again if needed. The fifth tree remained dark, but the tree itself was still green and vibrant, showing no signs of damage. None of the guildlords seemed to know if there was anything that he could even do to help the tree. Possibly there was not, and whatever Venass had done truly had killed the power the Elder Tree stored. If there was anything that could be done, he didn't yet know what that might be.

Rsiran rose above the trees, drifting through the otherwise empty darkness with only the faint sense of the power of the trees pushing on him. From above, he could still see their bright white light. Beneath them, he detected the blue light from the crystals. Blue and white. Heartstone and lorcith.

Seeing those metals made him wonder about shadowsteel. It wasn't pure, not that he knew of, which meant that it had to be forged. From what he'd detected of shadowsteel in the past, he suspected that it required the use of both heartstone and lorcith in its creation, and because of that, he *should* be able to detect it.

Nothing from this vantage told him what had happened to the crystal, and nothing from here told him about the connection between the Elder Trees and the crystals.

Rsiran returned to his body.

He, as well as the guildlords, had thought they could continue to keep the crystals safe. Even with one of the trees damaged, they had believed they could protect them. Had it been arrogance on his part? He'd grown too confident in what he could do, but the guilds had also reassured him that the crystals were in no danger.

Would something happen to the others?

If the missing crystal was tied to one of the trees, then it made sense that with the one damaged tree they would lose one crystal, but what if Ephram was right, and there was no association? If the crystals could move, could others be taken?

This entire area had to be protected.

That meant closing access to the chamber entirely. If no one other than Rsiran could Slide into the chamber, then sealing the doors might be enough, but doing so would require more strength than he possessed.

Could he use the power of the Elder Trees?

He'd only done so once, when Della had been injured.

This was a greater need, and one that he should have considered sooner, especially knowing that Venass had already breached the Elder Trees, and they had shown far too much capability with shadowsteel, which made it all the more likely they would reach the crystal chamber.

Rsiran stepped into a Slide and paused. Sliding from this room had once been difficult, but his connection to lorcith and heartstone made it so that he barely struggled. When he emerged, he was in the place between Slides and in the heart of the Aisl.

The other time he'd done this, he had emerged *within* one of the trees, but this time he didn't want to use the energy of only a single tree. He needed to draw upon what he could from all four of the remaining Elder Trees.

Unlike when Traveling, when he was in this place—in his physical body, the air smelled of a mixture of the bitterness of lorcith and the sweetness of heartstone. The blinding light that he observed while Traveling was now muted, but in his body, he felt it pressing on him with energy and warmth.

What had he done when he'd tried to heal Della?

Somehow he had used that energy. He used it now, but unintentionally, restoring strength he hadn't known he needed, letting it fill him. Could he draw upon more, and do so intentionally?

Rsiran *pulled* on the power that he felt around him.

As he did, the sense of it began to fill him. In some ways, it was much like what he did when *pushing* or *pulling* on lorcith, or even heartstone, but in other ways, it was entirely different. With the power he pulled on in this place, he had the sense that he could do anything, only he suspected that it had to be done in this place.

Could it impact the world outside?

Rsiran wanted to return to the crystal chamber where he could attempt to use this power in a way that would protect the crystals, but he couldn't Slide while holding this power.

An option existed, one that seemed impossible, but then so was what he was doing now.

If he could Travel from here, could he return to the crystal chamber while his body remained in this space between the Slides? If so, he could pull on this power and attempt to use it within the chamber.

Rsiran took a breath, continuing to *pull* on the power all around him, and attempted to Travel.

The sensation came as a shearing, almost painful as he separated from his body while imaging the crystal chamber. Did anything even happen? Darkness surrounded him, with none of the brilliant white light of this place, and none of the blue glow from the crystals telling him he had returned to the chamber.

But he still felt the power of the Elder Trees coursing through him.

Where was he?

Rsiran focused again on the crystal chamber, but detected no sense of movement.

Nothing but darkness remained around him.

Had he reached the crystal chamber?

He attempted to move, and felt a presence near him.

Not a single presence, but several.

As he did, he realized that he hadn't left the space between Slides. He might have Traveled, but he had not left that place. Had he come to where he intended?

If he had, where were the crystals?

Unless they didn't exist in the same fashion in this place. The Elder Trees were different here, more powerful, as if this was the place that fed all of their strength. Could it be that the crystals had *no* power here?

If so, would he be able to influence the physical world where he was?

He had to try.

The only thing he could think of doing was using a method similar to forging lorcith when he didn't know *how* he needed to accomplish something, letting the lorcith guide him. Listening to its song. Rsiran envisioned a ball of power sealing the crystals, and *pushed* the power that he held out. Slowly, that power eased from him, taking on the shape that he intended. A soft and steady hum emanated as he worked, and as the humming changed, he realized he had *pushed* the power as far as he needed and stopped, knowing he was finished just as he knew with the lorcith. The chamber was now sealed.

The darkness around him changed, taking on a faint shimmery color, a faint greenish hue that he wondered if it was imagined or real.

The energy that he had *pulled* into himself was spent, and he returned to his body.

Stepping out of the space between Slides, Rsiran noted the power from the trees. Did he damage the trees using their power? Would there come a time when the trees had nothing more to offer?

Those were questions for another time. Now, he needed to return to the crystal chamber and determine if anything he'd done even mattered.

The Slide pushed against him, much like heartstone alloy once pushed against him. Rsiran breathed a sigh of relief and shifted the Slide, emerging near the other guildlords.

"Where did you go?" Ephram demanded.

"I did something I should have done before. I sealed the crystals into the chamber. Now no one can reach them. Not even me."

Sarah gasped, the blood draining from her face. The other guildlords all stared blankly at him.

Only Ephram could speak. "But the Elvraeth…"

Rsiran turned to him. "Even the Elvraeth won't be able to reach the crystals."

At least, that was his hope. Until he found a way to keep them safe, he would maintain the protection. Only then could it be removed.

Rsiran tapped on Ephram's arm and guided him away. The alchemist guildlord followed hesitantly. "I need to know what the alchemists know about shadowsteel. It's more than you've shared."

"Lareth—"

"I know. It's a secret of the guild. But if Venass has managed to take one of the crystals… Shadowsteel is what threatens us the most. They have used it to attack me, to destroy the city, and the Great Watcher only knows what else they intend to do with it. We need to know how they make it so we can come up with some way to counter it."

Ephram squeezed his eyes shut. "There is no counter," he said softly. "We discovered it as a way to understand lorcith and heartstone, but when the earliest alchemists learned what it could do and how it could be used… the recipe was hidden. Locked away. Most within the guild forgot about it, but the guildlord could not." He met Rsiran's eyes, and there was almost an accusation there. "They should not be able to make it in such quantities. Even the earliest alchemists never discovered how."

"How did they discover it?"

Without blinking, he held Rsiran's gaze. "Secrets were taken from the Hall of Guilds that should have remained protected."

Rsiran blinked, taking a step back.

Could it have been *his* fault that Venass discovered shadowsteel? Was it *his* fault that the Elder Tree died?

If so, the responsibility for stopping Venass from using it was his and his alone.

But how would he find the missing crystal and focus on stopping Venass at the same time?

CHAPTER 21

"A DANGEROUS THING THAT YOU DID." Della stood near her fire, nursing a cup of her mint tea, an orange and blue-striped shawl hanging around her shoulder. A slender metal pin—grindl and iron, he noted—held her hair in place.

"It was necessary," Rsiran said. "I should have done it when we first realized the Elder Tree was dead."

He leaned on the counter, wiping his hand absently across the crushed powder of herbs that remained. The aroma of the mint tea reached his nose as he did, but there was a sharp note—either pine or something that reminded him of whistle dust—that mixed in as well.

She shook her head. "Not dead, I don't think."

"There's no power to the tree like there is with the others."

"Perhaps not the kind of power that you can see," Della agreed, "but the tree itself still lives. That gives me hope that it can some day be salvaged."

"How can Rsiran help the tree?" Jessa asked. She sat in a chair with her legs bent up, and her arms wrapped around them. Her eyes appeared tired, and her brow remained in a constant familiar crease of worry. She'd not found any sign of Haern. Rsiran hadn't expected her to.

"Ah, you ask questions that are beyond me."

"I thought you could See things like that," Jessa said.

"I can see many things, girl, but you have witnessed the limits of my abilities."

"No more secrets, then?" Rsiran asked. He pulled one of the canisters to him and opened the lid, inhaling a pungent odor before sealing it closed again.

"I think I still have a few things you could learn." Rsiran arched a brow. Della couldn't continue to withhold information from them, especially with what he had already learned. "Maybe not about the guilds or the Elvraeth—you seem to be getting plenty of firsthand instruction there."

Rsiran tapped on one of the jars on her counter. Inside was a thick liquid, one that reminded him of the vial that Brusus carried with him. What had she made for Brusus?

"Why was what Rsiran did dangerous?" Jessa asked.

Della sighed and took another sip of her tea. "The crystals were our people's first connection to the Great Watcher. Now that he's held one of the crystals twice, Rsiran knows that. They are the reason our people have the abilities we do."

"You mean the reason the Elvraeth continue to have the strongest abilities," Jessa said.

Della nodded. "The crystals unlock potential within those who hold them. Rsiran has experienced that as well."

Jessa shook her head and turned toward the fire, staring into it. When Rsiran had returned to his smithy from the crystal chamber, he'd found Jessa there. She had learned nothing about Haern's whereabouts, almost as if he had simply Slid from Elaeavn. Either he didn't want to be found, or something had happened to him. Rsiran knew that she worried about the woman who had come for Haern in the Barth and what she might have managed to do to him, regardless of Rsiran Sliding her from the city.

"The Elvraeth have more abilities to begin with. The rest of us without abilities never have that opportunity."

Della chuckled and Jessa jerked her head around to her. "How do you think the rest of our people manage abilities? Your Sight is pretty powerful. I think Haern would agree that his ability as a Seer is potent. All within the city have some aspects of the Great Watcher's abilities."

"Not all," Rsiran corrected.

Della frowned. "Perhaps not all. But most do."

"How?" Jessa asked. She didn't look up. "The Elvraeth don't mix with those outside the palace unless they're Forgotten, and then they're banished from the city."

"That wasn't always the case," Della said. "But doesn't change the importance of the question." She limped to the counter and gently pushed Rsiran to the side as she began mixing a few powders, humming softly under her breath as she did. "The crystals gave the first powers, and help maintain them. Without the connection to the crystals, it's possible that our people will be cut off from their abilities over time, much like what happens to the Forgotten who live outside the city." She tapped a thumbnail of powder into a cup. "That is the real punishment of banishment, regardless of what the council would have you believe."

"Evaelyn and Danis remained plenty powerful," Jessa said.

"They did, but what of Inna? What of the descendants of the Forgotten born outside the city? Those who lived here and were born here would not lose their abilities, but those too long away from the crystals find their abilities begin to fade. That is why your mother did not have the same ability as her father," Della said to Rsiran. "Were she born in the city, it is possible that she would have been born with the same abilities as the rest of the Elvraeth."

Rsiran hadn't spent any time thinking about what it might have been like had his mother been born within the city, and to a father who was one of the Elvraeth. Doing so would only lead to frustration. In that, he suspected he had only a hint of what Brusus experienced. Had his mother never been exiled, he *would* have been raised in the palace. Brusus had the abilities of the Elvraeth, something Rsiran couldn't claim, so his frustration had to be much greater than what Rsiran knew.

Thinking about what might have been got him nowhere. Better to realize that he was never meant to have lived in the palace, and better still to forget about his mother entirely.

Rsiran shook himself from those thoughts. "You're afraid that sealing off the crystals will lead to the same thing happening that happens to the Forgotten?"

Della paused as she lifted a spoon of scarlet powder that smelled of ash and fire to her cup. "I think it's possible." She tipped the spoon into her cup and stirred it around. Smoke rose from it and she inhaled slowly. "Equally possible is that nothing will change. You might have done nothing more than protect the remaining crystals. I cannot See the answer."

"Better than to risk losing another," Rsiran said.

"I agree. I wonder if the council will feel the same."

Rsiran sighed. The council hadn't yet been told what he had done, and even when they found out, there likely wasn't anything that they could do. Rsiran would have to be the one to remove the protection around the crystal room, and he wouldn't do that until he was sure the others would be safe, and the missing crystal returned.

"I did what I thought needed to be done," he said.

"That's not all that bothers you."

Rsiran shook his head. "I'm responsible for Venass acquiring shadowsteel."

Della paused and watched him. "Ephram told you this?"

"When I was looking for a way to stop Josun and snuck into the alchemist guild house, I took some things. I didn't know then what they were..."

Della's eyes went distant. "I cannot See." She sighed. "They would have discovered it, regardless. Danis is too crafty for them not to."

"Della—"

She shook her head and handed the smoking cup to him. The smoke caught his nose, and Della smiled when he grimaced. "What do you smell?"

"Fire."

"Too easy. What else do you smell?"

Rsiran took a cautious inhalation, drawing the smoke into his nose. Within the smoke, there were other odors, though they were faint. He detected a woody odor, and one that strangely smelled wet, like moss on a log, mixed with an earthy scent. Other than the smoke, the other odors all reminded him of the Aisl Forest.

The smoke helped clear his head in the same way that working at the forge often did.

"What is this?" he asked.

"You asked if there was anything that I still kept from you, and I told you there was. It's time you begin to understand more than your abilities, more than Sliding and the metals that you manipulate. Especially as we must find a way to stop shadowsteel."

"Why does that matter?" Jessa asked.

Della squeezed her eyes closed. "Because I See that Rsiran will go after the missing crystal, and he will find a way to destroy the source of shadowsteel. When he does, he must be prepared."

Jessa stared at him, her gaze begging for answers that Rsiran didn't have. He hadn't told her that he would search for the crystal, but what choice did he have? He knew how powerful the crystals were, and if one of them reached Venass… Rsiran didn't want to think of what they would manage to do with it.

"I think what Haern has been teaching me should be enough."

"Perhaps for what you have faced, but not for what you will. I don't know why, but I must teach you some of what I know of herbs and medicines."

Jessa stood and made her way over to the counter. "Why do you think that? You've never offered to teach before."

"I've taught before," she said softly. "And for the same reason, I fear."

"Do you See something about Rsiran?" Jessa asked.

The old Healer shook her head. "With his ability, I have never been able to See him well."

"Then what is it? Why do you think you must show him this now?"

"Because I See it of myself. If I don't, those you care about, and those I care about, will suffer. For this reason, I must show Rsiran what I know of medicines, and he must learn how those medicines can be used as poisons."

"Poisons?" he asked. When Della nodded, an amused grin crossed his face. "Like what Haern did?"

Della sighed. "Not *quite* like Haern, I suspect, but close enough that it might not matter. Regardless, you must pay attention to what I will show you."

"I don't have time for this," he said. "I need to be focused on shadowsteel."

Della touched his arm. "Trust what I See, Rsiran."

There was a pleading note to her voice that he'd never heard from her before.

What *else* had she Seen but not shared with him?

CHAPTER 22

The council chamber had an ominous air to it today. For the second time, Rsiran stood before the Elvraeth council, but this time, he actually worried about what they might say to him and how they might react to what he had done. And regardless of what they wanted, there was no way that he was willing to release the seal around the crystals.

He wiped his hands on his pants, smearing scarlet powder—idala root, he'd discovered—across the fabric. In the last two days, he had spent nearly every waking hour working with Della. She taught with a fervor and intensity, demonstrating powders to him, showing him whole plants, making him taste things both terrible and sweet, and drink concoction after concoction so that he knew the way they were supposed to taste. Last night, she had dragged him throughout the city, stopping in nearly a dozen different shops where she purchased her powders and herbs, so that he would know what to look for when he sought his own.

The only thing that Rsiran was certain of was that Della knew *far* more than he had ever suspected. Hours of teaching him likely barely scratched at the surface.

Then Ephram sent word of the council requesting a meeting with the guildlords.

His feet thudded across the tiles. His stomach roiled, though he didn't know how much of that was from nerves about presenting before the Elvraeth council for a second time, and how much came from what Della had asked him to drink moments before he had left. It had been a thick liquid and had seemed to deaden his nerves. Now, he only wished that it had worked better.

Luthan sat in the same chair that he had when Rsiran had first come to the chamber. The old man's eyes were cloudy, but it seemed as if they were less so than they had been that day. He glanced to Rsiran's pants, and Rsiran followed the direction of his gaze, noting all the stains from his time working with Della, and wished he had taken the time to change.

Yongar stood behind his chair, his hands gripping the back. His eyes narrowed as Rsiran entered. Sasha and the other woman sat in quiet conversation, and both stopped and looked up when he appeared.

The other guildlords and Naelm were not here.

"I presume you Slid here?" Yongar said.

"To the palace," Rsiran answered. He had walked from there. He enjoyed the fact that he no longer had to fear hiding his ability to Slide, and did so openly now. As a member of the guild, he enjoyed certain benefits, but both Sarah and Ephram told him that as the guildlord, he had nothing to fear from the Elvraeth. If anything, they had to worry about what he might do. "Does it bother you?"

He shouldn't ask the question in that way, but Josun had told him how the Elvraeth had tried to tamp out the ability to Slide. At the time,

Rsiran had believed it to be an ability granted by the Great Watcher, but now, he knew it to be a gift of the Elders, one that came from the ancient clans. For the Elvraeth to attempt to eliminate it meant that they tried eliminating one of the guilds as well.

"It is a dangerous gift. One that is meant for—"

"Careful with how you finish that statement."

Rsiran glanced over to Tia and she nodded. She wore a heavy wool cloak pinned at the neck with a broach. Sweat dripped from her brow and mud stained her boots. Where had she been?

"I think the Elvraeth have done enough to stigmatize the guilds," she went on. "Were it up to you, there would be no guilds, and then where would you be?"

"Probably the same place that we are now." Naelm strode into the council chamber with Ephram at his side. The Alchemist Guild guildlord stopped next to Tia, twisting his hands together and making a point not to look over at Rsiran. What had they been talking about before they came in? Whatever it was appeared to bother Ephram.

"Where we are is because of Venass," Rsiran said.

"Indeed? And how is it that Venass managed to find the Elder Trees?" Naelm asked. He took a seat and leaned forward, looking up at Rsiran with a dark frown. "The scholars have existed for decades, and never once have they managed to reach the heart of the Aisl. Before now."

Rsiran resisted the urge to glance over to Ephram. Had he suggested that to Naelm?

His bracelets went cold and Rsiran scanned the Elvraeth, his gaze settling on a wincing Yongar. Rsiran took a step toward him, ignoring the way that Ephram reached for him. "Is this how you work with the guildlords?" He stopped across the table from Yongar. Why was it that every time he faced the council, he let his temper get the best of him?

"You would Read me rather than ask? I warn you... if you attempt to Compel me, you will find a much more severe kind of pain than you experience now?"

Rsiran held Yongar with his gaze until the Elvraeth looked away.

He moved down the table, stopping in front of Sasha and the other woman. They both met his eyes briefly before turning away from him. Luthan nodded, and actually smiled. What did the old man See of him?

When he stopped at Naelm, the Elvraeth stood and leaned into Rsiran. "Do you think you can intimidate the Elvraeth council? You have barely been raised to guildlord. What gives you the right to threaten—"

"Threaten?" Rsiran asked. "I have not threatened the council. All I have done is show that you will not use your abilities against me, much as I don't intend to use my abilities against you."

He *pulled* on the lorcith sculptures near the back of the room, dragging them forward. They were exquisitely made, and there was a time when he would have wondered how the smiths had forged them.

"I might not have been guildlord for long, but I will not be intimidated by the council. And if I discover that you have attempted to Read or Compel any of the other guildlords, you *will* face my anger."

Naelm stared at him before nodding.

"What do you intend to do about the crystal?" Naelm asked. "As guildlord, I'm sure you're aware that the protection of the crystals is the domain of the guilds. Now that one is missing..."

Rsiran took a step back. Sarah and Gersh had arrived. Sarah watched him with widened eyes, but Gersh studied him the same way the Rsiran might study a lump of lorcith and try to determine what it could become.

"I intend to discover what happened," he said. Della was right that he would, but not because he worried about the people of Elaeavn losing their abilities. He feared what would happen elsewhere if Venass possessed them. "And find any who might be involved with them."

"The Elvraeth must be allowed access to the remaining crystals while you search," Naelm said.

"You can try."

Rsiran hadn't tested what would happen to the Elvraeth if they attempted to reach the crystals, but he could no longer Slide to them, and suspected that the barrier he had placed was potent enough to restrict the Elvraeth as well.

Luthan coughed and the other Elvraeth turned to him. "You may as well tell him that we have tried, Naelm. Better yet, ask him what kind of barrier he placed."

"We can't hold a Saenr with the barrier in place," Sasha said.

"Then we don't hold the Saenr until this is sorted out," Luthan said. "The only value to the ceremony is the potential to hold one of the crystals. If one is missing, how can we know if the Saenr succeeded? What if the missing crystal is the one required?" A concerned expression passed across his face, almost as if for show. "Would we retest those who fail?"

"That will anger the families," Yongar said.

Luthan coughed. "More than when the celebrant doesn't reach the crystal in the first place? How long has it been since anyone even reached them?"

Rsiran hadn't realized how difficult it was for the Elvraeth to even reach the crystals. Given that, how had one of them disappeared?

"Someone reached the crystals recently," he said.

The council looked over to him. Naelm spoke first. "I believe that *you* have reached them. The first of the guildlords to be able to do so." He shot an accusatory look past Rsiran to Ephram. "And they had been safe until then. Why do you think that is, guildlord?" he asked.

Rsiran clenched his jaw to keep from retorting. Something about standing in front of the Elvraeth—men and women he had once feared and admired—brought out a surge of anger. Maybe it was because of what he'd seen, and how they were so willing to simply abandon their own family, banishing them from the city, or maybe it was the staggering display of wealth hidden in the warehouses down in Lower Town, kept from the people of Elaeavn who might have benefited from what the warehouse contained.

"I think years of Elvraeth exiles have finally caught up to you," he finally said.

"You dare to blame the council for what is supposed to be the responsibility of the guilds?" Yongar said. "The guilds' purpose is to protect the crystals!"

"I blame the council for the Forgotten. I blame the council for Venass. The crystals would have been safe had neither existed. And I will find what happened to the missing crystal, and I will return it."

"And then you will restore access to them?" Sasha asked.

Rsiran shrugged. "I don't know."

He Slid from the council and emerged outside the walls of the palace.

Rsiran took a few breaths, trying to settle himself. Why had he allowed himself to get so upset by the Elvraeth? He should know better. As guildlord, they might not exile him, but that didn't mean they couldn't—or wouldn't—go after his friends. What would he do if they brought Jessa before the council? What of Alyse? Was his position such that he could protect them if it came to that?

He doubted that he could.

From here, the palace jutted out from the wall of rock. The towers rose high over the city, granting the Elvraeth a view that few within the city would ever have. From below, where it appeared the palace floated, it looked as if the Elvraeth remained above the people of Elaeavn.

It didn't have to be that way. It *shouldn't* be that way. Since learning of the Forgotten and of Venass, he had wanted nothing more than to keep them from harming him or his friends. But now that he had a position within the guild, he had a different set of responsibilities, wanting to protect the city. Didn't that mean he had to protect it from the dangers within the city as well as outside the city?

A flash of light told him someone Slid.

Rsiran waited, expecting Tia to emerge.

When Luthan did, Rsiran stood in shock. "You can Slide?"

The older man chuckled. He blinked, and his eyes cleared slightly, becoming a deeper shade of green. Did he Push, much like Brusus did to hide what he could do? "I understand you have already come across one among the family with this particular ability." He looked over at the palace and a troubled look came to his face. "Much like those among the guild possess abilities of the Great Watcher, there are Elvraeth with guild abilities." He sighed. "The council thinks that we must remain separate to maintain tradition, but separate has only gotten us to where we are and no further."

"Why did you follow me here?"

"So direct," Luthan said. "A trait that I admire, but one that puts you in direct conflict with the council, I think. You might have taken a different approach with the council, though I can't say whether the outcome would be any different if you had. The crystal. You intend to search for it." Rsiran nodded. "It is difficult to See anything when it comes to the crystal, though I suspect that has more to do with your presence than anything."

"How can you See anything?"

Luthan chuckled. "My Sight is not as bad as it seems, Master Lareth."

Rsiran shook his head. "That's not what I mean. You can Slide, so how does that not affect what you can See?"

"It does. I cannot See much about myself. A weakness to most, but one that has given me a particular gift at Seeing what others ignore. Much like when I attempt to See with you, Master Lareth. When I focus on you, there is nothing but swirling colors and darkness, but when I look to the side—" He turned his head so that Rsiran would be barely more than at the edge of his vision. "Then I can See more. You are difficult, regardless. I suspect that comes from the combination of your abilities, but perhaps not."

"Why are you telling me this?"

"Because you should know what you risk, just as you should know what is at stake."

"I know what I risk if I don't find the crystal, Luthan. I might not agree with the way the Elvraeth have ruled, but I understand the power of the crystals and the reason Venass can't possess them."

The elderly Elvraeth nodded slowly. "Venass. We overlooked them for too long, and then… then they developed the ability to obscure themselves from us. Now we See nothing when it comes to them. From what I can See, they do not possess the crystal."

Rsiran took a deep breath. Knowing that Venass didn't have the crystal provided some reassurance. "Can you See where it is?"

Luthan smiled. "The ability is not quite like that. I can't force it to work on what I want to See. When I think about the crystal, there's a brightness, an intensity that makes me wonder if we might be missing something. I will have to ponder what that means." He touched a wrinkled hand to his forehead and massaged. "It is not in Thyr. The brightness… I do not See it there."

"Where? If you can find it…"

"I can't pinpoint the location like that. It is not a map so much as it is… colors, I suppose. Flashes of blue in a field of white. I don't know what it means."

Rsiran thought that he did, but why would Luthan see the crystal in a field of lorcith unless Venass had claimed it?

But knowing that they hadn't acquired it yet gave them an advantage, but how much longer would they hold the advantage? At what point would Venass realize the crystal had disappeared? They had Seers whose abilities were augmented with lorcith and heartstone, men like Haern, who would likely know the crystal was now missing.

"I have to find it before Venass does," Rsiran said.

"I think you are right that they must not be allowed to possess the crystals, but that is not the warning I would give, nor the risk I imply."

"What is it then?"

"You should know what you risk by going."

"Which is what?"

"Delay. I See danger in delay. There is darkness linked to you."

Rsiran nodded. "Because I can Slide."

"This is different. Painful in some ways. A burning darkness that would destroy much. You are the key to ending it, I suspect."

Rsiran's breath caught. Could he be talking about shadowsteel? "How?"

"I don't know, only that anything that causes you to delay risks even more than the crystal."

CHAPTER 23

Rsiran swung the sword in a rapid arc, sweeping it in the motions that Haern had taught him, fending off the imagined foe. With each swing, he imagined that three swordsmen stood opposite him, and with each swing, he made an effort to not use his ability to *push* or to Slide.

He needed clarity of thought, but he could not have that, not with what Luthan had told him, and not with what he knew he needed to do: find the crystal. That meant leaving the city. Rsiran felt certain of the fact that the crystal would not be found within Elaeavn, but he wasn't entirely certain where else to look. It wasn't as if the crystal were heartstone or lorcith that he could simply use his connection to locate it.

More than that, he needed to decide if he would take Jessa with him.

Not taking her would leave her hurt and angry, but taking her put her at risk. He feared he'd be unable to protect her. After the attack on them in Thyr, he'd already seen what he would do when she was threatened. Rsiran no longer had the same hesitation when it came to doing what was necessary to protect those he cared about, but did he dare risk that needlessly?

The door to the smithy opened, and Rsiran quickly slipped the sword into his sheath and turned toward the door.

"Master Lareth," Luca said, standing in the doorway.

"Luca, I've told you before that Rsiran is fine." He wiped the sweat from his brow.

"I'm the apprentice and you're the master. That is how it is supposed to be."

"I'm not sure how it's 'supposed' to be. When I was apprentice, it was my father."

Luca's eyes widened, and for a moment took on some of the wildness that Rsiran had often seen from him before returning him to Elaeavn. As he lifted the sculpture of Ilphaesn to his ear and took a deep breath, the expression faded. "My father is gone."

Rsiran hadn't given much thought to Luca's lineage, but he should have. With his talent for hearing the song of lorcith, he obviously had smith blood, but Luca hadn't said anything about his family, only that he'd lived alone, forcing him to sneak into the Elvraeth palace for warmth. That was the reason he'd been exiled to Ilphaesn.

"Do you know what happened to him?"

Luca shook his head.

"Where was home for you before you went to Ilphaesn?"

Luca licked his lips and slowly lowered the sculpture, cradling it in front of him. "I had no home. Ilphaesn was my home."

He needed to be more careful with Luca. He didn't want the boy thinking that he had to return to Ilphaesn, risk losing the connection that he'd formed with him. They had made real progress over the last few months. Luca had grown with his forging skill, and had an obvious talent. Rsiran had only to draw that from him. "Where did you live before you lost your home?"

"I don't remember." Hair fell across his face as he looked to the floor. Luca spoke softly, his voice catching as he did.

How young must he have been to not remember his home? Could he really have lived on the streets that long?

But Rsiran had to believe that he could. There were others he'd seen, children in the very alley outside his smithy, who appeared to live on the streets. Rsiran Slid past them, never seeing them, not as he would if he had to walk. Even then, he wondered if he would pay as much attention to them as he should.

"You have a home now," Rsiran reminded him. "The smithy is your home. The guild is your family."

Luca briefly looked up. His fingers gripped the sculpture of Ilphaesn so tightly that his knuckles whitened. "Thank you, Master Lareth."

Rsiran sighed. He shouldn't have pushed Luca this morning. He had too much else that he needed to be focused on. Trying to keep his apprentice's insanity from returning fell fairly low on his list of priorities.

"Can you work on a project for me?" he asked Luca.

"For you?"

Rsiran nodded. He usually worked with Luca, but he needed to make a few stops before he decided what he would do about the crystal. "I think you're ready, don't you?"

Luca bit his lip. "I don't know. If someone asked you to make something, they wouldn't want me to be involved."

"I don't think Brusus will mind. And this is something I think you'll do well with. I would say that it's nothing complex, but when you're forging metal, anything can be difficult."

"What is it?"

"Pots."

"Pots?" Luca repeated.

Rsiran went to his bench and searched for another that he'd made, finding it near the back of the bench. "Like this," he said, holding it up. Rsiran had made the one he held in the months before Luca joined his smithy. It was not nearly as intricate as what he might make today, but then, with a pot, there wasn't the same need for intricacy. "Brusus would like a set for his kitchen. You can check with him on what specifications he might have."

"Are you… are you sure he won't mind?"

"Brusus? He'll be happy that I didn't forget. And honestly, I did. I'm hoping that having you do this for him will keep him from getting too upset with me for forgetting him." With Brusus so focused on the Barth, he gave little thought to what Rsiran went through, and that included not worrying about how Rsiran managed to find time for forging. Anything that Luca made that would help the Barth would satisfy Brusus.

Luca took the pot Rsiran held and studied it, turning it to the side, and listening. The lorcith had a soft song that Rsiran could hear, buzzing gently. What did Luca hear when he listened? There were times when Rsiran suspected that Luca might be more attuned to lorcith in some ways. Living within Ilphaesn for as long as he had must have given him a better connection. Even the short period of time that Rsiran was there had given him a greater understanding of it.

"I think… I will try, Master Lareth."

"Good."

Luca set the pot back on the bench and went to the forge where he began shifting the coals, quickly bringing them to a soft glow. He moved with a practiced confidence that brought a smile to Rsiran's face. After the time that he'd spent with the council, and after losing the crystal, it was good to have something that he could smile about.

"Do you remember where the tunnels deep within Ilphaesn went?" Rsiran asked, thinking of the connection he'd begun to suspect between Ilphaesn and the crystal chamber.

Luca paused as he set a lump of lorcith onto the coals. "The tunnels were dark, Master Lareth."

"I know they were dark. Do you remember where they stretched?"

Luca looked over his shoulder at him. "The song was everywhere, but I was told to stay where I could hear it the loudest. I was afraid to explore any further. Was that wrong?"

Rsiran shook his head. "Not wrong. Your answer was very helpful."

Luca smiled and turned his attention back to the lorcith. A part of Rsiran wanted nothing more than to work with the lorcith, to help Luca as they forged the pots for Brusus, but doing so would take away the chance that Luca had to work on his own. And Luthan's words echoed in his mind. "I See danger in delay."

Rsiran *pulled* knives to him from his bench and Slid.

He emerged deep within Ilphaesn. White light from the lorcith buried within the walls glowed all around him. A soft breeze seemed to blow through the tunnel, what the miners had called Ilphaesn's breath. The air held the bitterness of lorcith and a dampness for which Rsiran had never found the source.

He slid deep into the mine, where it reached toward the Aisl. Down to where he'd discovered the small chamber with the evidence that confirmed Venass had been there. Given the items he'd found there, items he thought belonged to a forge, he was certain they'd made shadowsteel here. But nothing remained to would point him to where they made the shadowsteel now.

Rsiran thought back to being in the hallway—tunnel— that led from the Hall of Guilds to the chamber that held the crystals. He'd sensed the mine, the lorcith and heartstone, and felt sure there was a connection to Ilphaesn.

After glancing around, he Slid further down the tunnel, moving a couple steps at a time until the tunnel straightened. Then he could Slide more easily, following it as it continued to stretch toward the Aisl, reaching deep beneath the earth.

Rsiran paused between Slides. When he focused on the lorcith, he could detect the tunnels. Did he have to see where he was going before Sliding? As he focused, a map of sorts formed in his mind from the space left when lorcith had been mined. He traced this forward, stretching as far ahead of him as he could, before Sliding again.

When he emerged, the tunnel narrowed. Where before it had been wide enough for two or three people to walk side by side, now the walls scraped against his shoulders. He could stand upright, but were he much taller, he would have bumped his head. Sliding any farther than this would have risked him injuring himself.

Rsiran focused on the sense of lorcith all around him once again, searching for how far the tunnel might stretch. It continued much farther, still stretching toward the Aisl, but narrowed even more.

Had the guild mined this deep into the ground, or was this the work of others? Rsiran continued forward, walking this time rather than Sliding, and was soon forced to duck so that he didn't smack his head on the rock. A little farther, and his shoulders were too wide to continue, yet he could tell the tunnel went on from where he was.

How would anyone have mined this?

There didn't seem to be a connection to the crystal chamber, though if this tunnel stretched farther, eventually reaching it, Rsiran wasn't sure he would be able to follow. Short of crawling along the ground—and he wasn't sure he could do that—this was as far as he could go.

At least that much had been answered, though he still had no idea how the crystal would have been removed from beneath the Aisl. And he still didn't know where to look for shadowsteel. If it *was* his fault that Venass knew how to create it, he had to be the one to ensure they no longer could.

But he needed help.

It troubled him that so many distractions kept cropping up keeping him from his main mission of stopping Venass from harming the city and those he loved. First shadowsteel, then his friends, and then Carth searching for Haern, and now the crystal.

Taking one last look around him, he Slid from the tunnels.

CHAPTER 24

"You asked Luca to make pots for me?" Brusus asked.

Rsiran stood at the table in the Barth. Alyse had brought him a tray of food, but he'd only picked at it. It was too early in the day for the tavern to be busy, but still a few people sat around tables. No music played—not before evening time—and other than Brusus and Alyse, none of the other servers worked. "You asked me. I asked Luca."

Brusus laughed as he wiped at the table, clearing it off. "You're becoming a real master smith, you know that? Now you've taken to delegating."

Rsiran shrugged.

"What is it?"

He sighed. "I'm… I'm going to have to leave Elaeavn for a little while," he said.

Brusus stopped wiping. "What do you mean you're going to have to leave?"

Rsiran glanced around the tavern. Even as empty as it was, he still lowered his voice. "One of the crystals is missing. I have to find it quickly."

Brusus whistled softly. "Damn. Thought you said they were safe?"

"I thought they were. Now the rest are."

"Now?"

Rsiran nodded. "I placed a barrier around them. Even the Elvraeth can't access them."

A hint of a smile crossed Brusus's face. "Bet that made them happy."

"I don't care whether they're happy or not. They wanted to blame me for what happened, and blame me for the disappearance of the crystal, but had they not been exiling people from Elaeavn all these years, I'm not sure that we would have been in this situation." He sighed. "And I have to do this quickly so I can get back to stopping Venass, but it feels like everything is set up to keep me from going after them."

Brusus glanced to the kitchen before turning his attention back to Rsiran. "How can I help?"

There had been a time where Brusus's help would have mattered, but sometime in the last few months, that had flipped. Now Rsiran was no longer sure what Brusus could do to help. "You can stay here and keep the Barth running smoothly," Rsiran answered. "Keep Alyse safe. And keep an eye on Luca."

"I'm not sure that I'm the right person to keep watch over that boy."

"I'll ask Seval to as well. I don't know how long I'll be gone, and he'll need someone to continue his apprenticeship."

Brusus grinned. "You're taking your responsibilities with his apprenticeship seriously, aren't you?"

"He's the first person trained in... maybe generations," Rsiran began, "who hasn't been told to ignore the call of lorcith."

"You didn't ignore it."

"I didn't," he agreed, "but that doesn't change the fact that I was told I should. I think about it sometimes. What it would have been like had I listened to my father and managed to ignore the call of lorcith. Would I eventually have lost the ability to hear it, or would I have ended up where I am, regardless? With Luca, he doesn't have to worry about being able to hear the call of lorcith. He's not being taught to ignore it as he learns, told how that is the key to what he can do as a smith."

"And he doesn't have to worry about the supply of lorcith, either."

Rsiran smiled. "Not that, either. It makes the knives I've made for you less valuable. I'm sorry about that."

Brusus waved his hand. "Ah, don't worry about it. I don't need the coin the same way I used to. I've got a reputable business now, you know."

"I've never asked… What did you do that got you into debt?" Rsiran asked. He knew how Brusus had owed Josun, and because of that, he had ended up taking on the job that had nearly killed him, and had pulled Rsiran and Jessa into Josun's plan, but not much of what Brusus had been into before that.

Brusus glanced to the kitchen. "That's a story for another time."

"Did it have to do with finding your mother?" He shouldn't ask, but he had often wondered how much of that search had played into what Brusus had done in the time before Rsiran had met him. They had faced the Forgotten, but as far as he knew, they hadn't found Brusus's mother.

Brusus turned back to face him, his eyes flaring a darker green. "Maybe once it was. Before. Now that we've learned what we have about them… I don't know if I want to know, Rsiran. Is that awful of me?"

Rsiran shook his head. "Not awful. And I understand. I've wanted nothing more than to understand my family, and where has it gotten me?"

"Chased. Captured. Nearly killed a few times over," Brusus said with a grin. "You're not really the best example of how to find out the secrets about your family, are you?"

Rsiran laughed. The laughter felt good, as did sitting with Brusus. Strange as it was, Brusus had been his first real friend. Growing up as a smith, even before his apprenticeship, he had spent his days in the smithy at his father's side. That hadn't left much time for friendships. Maybe that was why he valued his connection to Brusus and Jessa as much as he did.

"I'm not the best example of many things."

"I don't believe that, and you shouldn't, either. Seems to me that—" He looked up and his eyes paled. "Ah, see that? In time to boost your ego."

Jessa came through the door and sat next to them. She fixed Brusus with a hard stare, and he only shrugged. "What are you telling him?"

"Well, I *was* telling him how lucky he was to have found you, but maybe I'll tell him he needs to rethink that. A guildlord has options, you know."

Jessa swatted at Brusus, and he hurried away, smiling as he did. "Better get back to the kitchen. But, Rsiran, if you do find that you need anything, let me know. You have only to ask."

Jessa waited for him to disappear, shaking her head at him the entire time. "Damn man," she muttered. "Where have you been? I've been looking for you all over the city."

"The smithy. Ilphaesn. And now here."

"Why Ilphaesn?"

He explained what he worried about when he'd been in the crystal room, and then about what he'd discovered when he went to Ilphaesn. "I can't imagine how they managed to mine it out. There was barely enough room for me to walk through there sideways."

"Maybe it's a natural cave," Jessa said. "There are others like that."

"It's possible," he agreed. Ilphaesn had a few other places that were naturally made. Most of the mineshafts connected to them.

"You don't think so."

"The walls were smooth. I haven't seen that in naturally occurring tunnels."

"Maybe the guild sent their children in to mine," Jessa said, plucking a biscuit off his plate that he'd left untouched. "Or maybe there are tiny people that we haven't seen who hollowed out that mine."

"Don't have to be tiny," Rsiran said. "We're taller than those outside the city."

Jessa shrugged between bites.

"Why have you been searching for me?" Rsiran asked.

"Because of Haern and the crystal."

"Haern wouldn't have taken the crystal."

Jessa shook her head. "No, I don't think he would have. Haern didn't want that kind of power. If he did, he would have stayed with Venass. But what if the woman chasing him had been after it? You said that she had some kind of skill. That she managed to know when you were Sliding and was able to counter it."

The timing would have been right, but that didn't answer how she would have managed to reach the crystal. There didn't seem to be any access other than Sliding, but if she *had* been the one to take it, would he be able to get it back from her? She was talented—maybe more than what he could manage. And Haern suggested that she had a network of spies.

"She was skilled," Rsiran said, "but I didn't get the sense that she had come here intending to take one of the crystals."

"No. She came to take Haern."

"He left on his own," he reminded Jessa. And the timing couldn't have been any worse—they *needed* Haern now. If Rsiran could find him, then he could take the next step… either finding the crystal or learning what he could about shadowsteel—or both at once.

"That's what we think, but what if that's not what really happened? It's not like Haern to simply disappear like this."

"Really? I don't know Haern nearly as well as you, but it seems like that is the kind of thing that he *would* do, especially if he thought it would protect you."

"Like you?"

"Like…" Rsiran reached across the table for her, but she pulled away. "I'm not trying to run away to protect you."

"Aren't you? You think you need to find the crystal—"

"I *do* need to find the crystal."

"—but you think you can do it without me. Without Brusus. And that's not all that you're after, so don't even try to convince me of that." She glanced toward the kitchen. Brusus and Alyse came out together, him leaning toward her as he whispered something softly into her ear. Alyse smiled, so relaxed compared to the terse person that Rsiran had known when they had lived in their parents' home. Was it something that Brusus did that put her at ease, or was it simply getting away from their mother and her attempts to Compel her? "Did you intend to have anyone go with you, or will this just be more of the same?"

Rsiran leaned back, considering his answer. He had intended to act alone. Not because he wanted to be alone—the Great Watcher knew he would prefer to have Jessa with him—but because he didn't want to worry about what might happen to her. When working alone, there was the potential to Slide himself to safety without fearing what might happen to her. If she lost contact with him, or he wasn't able to reach her, or she lost the lorcith on her that allowed him to detect her, or… any one of countless other problems he could come up with. None of them made him feel better about taking her with him.

But he'd been alone, and knew what it was like. If she were with him, she might help him see things that he couldn't. Not because of her Sight, but because of her training as a sneak, and her experience.

"I can't do this without you," he said.

"You're not leaving me here… What?"

"I need you to come with me," he repeated.

"Damn right you do."

"But I'll need someone else too."

"I'm sure Brusus will help, especially since it's Haern that we're talking about—"

Rsiran shook his head, not sure that who he intended would even agree. "Not Brusus."

"Not Brusus? But think about what would have happened in Thyr had he not been there."

Rsiran closed his eyes. The memory of Thyr and the attack in the hall came to him far too easily. That had been the first time he had intentionally attacked someone, the first time he had used what Haern had taught him, and he had done it to keep his friends safe.

He opened his eyes and looked toward the front of the tavern where Brusus and Alyse sat at a table together, talking quietly. Brusus seemed to detect Rsiran watching and looked up, a tight smile on his face as he reached across the table and took Alyse's hand. Rsiran couldn't pull Brusus from his sister, much like he couldn't risk Alyse losing happiness now that she'd found it.

"Brusus belongs here now," he said. "He could help, but I don't know that he would be able to help nearly as much as we need."

"Who then? And if you say Sarah, I might stab you with your own knife."

Rsiran hid the smile that came to him. "I thought about asking Sarah…"

Jessa reached toward her belt, and Rsiran raised his hands, laughing.

"I think Valn might be upset if I don't ask," he said with a grin. "I've fought next to him. I can trust him, and he knows what shadowsteel can do. If Venass is involved, we need others who can fight well with us." Rsiran tried thinking about who else he might ask, but couldn't come up with anyone.

What did it mean that those he once had sought for help no longer could provide what he needed?

Jessa nodded. "Fine. Then when do you intend to do this?"

"I have a few more stops to make. Then we can go."

CHAPTER 25

The inside of Seval's smithy had much of the same appearance as Rsiran's. The massive forge along the back wall glowed hot, and the master smith had a piece resting on his anvil that he worked, turning in between each strike of his hammer.

When Rsiran emerged in the smithy, Seval barely glanced up to nod.

He walked to where Seval worked, and listened to the sound of the lorcith. There was a subtle satisfaction in the song, one that told Rsiran how Seval worked with the metal rather than forcing it. That made him smile, as did the fact that much of what the smith made was now with lorcith. Now that the flow of lorcith was no longer restricted, the smiths used lorcith in quantities that once would have seemed obscene, something that irritated the miners. Other smiths tried to listen for the song, straining to hear what they had once attempted to ignore, though most still hadn't managed to hear it yet. The fact that they tried meant that things were changing.

Seval paused as he hammered. "Look at the schematics and see if I've got this right." He tapped at the hot metal a few more times, flattening it slightly.

Rsiran made his way to the bench that ran along the back of the smithy, one much like the bench that Rsiran had in his smithy, to look at the roll of parchment held open with a few smaller forgings. Since Rsiran had been welcomed into the guild, Seval had spent time working with him on various aspects of running a smithy that Rsiran hadn't learned from his father, things like the proper mixture of oil in the quench, the best places to source coals, but most importantly, how to read schematics. He had never learned enough from his father to make him proficient, so Seval's willingness had been necessary for him to grow as a smith. He still didn't have the same skill as others in the guild, aside from his connection to the metals, but he was learning.

What Seval worked on appeared to be another forging for the Servants of the Great Watcher. The schematics showed a complicated series of blocks tied together with a length of chain. From the diagram, he could tell that Seval worked on one of the blocks.

"What is it?" Rsiran asked, turning back to Seval.

Seval rested his hammer on the forging as he paused. "Servants hired me to make this. Something for their temple, I suspect."

"You get a lot of work from them."

Seval wiped his sleeve across his forehead. "You would, too, if you would open your smithy for commissions. The word is out, Rsiran. Others want access to your work. The rest of the guild… we're considered second rate compared to this new smith."

Rsiran flushed. "When the others can hear lorcith, there won't be the same distinctions."

"Not sure that will matter. *I* can hear it now, and won't deny that it helps in ways that I never would have imagined, but that doesn't mean

I can make the same things that you do. Do you know that people visit your friend's tavern just to see that sjihn tree you made?"

He hadn't. The Wretched Barth had been busier, but that had been because of his sister's cooking, hadn't it?

"I didn't know," he said.

Seval smiled. "You've got some of the other smiths working harder, wanting to prove we can do the same quality of work."

"I don't want to be the reason there's competition within the guild."

"No? Seems to me that a little friendly competition is good. The master smiths understand that you have a different handle on lorcith than the rest of us. That's part of the reason you were welcomed to the guild without conventional training. And a few of us hope that we'll find a way to use lorcith in the same way that you can."

Would the other smiths be able to *push* on lorcith? He thought the ability was because of his smith bloodline, but with everything that he managed that was tied to the Elders, he was no longer certain.

"I'll show you as much as I can," Rsiran said.

Seval struck at the metal a few times before carrying it to the coals to heat it once more. "I know you will. In some ways, you're the best guildlord the Smith Guild has had in years."

"I'm not sure the council would agree," Rsiran said.

Seval's eyes widened slightly. "The council?"

He debated how much to share with Seval, but the man was a friend. "I had to present myself to the council when raised to guildlord."

Seval wiped his hands on his thick leather apron. "Suppose that makes sense. Guildlords serve as something like the council, even though we sit beneath the Elvraeth."

"I don't believe that," Rsiran said. "The guilds are at least their equal. And I worry about what the Elvraeth intend, Seval. They aren't pleased with me right now. With any of the guilds. Those in the guilds fear them, when we don't have any reason to."

Seval smiled. "Maybe *you* don't, but the rest of us… We only have a single talent and whatever the Great Watcher gifted us. That sits us beneath the Elvraeth." He shrugged and pulled the forging from the coals and brought it back to his anvil. "We've always had the guilds to protect us, and the guildlords to deal with the Elvraeth, but there has never been a question about where we belong."

Seval continued working at the metal, but paused to tip his head as he seemed to listen while hammering it.

Rsiran wouldn't argue with Seval. His time as guildlord hadn't been long, but he'd seen the way the council treated the guilds, just as he had seen the importance of the Elder Trees and their ties to the people of Elaeavn. The Elvraeth might have the crystals, but the guilds had access to a power just as great. It was the reason the council feared losing power, and the reason he had to keep the guilds unified.

"I need your help with something," Rsiran said.

"Of course."

"I need to be gone for a time. Will you work with Luca?"

Seval looked up between strikes with his hammer. "I'd ask where you were going, but seeing as how you didn't offer, I suspect you either can't share or don't know."

"Don't know," Rsiran said.

Seval nodded. "My smithy could use a good apprentice, especially after what happened with the last one…"

"Luca will be pleased. I think he'd prefer you over me, anyway."

"When he reaches journeyman, he'll rotate through each of the master smiths."

How would Luca do with that tradition? He could hear the lorcith better than any of the master smiths, and if anyone would be able to learn to use the potential of lorcith, to *push* on it, it would be Luca. What would happen if Luca's ability rivaled Rsiran's? The other smiths might not have as much that they could offer him.

Seval set his hammer down and looked at Rsiran. "So. Is all of this your attempt to ignore the request to take back the Lareth smithy?"

"I…" He hadn't thought much about the request. There had been too much going on for him to focus on that. "After this is over, I'll consider."

"Don't consider," Seval said. "Do it. We need a Lareth in that smithy. More than that, we need to have the guildlord closer. When you're down there… not as many want to take the time to reach you," Seval said. "And we need you, Lareth. You're good for the smiths. I know you still have a hard time believing it, but it's the truth."

"I'll think on it," Rsiran said again.

Seval watched him a moment and then nodded before turning back to the cooling lump of lorcith on his anvil. "Send Luca whenever you need. I have a pile of projects that he can help with."

Rsiran wanted to say something more rather than leaving on this note, knowing that Seval wanted more from him, but what could he say without committing to something that he wasn't sure he could, or wanted to do.

Focusing on the different lorcith collections in the city before finding the one that he sought, Rsiran Slid away from the smithy.

He emerged on the edge of the Aisl Forest. The earthy scents struck him first, but the overwhelming stillness followed. Somewhere near here was the hut where Brusus had held his father after Rsiran rescued him from Asador. Why would Valn be here?

Lorcith flickered and reappeared.

Rsiran spun, preparing to *push*, when Valn emerged from his Slide about ten paces away. A sheen of sweat covered his face, and the hardness of his green eyes matched the frown on his face. He gripped a sword tightly, as if ready to swing.

"Practice?" Rsiran asked.

Valn grunted. "Damn, Lareth. I could have attacked you."

"You could have, but you didn't."

Valn slipped his sword into his sheath. He was a lean man, and his dark hair matched his expression. A thin cloak covered his shoulder. "I didn't." He turned and gestured to the small clearing that spread around them. A few sjihn trees grew here, but they were small compared to those found deeper in the forest. Oaks and elms rose up in between. "After what happened in Thyr, I've been trying to prepare for the next."

"I don't know what we can do to prepare for shadowsteel other than try to understand it."

"We *could* stop the bastards from making it."

Rsiran's expression soured. "If we could figure out *where*."

"Isn't that what you're supposed to be doing?"

"I tried." He didn't want to admit that he'd Traveled to Venass, not after how they had struggled as much as they had in Thyr. "And I think it's my fault they know how."

He hated admitting that, but Valn deserved to know.

"I doubt that."

"I took something from the alchemists once."

Valn snorted. "And you think it's the key to shadowsteel? If Ephram lets you believe that… it would be *his* fault then, Lareth. The guildlord is supposed to protect that sort of thing." He shook his head. "That's what brings you out here for me today?"

"Not all of it." Having Valn dismiss his concerns felt… freeing in some ways. Maybe others wouldn't blame him, either. "I was hoping that you might help me with something. It'll be as dangerous as Thyr."

Valn's eyes narrowed. "Never easy with you, is it? And this is about shadowsteel?"

Rsiran turned so that he faced the distant Elder Trees. He could practically feel them, especially now that he knew the power the trees possessed could be used. "Not this time. Not entirely."

Valn frowned. "You're talking like a guildlord now. I think I liked you better when you were just Lareth."

Rsiran forced a smile. "When the Elder Tree was damaged, I worried what that meant, and what might happen to the crystals."

"The guild watches them," Valn said. "*I* watch them when I'm assigned."

"The guild watches, but even that was not enough."

Valn lowered his voice to a whisper and leaned toward him. "You're not telling me what I think you're telling me."

Rsiran nodded.

"The crystals are gone?"

"Not all. We don't know when, or how, but one is missing."

"The others—"

"Are protected. I used the power of the Elder Trees to protect them. I should have done it sooner, but didn't know I could." He flushed with the admission. Had he only attempted it sooner, done what was needed as guildlord, the crystals would have been safe, but he had not. He'd been too focused on looking for the shadowsteel forge... and his father... and Danis.

"Great Watcher," Valn whispered. "Was it Venass? How'd they get into the city?"

"I don't know. I have to assume that it was. That's why I need your help again. I think it's up to the two of us, and Jessa, to find the crystal and return it to the city."

"But if it's Venass, we won't know, will we? Any time we've found any of their people, we've ended up killing them. Can the council help?"

It was a measure of how much the crystal meant to everyone that Valn was willing to ask the council's help. "In their own way, they will. They've told me that it's not in Thyr," Rsiran said. "Beyond that…"

Luthan hadn't been able to See that. The crystal was out there, blue amid a field of white.

Rsiran believed that he could find it… and wondered if one of the councilors—likely Luthan—would need to come with them. He hadn't considered bringing the old man with him before, but if he would come along, they might be able to at least match the power that Venass possessed.

"Beyond that what?" Valn asked.

"Beyond that, I think we'll need more help than I suspected." He turned back to Valn. "Will you help with this?"

"With the crystal? I'm of the guild, Rsiran. That is why we exist—to protect the crystals. More than that, I'm with you. I'll help."

Rsiran let out a relieved sigh. "Thanks. And Sarah—"

"She'll want to come, too. I'll talk to her. We'll get this solved, and then we'll figure out a way to deal with this shadowsteel they use too. You don't have to do this on your own, Rsiran."

He nodded, thankful that Valn was willing to help, all too aware of how his friends had changed with the shifting of the attacks. He still had Jessa, but Brusus was gone, as was Haern. Now he had to rely on others he didn't know nearly as well. That made him nervous, but the guilds had to work together, even if that cooperation didn't come from the guildlords.

CHAPTER 26

The flame flickered in the hearth of his smithy, piercing the darkness. Rsiran stood with Valn and Jessa, collecting knives from his table and strapping them to his belt, and stuffing a few of the smaller knives into pockets. He belted on the sword and hesitated when looking at the shield. Haern hadn't taught him how to use it, and he worried that he might look ridiculous carrying it.

"Just bring it, Lareth," Valn said. He stood next to Rsiran at the bench, testing a few of the remaining knives before settling on a pair of long, lorcith-made blades.

"He'll probably hurt himself with it somehow." Jessa rolled her lock-pick set into the leather carrying sleeve and slipped it into her pocket. She patted her belt and nodded to herself, as if pleased to find the knives still sheathed there.

"I'm not really sure how to use a shield, but the lorcith wanted me to make it." That was important to him, especially since he didn't really know why he'd made it.

"The metal wanted you to make it?" Valn glanced from Jessa to Rsiran, an amused expression on his face.

"Yeah, that's how I reacted the first few times he told me that," Jessa said. "You get used to it. And most of the time it's right." She tapped her bracelets and winked.

Valn glanced at his wrists a moment. "I'm not even certain these work."

"Ours work. Not sure about yours yet, either," Rsiran said.

"You said they'd go cold." Valn twisted the narrow bands of lorcith and heartstone around his wrists. "Hasn't happened when we've fought Venass."

"Yet," Rsiran said. "If they try to Read or Compel you, you'll be thankful you have them."

"So who's this other person we're waiting on?" Valn asked.

"Hold on," Rsiran said, offering his arm.

"Lareth—I can Slide myself."

"Not here."

Valn frowned and grabbed onto Rsiran's arm. Jessa took the other.

Rsiran *pulled* them into a Slide. In addition to saving his energy, it had the added benefit that it couldn't be tracked easily. Sarah had not been happy to learn that she wasn't invited on this trip. He didn't think she would follow them, but he didn't want to risk her influencing his Sliding, either.

They emerged in an upper hall of the palace.

Blue light glowed around them, the heartstone lamps similar to the alchemical potential that he saw from heartstone. A long, plush carpet ran the length of the hall. Three ornately decorated doors were set into the walls.

"How did you know where to take us?" Valn asked.

"I've been here a few times."

Valn glanced at the doors. "To the palace?"

"I wasn't invited the first couple of times."

Valn fought back a grin. "Does the council know that their newest guildlord Slid inside their palace?"

"They know."

Rsiran spun. Luthan stood behind him carrying a satchel over his shoulder and wearing a traveling cloak. His rheumy eyes were clearer than the last time that he'd seen him. "Luthan. I came for you—"

Luthan leaned to the side and glanced past them. "Yes. I Saw that you would."

"I thought you couldn't See anything when it came to you. Or to me."

Luthan smiled. "We're not the only ones here, are we now, Master Lareth. And I think it is time that you depart if you don't want others to find you here. Tanis may be young, but she has particular talent, especially when it comes to Seeing."

Rsiran hesitated. It might be helpful to have another Seer with them, but that risked too many of the council. Taking Luthan was a great enough risk as it was.

"I need you to help. With what you can See—"

"My place is here," Luthan said. "And there is no way I can leave without others noticing."

"You can't go out of the palace?" Rsiran asked. "But you Slid to me from the palace!"

"Outside the palace. I walked first."

Valn shot Luthan a questioning look. "You can Slide?"

"Not all have lost the ancient talents," Luthan said. Turning to Rsiran, he shook his head. "Unfortunately, unlike you, I cannot Slide beyond the walls of the palace. The travelstone prevents me."

"Travelstone? Is that the same as heartstone?" Jessa asked.

"Perhaps once, but when the first builders added it to the rock that became the palace, it turned into something that Master Lareth should not have been able to Slide past." His eyes went distant a moment, and he turned to Rsiran. "Master Lareth—will you Slide us from here?"

Rsiran held out his arms, and all three of them grabbed on. He *pulled* in a Slide, drawing them away from the palace and emerging in the heart of the Aisl Forest.

The massive sjihn trees rose around them. These were not the Elder Trees, but they were close enough that Rsiran could feel the pull from them. All he had to do to access that power was step into a Slide and pause in the place between. The temptation to use that power against Venass was there, but so far, he hadn't risked it. Doing so felt like a violation of the Elder Trees, as if they wouldn't want to be used in such way.

"Why this place?" Luthan asked.

"You knew I was coming," Rsiran said.

Luthan glanced from Rsiran to the others with him. "There are things that I Saw that told me those close to you were coming. This woman," he said, motioning to Jessa, "and your Sliding friend. I Saw that they would come to the palace this evening. I saw that it was tied to stopping shadowsteel, though *how* remains unclear."

"You Saw us?" Jessa asked.

Luthan nodded.

"Then you would have known the other times we came," she said.

Luthan nodded again. "Master Lareth's protection can only extend so far. Like many things, there are limits."

She looked to Rsiran. "What about when Venass tries to See us?"

"Venass would not have Seers like me." Luthan didn't sound as if he boasted, making it as a statement.

"They had Haern," Rsiran said.

"And he is not like me."

"No?" Jessa asked. "We've seen the way that Venass augments their Seers abilities. They use lorcith and heartstone to make their Seers more powerful. Do you really think that you're still more skilled than them?"

"And shadowsteel," Rsiran added.

"Interesting that they use the implants to somehow harness abilities of the Elders to augment those of the Watcher," Luthan said.

"It also grants abilities of the Elder," Rsiran added. "They can manipulate lorcith."

"As well as you?" Luthan asked.

"Not as well as me, but the point is that they—"

"Much like with your lorcith, they might add to their ability, but I do not think they could reach the same level of skill as someone born to it."

"Haern was born to it," Rsiran said.

"He was born with some talent, but strength is another thing entirely."

"How do you know?" Jessa asked.

"There are many things that I can See. Strength is but one." Luthan gazed up into the trees. The sjihn trees here stretched high overhead, spreading their branches wide. The bases of the trunks were nearly a dozen paces wide, but still half the size of the Elder Trees. "They are here?"

"These aren't the Elder Trees," Rsiran said.

"I can See that they are not. You fear showing me the trees?"

"You can Slide. You have the same right to them as I."

"Lareth—" Valn started. "He's not of the guild."

"The guild doesn't own the trees, either, Valn. It's like the crystals with the Elvraeth."

"Still you won't bring me to them," Luthan said.

"That's not why we're here. I stopped here for a different reason."

Valn watched him, a curious expression on his face. "What might that be?"

"Yeah," Jessa added. "What?"

"Wait for me."

Jessa frowned but nodded.

Rsiran took a step into a Slide and paused, stopping at the place in between in the midst of the Elder Trees, needing to determine if he could hold onto this power. If he could, there would be something that Venass didn't yet understand, and wouldn't be able to counter.

As he stood here, he *pulled* power to him, letting it fill him. Rsiran *pulled* on more and more, drawing all the strength he could until it practically seeped back out through his pores. He held onto it, and then Slid back to the Aisl and the others.

Stepping out of the Slide, the energy from the Elder Trees washed away from him, slipping free as if it couldn't exist in this world. He felt invigorated, strengthened, but couldn't hold onto the power as he wished he could.

"What did you do?" Valn asked.

Jessa watched him, seeming to know what he did. "Did it work?"

He shook his head. "I didn't think that it would, but I wanted to know for sure, especially this close."

"Did what work?" Luthan asked.

"Are we ready?" The other advantage of Sliding to that place alone was that Luthan wouldn't be able to See where he went. Rsiran needed him, but could he trust him? Della and Brusus might be Elvraeth, but Luthan was different. Not only was he Elvraeth, but he sat on the council.

"Where do you think we start?" Valn asked.

Rsiran nodded to Luthan. "I thought that our Seer might be able to guide us."

"It doesn't work like that, Master Lareth. I might be able to See aspects of the crystal, but as I believe I told you before, it is not a map."

"What can you See? There has to be something that gives us an idea of where to start."

Luthan watched Rsiran for a moment, hands clasped in front of him. He seemed as if he wanted to argue, but nodded, his cloudy eyes going wide as he seemed to stare through Rsiran.

"This is a mistake," Jessa said to him.

"We need their help."

"Sure. Valn's help," she said, nodding to where Valn paced slowly in a circle around them. He kept one hand on the hilt of his sword, and tossed his gaze around him. "But you brought one of the members of the council with us."

"He agreed to come."

Jessa watched Luthan. "For what reason? The only thing we know about the Elvraeth is what they've been willing to do to others of their family. What happens if he decides that he is done helping? Or if you find the crystal, and he wants to claim it for himself?"

"Luthan wouldn't do that—"

"Are you sure? Can you be sure what he'll do? What if the only reason he agreed to come was so that he could make sure he got access to the crystal?" She squeezed his arm, forcing his attention back to her. "There are other Seers we could have asked, Rsiran. Haern or Della would have helped."

"Della doesn't leave the city," Rsiran reminded her. "And part of this is about finding Haern while we search for the crystal."

"I still don't like it."

"I know," he said.

Luthan let out a sharp breath and turned to face them.

"What did you See?" Rsiran asked.

Luthan touched crooked fingers to his forehead. "What you ask of me is difficult, Master Lareth."

"I understand, but even you have to know how important it is for us to prevent Venass from taking the crystal."

"Even me?" Luthan asked.

"Elvraeth," Jessa clarified.

"I'm not sure what you intend by that statement."

"I intend," Jessa said, starting forward. Rsiran had to grab her arm to keep her from getting too close to Luthan. "I intent to point out that the Elvraeth sat in the palace and did nothing while the rest of Elaeavn was attacked. You did nothing when Venass entered the city. Nothing when they hurt people of your city. Nothing to stop them."

Luthan glanced over to Valn who had stopped pacing and watched Jessa with interest. "The guilds ensure that we have capable protection."

"The guilds?" Jessa sputtered. "Just because they provide the constables, that doesn't mean they provide any real protection. Think of what you could have done to help in the attack."

"What form would that have taken," Luthan asked. "Would you have me Read Venass? I think I would find that difficult. Perhaps you would like my Sight?" He smiled as he said it, stepping closer and making his eyes somehow appear even cloudier. "Would you like my ability as a Listener? The only thing that *might* have been beneficial would have been Seeing, but even in that, what I could See told me that I was unnecessary." He turned to Rsiran. "The guilds forget how they have protected our people through the years. They forget their purpose. Thankfully, Master Lareth has not."

He turned away from them. "Now, if we are about done with discussing what I have not done, let me tell you what I might be able to do. There is a place I See."

"What kind of place?" Jessa asked.

"One that is tied to you," he said, nodding to her. "Cort. That is where we must go."

CHAPTER 27

The Slide took them out of the Aisl Forest and to Cort. Rsiran emerged on a grassy plain overlooking the city. In the darkness of night, some candles flickered in windows, like stars in the sky, but the rest of the city remained dark. The sliver of moon overhead wasn't enough to light the city.

Much was dark around him. Were it not for the lorcith and heartstone his companions carried, he wouldn't be able to see anything.

"That's Cort?" Jessa asked.

"From what I remember," Rsiran said.

Valn stared into the darkness. "That is Cort. A strange city, and dangerous."

"It didn't seem dangerous when we were there before," Rsiran said.

Valn turned to him. "You mean the market where we were attacked for asking questions?"

"We didn't know there were that many of Venass here," Rsiran said.

Valn shook his head with a smile. "Still don't think we should go in at night."

Rsiran laughed softly. "We have to for the crystal." Turning to Luthan, he asked, "What do you See here?"

Luthan blinked. "It is hazy."

"I thought you said you were a powerful Seer," Jessa said.

"I am, but Master Lareth exerts an equally powerful influence. There is only so much that one Sees when he is involved. As I have told him, there are ways to See around it, but they are difficult even at the best of times, and often the meaning is obscured. What you are asking—wanting me to understand what I See immediately—requires great focus."

"Then how are we—"

Rsiran touched her arm, and she turned her frustration to him.

"You have the four of us hunting for the crystal, Rsiran, when it should be all of Elaeavn looking."

"If all of Elaeavn looked, what would happen if someone else found it first?" he asked softly. "What would happen if someone who sides with Venass or sympathizes with the Forgotten discovers the crystal first?"

Jessa clenched her fists, but nodded. "Fine."

She turned away from him and stared down into Cort.

Luthan made his way over to Rsiran. "I thought you said the Forgotten were disbanded?"

He turned to the Elvraeth councilor. "I haven't said much of anything about the Forgotten to the council."

"You did not, but the other guildlords presented to the council how the threat of the Forgotten had been neutralized."

"We stopped their leader," he said. "Evaelyn Elvraeth."

He watched Luthan for a reaction, thinking that Luthan might be upset at his mentioning her name, but he only nodded. "Said to be a powerful woman. A Reader of much skill."

"Not only a Reader," Rsiran said. "She Compelled as well."

"A dark ability," Luthan noted.

"Careful using those words around Rsiran," Jessa said.

Luthan slipped his hands up the sleeves of his cloak as he watched Jessa. "I meant no offense. Only that using the abilities of the Great Watcher in such a way leads to—"

"To darkness?" Rsiran asked. "Like Sliding?"

Luthan smiled. "I think you know that I would never make the accusation that Sliding is a dark ability."

"Some of the Elvraeth had," Rsiran said.

Luthan glanced to Valn before turning back to Rsiran. "How long have you been guildlord, Master Lareth?"

"A few months."

"And how much time were you a part of the guilds before that?"

Where was he going with this? "You know how much time."

"Yes. You were not part of the guilds before you became guildlord. You were barely a part of the city, a man with barely any abilities given to him by the Great Watcher, and nearly exiled by his father."

"You had better have a point," Jessa said.

"Trust that I do. You say that you're descended from Danis Elvraeth, which should have given you the same connection to the Great Watcher as I have. Your Lareth bloodline ties you to the ancient smiths. You could trace those connections back centuries were you to access the archives."

"I know all of this," Rsiran said.

"You know all about your heritage, but you know next to nothing about the guilds and the Elvraeth. When you accosted the council, I thought that perhaps you knew more than you did, but the more time I spend with you, the clearer it becomes that was incorrect. Your anger stems from what you experienced, not from traditional rivalries."

"Rivalries?" Valn asked. He had turned his attention away from Cort and now watched Luthan with a hot intensity. "Is that what you would call it when the Elvraeth tried to eradicate an entire guild?"

Luthan watched him carefully. "I share the same gift, young man."

"You might share the same gift, but you're part of the reason that those of the guild haven't been able to Slide openly for years. You're the reason that people view what we can do as—"

Rsiran gently *pushed* on the lorcith Valn wore, nudging him back a few steps. He had continued to stalk toward Luthan, and was nearly to the point that he looked as if he might attack him.

"Easy, Valn," he said. "That's not why we're here."

Valn glared at Luthan a moment longer and then shook himself, forcing a smile onto his face. "You're right, Lareth. That will be later."

Rsiran glanced at Jessa, but she kept her focus on Luthan. "What do you See in Cort?" he asked again.

"Not in Cort, but outside. I could show you, but I will need to travel there myself, I think."

Rsiran reached into his pocket and pulled out a lorcith coin, much like the one that they'd slipped to Haern. He handed it to Luthan, who took it and held it up to the faint glimmer of moonlight.

"This is not approved currency," Luthan noted.

"It's not currency at all. You carry it with you, and I'll know where you go so that I can follow."

"Even something so small as this?" Rsiran nodded. "At what distance?"

"Far enough," Rsiran said. From here, he could still detect the coins Brusus carried all the way back in Elaeavn if he needed.

"Interesting. I would ask more about your abilities if we had the time."

"I have no abilities of the Great Watcher," Rsiran said. "So I doubt that you would find me all that interesting."

"On the contrary, I think that is the exact reason that I *would* find you interesting." He slipped the coin into his pocket and closed his eyes. With a soft shimmer of light, he Slid away from them.

Rsiran waited for him to emerge, and it took a moment for him to locate where he'd Slid. The coin seemed to be not all the far away, a quick flash of lorcith that disappeared again. Rsiran waited for it to reappear, but it did not.

He Slid forward a step, straining for lorcith, but found no sign of the coin.

"What is it?" Jessa asked.

"The coin didn't return," he said.

"What does that mean, Lareth?"

"I don't know. Maybe he emerged someplace that I can't detect."

"What kind of place would that be?"

Once he would have claimed that a lorcith mine might prevent him from finding the coin, but with his heightened sensitivity with lorcith, even that was unlikely to prevent him from finding it, especially something that he had forged. For it to disappear meant that it had either been destroyed, or there was some way of masking it.

"There aren't many places like that," Rsiran said.

"Can you find him?" Jessa asked.

"I can find where he was. From there…" From there, he would have to see if there was anything that would give him an idea about where Luthan had disappeared. He held out his arms, and Jessa and Valn took them. Then he *pulled* himself into a Slide.

He emerged inside a small brick building. Smoke trailed from a fading fire, embers still glowing in the hearth and the scent of ash on the air. The room was empty.

"He came here?" Jessa asked.

Rsiran readied a pair of knives, preparing to *push* them if needed. He hadn't expected Luthan to disappear on them like this.

Maybe he hadn't. Could something have happened to him?

"Do you see anything?" he whispered to Jessa.

She shook her head. "There's no one here."

"There had been," Valn said. "Fire. The bed," he said, motioning to a mattress with sheets pulled to the side. "The food."

Rsiran hadn't seen the plate of half-eaten meat resting on the ground near the mattress.

"Is this in Cort?" Jessa asked.

"We didn't Slide very far, and we were on the border of Cort before we did."

Valn stopped at the door of the small building and pulled it open a few inches. He peered through the crack, then jerked his head back. A knife struck the wood where Valn's face had been.

Valn swore softly and Slid.

"Rsiran—" Jessa started.

"Stay here," Rsiran said. "Stay safe."

He Slid outside the building, following Valn.

As he emerged, he *pushed* on a pair of knives, sending them away from him, choosing heartstone knives. There weren't as many people able to manipulate heartstone the same way that Venass could with lorcith. His grandfather had managed, but he had been the only person that Rsiran had met with such an ability.

Valn lay on the ground nearby in a heap.

Rsiran heard a soft whistling, and Slid.

He emerged back inside the building with Jessa.

"What is it?"

"Don't know. Watch over me."

He separated from his body, Traveling outside the small building. As he did, he could see that Valn still breathed. A knife protruded from his back. Rsiran moved, searching for who might be outside, cursing himself for his stupidity. He should have Traveled before doing anything, especially when he didn't know what he might find.

In the shadows, he found a man.

The man held a clutch of knives, each made of slender steel. Were they lorcith—or even heartstone—he would have been better able to stop them. A hood covered his face, keeping him in shadows, but from his wrinkled hands, Rsiran knew that he was an older man.

Was there anyone else in the street?

He moved along the rest of the street, searching for signs of others, but found no one.

Rsiran returned to his body and then Slid, emerging behind the man, who spun, as if expecting Rsiran.

Rsiran *pushed* on a pair of knives.

The attacker rolled, both knives missing. As he did, he flipped his knives toward Rsiran, sending five streaking toward him. Rsiran Slid, emerging near Valn.

"I don't want to harm you," Rsiran said.

"Seems that you do," the man said. He had a deep, strong voice, and stepped toward the shadows clutching a pair of knives.

Rsiran prepared to Slide. He could take Valn with him, but might need to Slide quickly if this man attacked again. "What did you do with him?"

The attacker shifted. Rsiran *pushed* on a pair of knives to remove the darkness. The light still didn't penetrate the shadows around the man, as if deflected off the cloak he wore. "Who?" the man asked.

"The one who preceded me."

"I warned him that if any returned, I'd kill them. I've faced your kind before."

"What kind is that?"

The man grunted. "Hjan. They haven't killed me yet."

Rsiran prepared to Slide, nudging his toe closer to Valn. He needed to get him healing. Even as he stood here, he could tell that his breathing slowed.

"I'm not with the Hjan. And I'm not with Venass," Rsiran said.

"The last one said the same right before he tried to send a pair of knives my way. So I think I'll err on the side of finishing you off like your friend. Won't be long for him now."

Valn barely breathed now. The knife didn't look like it had penetrated too deeply into him, but what if the man had poisoned it?

"I'm going to take him and leave."

"Can't let you do that, either. Don't think I can have any more of your type searching for me."

"I don't even know who you are!" Rsiran said.

The man stepped forward and whipped a pair of knives toward Rsiran. He had to Slide behind him to avoid them. When he emerged, the man had already spun to face him, as if anticipating where he would emerge.

It was the same as the woman Carth had managed.

He needed to move quickly, or Valn would die. Rsiran didn't want to be the reason he died, and so soon into their search for the crystal.

Could he grab the man the same way that he'd grabbed Carth?

Rsiran Slid three times in quick succession. Each time the man turned to face him. Twice, knives came whistling toward him as he emerged. How many did the man have?

If he kept Sliding, would the man eventually run out of knives?

But Valn would run out of time if he did, and Rsiran was still no closer to reaching his attacker.

With the next Slide, he emerged and felt someone behind him.

He spun around, fearing that he'd made a mistake.

And nearly dropped the knives he carried. "Haern?" he asked softly.

CHAPTER 28

"Damn you, Isander, drop the knives," Haern called, thrusting Rsiran behind him.

"What are you doing here?" Rsiran whispered.

"Not yet," Haern said. He stepped away from Rsiran, into the faint light of the street, making no effort to hide himself from the attacker that he seemed to know.

The other man hesitated, then moved away from the shadows. "You know my name, but I don't recognize you."

"Because it's been more than a few years since you saw me. I was only a boy then. A couple of decades ages a man."

"Twenty years. If you're who you claim, you're supposed to be dead."

"Supposed to be, but I'm not. Now drop the damn knives, Isander. These people mean you no harm."

"Hjan tricks," Isander said. "I've seen them before."

"This is no Hjan trick. And the boy you're facing might be the key to taking down the Hjan for good."

"Others have tried and failed."

Haern grunted. "Others. You mean like Carth? She came looking for me."

"If Carth came for you, then you truly *should* be dead."

"I have friends."

"The man I knew twenty years ago had no friends."

"Like I said, a couple of decades changes a man." Haern stopped in front of Valn and nudged him. "Terad?"

Isander nodded.

"Any narcass?"

"Not here."

"Damn." He turned to Rsiran, ignoring Isander. "Sorry, Rsiran. There's nothing that can be done for Valn, not with terad at this point. Even Della can't—"

Rsiran didn't wait for him to finish. Now that he knew Haern was here, Jessa would be safe. Haern wouldn't let anything happen to her. He Slid to Valn, emerged to grab him, and stepped into a Slide before pausing in the place between Slides.

The Elder Trees surged around him.

Rsiran *pulled* on that power, drawing it to him as quickly as he could, and then *pushed* it into Valn. Would it work for him the way that it had for Della?

The other option involved Sliding back to Elaeavn and hoping that Della could do something that would help him, but he doubted there was time.

Nothing changed for Valn.

He continued *pulling* on the power from the Elder Trees, and *pushing* it into Valn, drawing more and more of the energy from this place.

Nothing changed.

"No!" He grabbed the knife from Valn's back, and almost threw it to the side, before deciding that he couldn't leave anything in this place.

He didn't know how that would affect this place. Maybe it wouldn't do anything, but the possibility existed that leaving anything here risked damaging the power.

Instead, he took one of his knives and *pushed* the lorcith around the steel blade, sealing whatever poison might have been used inside.

Drawing on more power, he continued to press it into Valn.

Valn took a breath. Then another. He coughed, and a bubble of bloody phlegm came to his lips as he blinked open his eyes. "Lareth?"

"Yeah."

Valn sat up, resting on his arms for support. "Where are we?"

"This is the place between Slides."

Valn jerked his head around. "What do you mean the place *between*? There is no place between!" His strength already seemed returned. Valn stood and reached for his back, scratching where the knife had gone in as he looked around.

"When you Slide, what do you see?"

Valn shook his head. "Flashes of color. That's it. Nothing that would make me think that we traveled through anyplace else in the Slide."

Rsiran took Valn's arm and Slid, returning to the building. Jessa let out a relieved sigh when they emerged and ran to him.

"What happened? I could see you Sliding out there, fighting someone who seemed to anticipate where you would come out, but then…"

"Then Haern appeared," Rsiran said.

He Slid back outside and found Haern standing in front of Isander. Isander looked up when Rsiran emerged and a pair of knives appeared in his hand.

Rsiran tossed the lorcith-encased knife at Isander's feet.

"Where did you go?" Haern asked.

"The only place where Valn might have a chance," he said.

"That was terad toxin," Haern said. "There wouldn't be anything that Della could have done to help him. I'm sorry—"

Haern cut off when Valn emerged from the house, holding onto Jessa's hand.

Haern glanced to Rsiran, his eyes narrowing as he did. He touched the scar along his cheek where Venass had placed the lorcith plate, the one that had augmented his ability to See. Was he able to See anything now?

"What did you do?" Haern asked.

"Another time. Why are you here?" Rsiran asked.

"I Saw that I needed to be. Thought it was tied to Carth appearing, a way to keep you and the others safe. Now I'm wondering if that wasn't the case at all."

Rsiran nodded toward Isander. "You know him?"

"Isander is the one who taught me some of the first things I needed to know about being an assassin."

"Are you with the Hjan then?" Rsiran asked Isander.

"I think that I've made my feelings toward them clear."

"Then you're just an assassin."

Isander laughed and stuffed his knives into hidden pockets and up his sleeves. "Don't say that with such judgment. There are plenty of people who this world would be better off without. That's the role that I play."

"Why are you here?" Haern asked.

"Doesn't matter," Rsiran answered. "Where is the man who was here before me?" he asked Isander.

If Isander had been here and attacked Luthan, that would explain why he had Slid away, but not where he might have gone. He focused on the lorcith that Luthan had taken with him and still didn't find it. Either he had abandoned it, or he was someplace where Rsiran couldn't detect it. That possibility bothered him the most. He had grown accustomed to his increased sensitivity to lorcith, and not being able to detect it didn't give him much faith that he'd be able to find it if he needed to for Jessa.

"As I said, anyone of the Hjan would be attacked."

"He wasn't of the Hjan. He is one of the Elvraeth councilors."

Haern started to laugh. "You brought one of the Elvraeth with you?"

Rsiran nodded. "He's supposed to be a skilled Seer. With what we're after, we needed a Seer."

The laughter stopped. "What's his name?"

"Luthan Elvraeth," Rsiran answered.

Haern tapped on his scar and shook his head. "Luthan," he repeated softly. "What are you playing at, old man?"

"You know him?"

"Knew him might be more accurate."

Isander stalked over, and near enough that Rsiran could *push* a pair of knives at him. After the attack, and what he'd done to Valn, a part of him wanted to attack Isander, but then the man seemed interested in fighting the Hjan, which meant that he opposed Venass. They needed allies in the fight with Venass, and if he could fight anything like Carth—and maybe get Carth's network to help—maybe they would have more aid than he realized.

"What did you do to him?" Rsiran asked the man.

Isander pulled back the hood of his cloak, revealing a weathered face with a neatly trimmed white beard that matched the hair on his head. *This* old man was the one who had given him so much trouble? A sly smile played at the corners of his mouth, as if he knew what Rsiran was thinking.

"I haven't seen any old man. Besides myself, of course," Isander added.

"He came here and then disappeared."

"What do you mean he came here?" Haern asked.

"Luthan Slid here and then Slid somewhere else. I'm not sure where he went."

Haern jerked his hand toward the house where Valn and Jessa still stood in the doorway. Valn held an unsheathed sword, and kept his focus on Isander. "Came here?"

Rsiran nodded. "Briefly. Then he disappeared."

"You tracking him with lorcith?"

"I was."

"Maybe he left it behind."

"Like you did?" Jessa demanded, coming from around Valn and smacking Haern on the chest. "You disappear like that and you think that we—*I*—wouldn't worry?"

Haern grabbed her wrists before she could hit him again. "I knew you would worry, but I knew *I* would worry more if I remained. I had to leave Elaeavn. I Saw it."

"That doesn't change that you should have told us."

"I can't protect you from what's after me. Don't think that Rsiran can, either." He glanced to Rsiran and shrugged. "Sorry about that, boy, but it's the truth. Something like the Forgotten or Venass you can almost see coming. But what's after me… You won't know it was ever there. Can't risk Jessa for what I done."

Jessa made as if she might strike Haern again, and he took a step back. "What makes you think you get to decide that for us? Hasn't what's happened with Rsiran shown us that you can't work alone like that? We're stronger together, Haern."

"You know I made a promise to your father."

"Yeah? And I made a promise to *you*."

Rsiran hadn't heard that before. What kind of promise had she made to Haern?

Haern cast his gaze around them before settling back on Jessa. "I let you in on this and you're in a different kind of danger. There's no Sliding away from it. Nothing your Sight will keep you safe from. This… this comes when you're not watching. A person passing you in the street. A stranger at the Barth. Even could be someone you know." He glanced to Valn as he said the last. "Her network is extensive, and she's more dangerous than you can imagine."

"And running will keep you safe?"

"Don't care about me," Haern said. "It's never been about me. Not for a long time. It's about a promise I made, and about keeping you safe. Now that he's here," he said, pointing to Rsiran, "I don't worry quite like I did. But with this… it meant I *had* to go."

"Damn you, Haern! We care about you, too."

Isander started laughing then.

Jessa looked at him, eyes holding the hurt she felt. Muscles in her shoulders tensed, and Rsiran wouldn't have been surprised if she tried to attack him. "What's so funny to you?" she demanded.

Isander's smile only widened as he looked at Haern. "When you said you'd changed, I didn't know you'd changed this much. Could it be that the deadly Haern of the Hjan actually has people who care about him?"

Haern turned toward Isander and grunted softly. "Unfortunately."

Isander laughed again. "Ah, come on, all of you. Let's drink a bit before you go searching for whatever it is you think to find."

Isander led them into the building, which turned out to be his home. Haern followed him, and then Valn. Jessa glanced from Haern to Rsiran before going with him. Rsiran lingered, uncertain. They needed to find Luthan before going after the crystal, but he had no idea where to begin. Without knowing what happened to the lorcith coin, he had no way of tracking him.

They might have Haern back, but they were no closer to finding the crystal than before. And with every setback, he felt the growing pressure of the Venass threat as it chased him. Eventually, it would catch up to him, and if he didn't figure out how to stop shadowsteel in time, there wouldn't be anything he could do.

Taking another look down the street, he followed the others into Isander's home.

CHAPTER 29

Smoke drifted from the hearth and a familiar scent brewed in the teakettle sitting on the coals, that of mint and spice that reminded him so much of what Della brewed. The home was too small for all of them to sit comfortably, so Rsiran stood along the back wall and decided that was the better place, anyway. He could more easily watch Isander this way.

The old man moved with a fluid sort of grace, one that belied the age that the gray in his beard and the wrinkles around the corners of his pale blue eyes revealed. And Rsiran had seen him with the knives. The man was deadly, possibly more than most of the Venass he had faced. At least Venass made the mistake of carrying lorcith weapons. Isander made no such mistake.

"Why did you come to my home?" Isander asked as he stood at the hearth. He lifted the kettle and poured a mug of tea, offering the first to Valn.

The guild member took the mug and sniffed it carefully.

When he didn't drink, Isander smiled, took the cup from him, and took a quick sip. "I think after what you've been through, you might appreciate something soothing."

Isander handed the cup back to Valn. This time, he accepted it using both hands and took a careful drink, then lifted it up to his nose so he could inhale the fragrant aroma.

"We came because we're searching for the man who was with us," Rsiran said.

Isander looked over at him, the wrinkles around his eyes deepening, making his gaze appear harder, more angry in some ways. He nodded. "I know why *you're* here. At least, why you claim to have come. But why is Haern here?" He handed a mug of tea to Jessa and then to Haern. After pouring one for himself, he set the kettle back onto the coals without offering one to Rsiran.

"I told you why I came," Haern said. He held the mug of tea, but didn't drink.

"You Saw something that prompted you to come for me."

Haern nodded.

"I haven't seen you in decades and now you return."

"Can't I need the help of my mentor?"

Isander grunted. "I think you outgrew me long ago, Haern."

"I'm not sure that outgrown is how I would describe it. I was impulsive then, and thought I knew more than I did."

Isander nodded. "Both are accurate."

"Had I not left, I might never have ended up with the Hjan."

Isander frowned. "Do you really believe that after everything you've learned?"

Haern looked into his cup and shook his head. "No."

"Ah, now I see. The man I knew truly is gone, isn't he?" His frown changed to a wolfish grin. "Was it a woman? The gods know my last student lost his way because of a woman."

Rsiran had never heard Haern mention any woman other than Jessa, but didn't know what really had prompted Haern to leave the Hjan. What had changed for him?

Haern ignored the question as he changed the topic of conversation. "Didn't know that you took on another student."

"You think you were the only one I would teach?"

Haern shrugged. "I liked the idea that I might be unique."

Isander laughed. "You are. The only one I've ever met who might be as good with knives as me."

"Your other student didn't learn knives?"

"Knives, yes. But he preferred other means."

"Who is he?"

Isander shook his head with a smile. "That's not for you to know."

Haern met Isander's eyes, and neither man looked away. "I Saw something here. That's why I came."

"Did it involve me?" Isander asked.

Haern nodded. "Otherwise, I wouldn't have come."

"So you didn't just want to seek advice from your old mentor?"

"I'm not that man anymore," Haern said.

"No. You seem to be a different one. But you've taught this one," he said, nodding to Rsiran, "haven't you? The way he uses his knives… that's something you picked up from me."

Haern nodded. "I've worked with him some, but there's only so much I can teach him. His abilities are much different from mine."

"So I've seen. Almost like the Hjan that have come through here."

"That's the second time you've said that." Rsiran stepped away from the wall. They couldn't simply stand around while Haern and Isander caught up on twenty years, not while the crystal remained missing, and Luthan had disappeared. They had to find him, and find what happened to the crystal. Now that they had Haern back, he could even help. "Why would the Hjan have attacked you?"

Isander took a sip of his tea. "The Hjan have always attacked me. They see me as a threat."

"You are a threat to them," Haern said.

"The Accords kept us neutral," Isander answered.

"What changed then?"

Isander's eyes narrowed. "I don't know. The one who chases you might have answers, but something changed."

"How long ago?" Haern asked.

"About a year. Maybe more. The Accords kept us at a tenuous peace."

"What are the Accords?" Rsiran asked.

"Treaty between the Hjan and C'than," Isander said. "One the Hjan sought, and then broke."

C'than. Rsiran had heard that name before. "You're like her," he realized. "Carth."

Isander shook his head. "I can't make that claim."

"Where is C'than?" Jessa asked. "I've never heard of it."

"Few have. It's not like Venass where they wave their tower proudly. Were they not so damned powerful, they might be interesting," Isander said. "The C'than prefer a more secretive approach."

"That's why Carth has spies?"

Isander shook his head.

"What then?" Rsiran asked.

"It's not for me to share. Unless you are of C'than, you can't understand."

Rsiran looked over to Haern. "Are you of C'than? Is that where you learned what you did?"

Haern looked away from Isander. The other man stared at Haern, his eyes blazing with heat. "I was of Hjan," Haern said.

"Because you were impatient," Isander said. "You could have learned. You could have stayed with me. In time, they might have called you."

"They were never going to call me," Haern said.

"Because you didn't believe."

"No," Haern said. "I Saw that they would not. There was only one way for me to learn what I wanted at that time, so I took it." He looked up and met Isander's eyes. "I paid the price for what I did, and have been paying it every day since I left."

Isander watched him for long moments. "I can't call her off, Haern. I don't have that authority."

Haern nodded. "I didn't think you did."

"That's not why you came, then."

"It's not."

"Why then?"

He nodded to Rsiran. "Like I said, I Saw something. Now that Lareth is here, I think I know what it is. You need to help us—help him—so he can face the Hjan."

"From what I saw, he doesn't need my help with facing the Hjan."

"He's got some ability," Haern admitted, "but he still needs help. There are things the C'than might know that could help him."

"You know I can't do that, Haern."

"Why? The Accords have been broken, and all of the Hjan come for him."

"For him? What could he have done that would have gained the attention of all the Hjan?"

"For starters, he stopped an attack."

"That's not reason enough for the Hjan."

"No," Haern agreed. "The reason he needs help is that his grandfather leads Venass."

Isander stiffened and set his mug down. "Danis?" he whispered. "He's your grandfather?"

Rsiran nodded.

"Gods. You're lost, then. Too bad. I was starting to like you."

CHAPTER 30

R SIRAN STOOD OUTSIDE OF ISANDER'S HOME, Jessa at his side, watching the street. Nothing moved. A few other doors down the street remained closed, and in spite of all the noise from the attack, they hadn't seen anyone appear. Either this place was accustomed to such things, or the homes were empty.

The sky had begun to lighten in the time that they'd been in Isander's home. A knot of worry twisted his stomach that only partly came from his fear for what might have happened to the crystal. Hearing Isander speak so callously about his grandfather—even though he knew what his grandfather might do—had affected him more than he would have expected.

Rsiran glanced to Jessa. "It's time for us to go."

"Where? We don't even know where we can look, Rsiran. Without Luthan, we don't have any way of knowing what might have happened to the crystal."

And even that hadn't been guaranteed. Luthan had been able to See *around* him, and that had been the way that Rsiran thought they would come up with answers, but without help, they would just be blindly searching. What good would that do anyone?

Maybe the crystal really was gone. How it disappeared and where it was in that "blue in a field of white" was anyone's guess.

How long before Venass discovered it? How long before they were able to use the power of the crystal against Elaeavn, and add that to what they could do with shadowsteel?

Not long, he knew. Once they discovered that it had disappeared—if they hadn't already—they would come after it, bringing every power, skill, and weapon they could to possess it. Which meant that Rsiran had to be ready to bring everything he could against them.

"Maybe Haern can help us," he suggested.

"Haern doesn't have nearly the same skill as Luthan. He hasn't ever since he left Venass."

Haern stepped out of the shadows of a pair of nearby buildings. Rsiran hadn't known that he was even there, and the shimmery cloak he wore—so similar to the black shirt they'd found in his house—caught the light and reflected it.

"Why did you really come here?" Jessa asked Haern as he approached. "If it wasn't for us, why did you come?"

"After Carth appeared in Elaeavn, I knew I needed to leave. I thought Isander might be able to help…"

"Why won't he help you?" she asked.

"Because I abandoned what he tried to teach me and went to Venass."

"Why?" Rsiran asked.

Haern shook his head. "I didn't know anything about Venass at the time. I was on a job with Isander and one of the Hjan recruited me. I saw what he was capable of doing and wanted the same level of skill." He sighed. "You can't know what it's like to have nothing and be offered everything. That was what I had. What I was."

"You were a Seer," Jessa said.

"And what does that do for someone not Elvraeth? They're the only Seers worthwhile. And I was promised more than Seeing."

"What did they promise you? What would you have wanted that would have made it worthwhile?" she asked.

"Jessa—"

"Don't, Haern. I've seen what they've done. I didn't realize that you were so willing to sacrifice others."

"I'm not that person anymore."

"Why? You didn't tell Isander, but why? What changed?"

Haern closed his eyes. "I did something… It doesn't matter. Not anymore."

Rsiran waited to see if he would say anything more, but he didn't. "Can you help us?"

"Not if you needed Luthan."

"One of the crystals is missing, Haern. Luthan said Venass didn't have it yet. But we need to find it before they do. There has to be something your Seeing can help us with."

Haern looked over to Isander's house. "Not that way, but maybe there's another."

"What way?"

"When something is stolen, there's either a use, or there's a market. If Venass doesn't have it, maybe we can look for a market."

"How do you intend to look?" Rsiran asked.

"Isander won't like it, but he's going to have to help." Haern flung open the door to the house.

Rsiran followed, expecting to see Isander inside, still sitting by the hearth drinking his tea, but the fire in the hearth had burned down to embers, and a lazy trail of smoke swirled around it, but nothing else moved.

"Damn him," Haern said.

"Where is he?"

Haern shook his head. "Gone. Damned man is gone."

"Are you sure?" Rsiran asked.

"Can't See him. And I did when he was here."

"Why would he have disappeared?" Jessa asked.

"Because we found him. And he thinks the Hjan are after him. Considering what we know, that's likely to be true." Haern grabbed an iron poker from next to the fire and jabbed at the embers as he threw on another log. "Thought that he might help me, but that was too much to hope for, I guess."

"Your idea won't work without him?"

Haern sighed. "It'll work, but it won't be quite as easy or as neat."

"Why do you say that?"

Haern glanced from Jessa to Rsiran. "Because it requires that we get someone on the inside who can get access."

"Not you?"

Haern tapped his scar. "Once that might have worked, but I'm not the same person that I was."

"What do you intend, Haern?"

Haern closed his eyes. "That's the part that I can play. We're going to make a trade."

* * * * *

"I don't think this is a very good idea," Jessa said.

They sat on the rooftop of a flat-topped building in Cort. The streets below were still noisy in spite of the late hour, and the air carried with it the stink of filth that he never got from Elaeavn.

"I don't, either."

"If she helps with this, why can't she simply help us find where the crystal might be?" Jessa said.

Haern raised a finger to his lips. "She might know. That would be the best-case scenario. But if she doesn't, then this is our other option."

"You're giving yourself up," Jessa said.

"Not yet."

Jessa peered around the buildings. From where they crouched, they could see the tops of all the neighboring buildings. "Still don't like it."

"I don't expect you to," Haern said. "Now quiet. Keep your eyes open—"

"Yes. Keep them open," came a voice from behind.

Rsiran Slid toward the sound of the voice, emerging with a pair of knives already *pushed* out from him.

The woman stood across from him wrapped in a dark cloak that drew the night around her. A soft smile pulled at the corners of her mouth. "Careful," she said.

How had she managed to sneak up here without them knowing? He didn't think that she could Slide, but then, she had managed to detect his Sliding before, almost as if she had some thenar ability.

Haern rose and held his hands in front of him. "We came willingly, Carth."

"Seems that way, but you have the numbers, don't you?"

Haern grunted. "Do we? I imagine you have a dozen of your people surrounding us."

"Haern, you think too much of yourself. There's no need for a dozen when only a few will suffice." She nodded to Rsiran. "Guildlord. Good to see you again."

Rsiran blinked, unable to hold back the shock that he felt. Even in Elaeavn—and even among the guilds—his position as guildlord wasn't well known. For her to know of his position meant that she *was* every bit as connected as Haern suggested.

"Thank you for coming," Rsiran said.

"I didn't come for you," Carth answered. "I came for Haern."

"And Haern came for me."

Carth raised a hand.

Rsiran pushed a dozen knives all at once. They surround Carth, all from different angles. "You might be fast, but how fast are you?"

Carth smiled and lowered her hand. "Interesting. And yet you claim you're not of the Hjan. I would imagine they are most interested in you."

"They might be interested, but they're not about to get to me."

"I hope so, guildlord. You and I have much to discuss when this is all settled." She touched the tip of one of the knives he held hovering in front of her. "Now, if you wouldn't mind removing this. I would hate for you to sneeze and send these through me."

Rsiran *pulled* the knives back but kept them in the air, ready to move if she threatened to attack.

"I came here. I think you have little to fear from me."

"You came for Haern. That's reason enough for me to fear," Rsiran said.

Carth made a small circle atop the roof. From the light glowing off his knives, Rsiran noted that her eyes darted around her, as if seeing things that even Jessa couldn't see. What powers did she possess? Not abilities—she was not of Elaeavn—but she possessed power of some kind that made her difficult for him to attack.

"What is this, Haern? You sent word that you'd meet. I should know better than to trust the word of one of the Hjan."

"I'm not one of the Hjan." He moved past the knives Rsiran held hovering in front of her, standing within the ring of knives. "As I told you in Elaeavn, I've changed."

"And as I said then, men don't change."

"This one did."

Her eyes flicked to Rsiran and then Jessa. "You came. And now you've attacked me. That is a mistake."

She whistled, a sharp sound against the night.

Haern spun and motioned to Rsiran, but he wasn't fast enough.

Three women appeared, each dressed much like Carth with long cloaks, and surrounded Jessa. Carth stepped forward, a knife pointed to Haern's back.

"Now, guildlord, I think we can talk."

Rsiran glanced to Jessa. She stood motionless. One of the women, with short dark hair and a slender face, held a knife beneath her throat. The other two stood behind her, each holding an arm.

He might be quick, but could he reach her in time? Even if he could, he doubted that he could reach Haern in time. If he acted, someone with him would die.

Rsiran *pulled* the knives back to him.

Carth nodded, and the knife beneath Jessa's neck was pulled back. She continued to hold the one in Haern's back.

"Carth—" Haern tried taking a step forward, but she jabbed her knife at him, quicker than Rsiran would have been able to Slide, and Haern winced.

"You came, but you did not come," Carth said. "Tell me why."

"Others are in danger," Haern said. "I... I thought you could help."

A hint of a smile pulled on Carth's mouth. "Haern of the Hjan thought that he would ask for help? That, I think, is interesting. Tell me, Haern of the Hjan, *why* do you think I should help you?"

"You wouldn't be helping me. You'd be helping them." He nodded to Rsiran and Jessa.

"Seeing as how they came with you, it appears that helping them would be helping you."

"Help them, and I will come with you willingly."

Carth laughed softly. "I think that you'll come with me willingly or not."

Haern twisted, moving in a blur, and spun around, a pair of knives suddenly appearing in his hands. He flicked two of them at the women holding Jessa's arms, and caught them in their foreheads, somehow managing to hit them with the handle of the blade. As they fell, Jessa jerked free and ran to Rsiran.

The other woman lunged toward them. Rsiran *pushed* on his knives, and she stopped.

One of the fallen women moaned softly. Rsiran glanced at them, realizing that Haern hadn't killed the other two women.

"Call off the others." Haern spoke in barely more than a whisper. "I might not still be with the Hjan, but that doesn't mean I don't recall my training."

Carth made a motion with her fingers, and the woman still standing jumped back, grabbed the other two, and dragged them off the rooftop and into the darkness.

"You will talk. I will listen," Carth said. "When you are done, you will come with me, willingly or not. Even one of the Hjan can't outrun me forever."

Haern nodded. "Fine. As I said, we need your help. One of the Great Crystals of Elaeavn is missing, and we need to recover it."

Carth's eyes twitched, more emotion than she'd shown before. Haern had hoped that Carth might have heard something that would tell them where the crystal might have ended up, but the show of emotion from her made it likely that she hadn't heard anything.

"Such a thing would be incredibly valuable."

"It would be."

"Powerful as well, if the stories about it are true."

What kind of stories had Carth managed to hear about the crystals? He hadn't even known they existed until relatively recently.

But Venass had. And the Forgotten. It was possible—likely, even—that others knew about them as well.

"Stories would not do them justice," Haern said.

"Why should I help you retrieve this crystal?"

"Because Venass seeks the crystal, and I fear how powerful they would manage to become if they succeed."

Carth sniffed. "No doubt the Hjan would use something like that in dangerous ways, but helping you might be equally dangerous."

Haern nodded to Rsiran. "That's why he's here."

"Explain."

"The guilds protect the crystals. Or had, until Venass damaged one of the Elder Trees. Rsiran needs to return it to the guilds' protection."

Carth studied Rsiran. "It seems the guilds can no longer protect the crystals. Perhaps it is time for alternative protection to be arranged. How do you know the others are safe?"

"They are safe," Rsiran said.

"Like the one that you lost?"

He shook his head. "I have placed additional protection around the others. No one can reach them."

Carth glanced from Haern back to Rsiran. "You hoped that I would have heard something about this crystal."

Haern nodded. "I thought it was possible."

"Interesting. I have not. Now that I know it's missing, I will discover all that I can."

"That would be valuable," Haern said.

She considered Rsiran. "I am not certain that I will share with the guild. They have lost the crystal once. If I recover it, I will find a way to keep it safe from Venass."

Rsiran fought the urge to tell her how unlikely it was that she would be able to protect the crystal. The guilds and the Elder Trees had kept them safe for hundreds of years. Now that he knew how to use the power of the Elder Trees, Rsiran thought that he could keep them safe, but first he had to get it back. Which meant using whatever help they could get.

"That means you won't help," Rsiran said.

Carth barely looked at him. "I have not decided the extent of the help I will offer"—she turned her full attention on Haern—"but tell me, Haern of Hjan—why should I do this for you?"

"You want me to pay for a crime you claim I made."

"There is no claiming. It is your crime."

Haern's face flushed slightly. What had he done that he hadn't shared with them? This was a part of Haern's plan that Rsiran understood the least. Somehow, Haern had to convince Carth that she could trust that he would go with her when this was all over. If he couldn't accomplish that, the rest of the plan would not work.

"You want me. Do this for us, and I will go with you willingly. I will answer for whatever crime you say."

"It is an interesting plan," Carth said, "but it requires that I trust you, Haern of Hjan."

"Not that you trust *me*, Carth. It requires that you trust Rsiran."

"I don't know him."

"No. But you know his grandfather. A man who he despises and nearly killed once, and a man that Rsiran would do anything to keep from reaching the crystal."

"Why does that matter to me?"

"Because his grandfather leads Venass."

Carth took a step forward, eagerness gleaming in her eyes. "Danis? You can help me reach Danis?"

Rsiran glanced at Haern before turning to Carth. "I don't know if I can help you reach him. I don't know where he is anymore."

"That is not a concern. *I* know where to find Danis."

"You can't reach him, can you?" Haern asked.

"He is well protected. Drawing him out would take something I do not have."

"Something like his grandson," Haern suggested.

Carth nodded. "If the guildlord helps with this, then I will agree. I will need some time, and then I will come to you."

With that, she jumped, leaping higher into the air than Rsiran believed possible, and disappeared into the night.

"What now?" Jessa asked.

Haern stared into the dark. "Now, we wait."

That was the answer Rsiran feared. How long *could* they wait?

CHAPTER 31

THE KNIFE TORE THROUGH THE AIR, whistling past his cheek. Rsiran ducked, Sliding away from the knife so that it barely missed. Another followed, and another. Each time, he Slid away, and each time he emerged, Haern seemed to know where he would be and threw another knife.

None were lorcith forged. Haern had gone back to steel, determined to prove to Rsiran how to work with metals that he didn't have the same affinity for. Already, he'd been cut nearly a dozen times. Were it not for the fact that he'd learned he could Slide to use the power of the Elder Trees to heal him, Della would have been upset with them.

Rsiran spun, *pushing* a dozen knives in all directions around him. None of them hit, so he *pulled* them back. Somehow, Haern still managed to evade him.

Since returning to Elaeavn after meeting with Carth, Haern had fought with a determination that Rsiran had never seen from him before. He had always come off as deadly with his knives, but now he was frightening. In some ways, he reminded Rsiran of when he'd faced Isander. In others, he had a terrifying skill all his own.

Rsiran Slid, this time emerging in the branches of one of the trees. Sliding into the trees was dangerous, and put him in some danger, especially if he miscalculated the distance. There had been one time that he'd misjudged, and emerged on the branch only to have it crack and break, dropping him to the ground. Had he not Slid again, he might have been injured, but he'd managed to *pull* himself away at the last moment.

From this vantage, he studied the ground below. Haern would be in the forest somewhere, likely wearing the black shirt that bent the light, making it difficult to determine where he hid.

Rsiran skimmed his gaze across the forest, looking as Haern had instructed for anything that might seem out of place. He kept his eyes mostly unfocused, not letting his gaze linger in one spot for too long. Doing that only made it more likely that he would miss others that would give him the insight he needed.

Nothing moved, and nothing appeared out of place.

Rsiran sent five knives sweeping around the forest, giving off a soft glow that helped him search. Still there was nothing. Haern was there, but he remained hidden.

Could Rsiran draw him out?

Movement exposed him, and risked Haern sending one of his knives through him. They were dulled so they couldn't cut too deeply, but they still hurt, regardless of whether he was able to reach the power of the Elder Trees.

But if he stayed here, he wouldn't find Haern.

Rsiran Slid, making a point of moving noisily.

When he emerged, two knives whistled toward him.

Rsiran Slid again, emerging where he'd seen the knives come from. This time, he found Haern.

He clung to the trunk of a tree, nothing more than a shadow lingering against the bark. Rsiran flipped a pair of knives, sending them handle first.

Haern jumped out of the way before they hit.

Rsiran Slid as Haern moved, emerging with his sword drawn, slashing at him. Haern was forced to roll, and brought his sword up, but not before Rsiran managed to *push* a pair of knives that he held to either side of Haern's head.

Haern dropped his sword and held his hands out. He let out a shaky breath. "Damn. Getting faster, aren't you, Rsiran?"

"I'd say the same about you." He helped Haern stand and then *pulled* all the lorcith knives that were scattered around the forest back to him. As Haern had stopped carrying lorcith when they sparred, they were all his.

"I'm not getting faster so much as I'm shaking off rust," Haern said. "Still not back to where I used to be. Closer than I've been in years, but…"

"You want to get to that point before you go with Carth?"

"Not sure that it matters," Haern said.

Rsiran tucked the knives he'd *pulled* to him into his pockets and the strap sheath he wore around his waist. Two went in wrist sheaths that he'd fashioned. He'd found that it was easier to *push* knives from those sheaths, but he needed to come up with a way for them to hold more than a couple of knives.

"Why does she want you, Haern?"

"Rsiran—"

"I know you want to keep your past to yourself, but this involves us now."

"No. It involves me," Haern said. He slammed his sword into his sheath and glanced around the heavily wooded area.

In the last few sparring sessions, Haern had moved them away from the clearings, wanting to test Rsiran more and more. The next step involved actually fighting through a city. Not Elaeavn. It wouldn't do for one of the guildlords to be discovered Sliding through the city throwing knives at another.

"And we're supposed to let her take you."

"If she upholds her end of the bargain, then yes."

"I don't think that Jessa will let that happen, regardless of what you might have agreed to."

"You can't let her come after me. She comes after Carth, and she'll only end up getting hurt or worse."

"Then convince me why we should let Carth take you. What did you do? Had to be pretty bad for her to chase you all these years."

Haern smacked the trunk of the tree and started walking. "I was one of the Hjan, Rsiran. There are things I did then that I can't undo. That's why Carth wants me."

Rsiran Slid and emerged in front of Haern. "What, then? The way she made it sound was that there was something particular that you did."

Haern clenched his jaw and looked away. "There was more than one particular thing. When I left Isander, I wanted nothing more than to reach the Hjan. They recruited me, but I had to prove myself. I didn't understand at the time that they used me."

"Used you how?"

"To understand it is to understand that there is history between the Hjan and C'than. The Hjan are assassins serving Venass, and we know what Venass wants."

"Power," Rsiran said.

Haern nodded. "Well, the C'than want power as well, only... only they go about it differently. Not through death, but through subterfuge and control. They use knowledge to work their power."

"Spies."

"Spies," Haern agreed. "A network deeper than even the Hjan could ever penetrate. They tried. The C'than have existed for centuries, longer than any outside even know. Venass is relatively new. They claim scholarship, but that's a front for something else. And the Hjan have long sought the influence the C'than command, but they do so through violence."

Rsiran watched Haern. The older man rubbed at his cheek, touching the scar that he'd earned from joining Venass. "What does knowing this have to do with what you did?"

"It will help you understand and know what needs to be done. I thought you soft, but I've seen that you'll do what's needed to keep those you care about safe. Maybe not the same way that I would do it, but you take the steps that are needed. That's all I can ask."

"Then why are you telling me?"

"Because you'll need to convince Jessa. I don't think she'll listen to me, not about this. She's got it in her head that she owes me something."

"You saved her. Isn't that reason enough for her to think that?"

Haern grunted. "Saved her. I took her from filth, and brought her to a different filth. Sometimes, I wish I never returned her to Elaeavn."

The forest began to thin and Haern hesitated, turning to Rsiran. "If this were only about me, I wouldn't have any qualms about hiding. Don't matter what Carth wants. But it's not about me. Guess it never was. Should've Seen that, I suppose, but then I took that damn thing out." He smacked his cheek.

"Haern?"

"Let me finish. You have to understand. Not only because you've been chased by Venass and you're stupid enough to think you can chase them, but because now, we got Carth involved. You need to know what she is. Who she is."

"I thought you said she was of C'than."

"That woman is of C'than, but she's different. Isander serves the C'than. There are others, more than I know. Like I said, they deal in secrets, so it's not surprising that there are so many secrets around them."

Through the trees, Rsiran could make out the faint outlines of the city as buildings began to become clear. Haern walked more slowly, as if each step pained him to take.

"Haern, enough about them. What did you do?" Rsiran asked Haern. He had managed to avoid answering the question so far, but Rsiran needed to understand.

Haern sighed and leaned against the trunk of an elm tree. "Let me finish, and then I think you will understand. I'm almost there, I promise. The Hjan have wanted the C'than network. They've wanted access, and if they couldn't have that, they wanted to remove it. So they started to attack. The problem was, the C'than have talents of their own. Think you saw that with Isander."

"And Carth," Rsiran said.

Haern nodded. "Don't know what their secret is, only that they have some talents that are different from what we have here in Elaeavn. Nothing like our gifts from the Great Watcher, or even your other abilities. When the Hjan started to attack, they thought to eliminate the C'than, but couldn't. Both sides fought. Many died. Finally, the Hjan and C'than came to an accord, a peace treaty of sorts. Had they not, the Hjan and C'than would have been at war, but Venass and the C'than Trivant—their leaders, sort of like the Elvraeth council or the guildlords—managed to reach an agreement."

"They left Venass to get more powerful?"

"Don't know that they understood all of what Venass is after. In spite of everything that we've faced, I don't think we do, either. You might have faced your grandfather, and you've seen the lengths that they'll go to to defeat their enemies, but Venass... well, they call themselves scholars for a reason. Venass has always been about knowledge. In that way, they're more like the C'than than they'd like to admit."

"Why haven't you told us this before?"

"What does it matter? The Accords stood for nearly fifty years, Rsiran. Nothing that we were going to do would disrupt that."

"Maybe not, but Carth is pretty interested in Danis. She wouldn't pursue him if she wanted to maintain the Accords."

Haern nodded thoughtfully. "That was my thought, too. That's why you need to know this. If the Accords are broken, then there's a different war. Probably the reason Venass decided to move on Elaeavn after all these years. They must figure they can take down the Elvraeth, but they fear the C'than. As should you. Which is why you can't come for me when I go to Carth."

Rsiran shook his head. "You still haven't told me why she wants you."

"I've told you enough."

"Not enough for Jessa. Haern, you know that she'll want to come after you, regardless of what you say, and regardless of the danger that might exist. She wants to keep you safe, the same way that you want to keep her safe."

"She can't. This time, she can't."

"Why? What was it?"

Haern pulled a knife from his sheath and began flipping it around. "Had I been smarter, I could have stayed with Isander rather than joining the Hjan. I would have learned more than the Hjan ever could have taught, but I was young, and dumb. Thought I knew more than him."

"What did you have to do?" Rsiran asked. "That's it, isn't it? They made you do something to join them."

"They needed a demonstration of my skills. Said that I needed to show them why I should be considered for the Hjan. Gave me a target, and… and I took it."

"Who was it?"

"My target was a woman who worked for the C'than. Not like Carth. Not sure I would have been able to face someone like her with my meager abilities at that time, but one of their assets. I went after her, and killed her for the Hjan. They claimed me, offered me their protection when the C'than came after me, and claimed ignorance about the killing."

Haern's voice trailed off as he finished.

"Carth wants you for something that you did to join the Hjan?"

"To her, I violated the Accords. I wasn't part of the Hjan then, but they used me to violate the Accords."

Rsiran swallowed. He couldn't imagine what Haern had gone through, the willingness to kill so that he could gain access to the Hjan. What would have driven him to do that?

"I deserve what's coming to me," Haern said. "Don't like it, but can't deny that I deserve it. I was too willing to do anything to get what the Hjan offered. The Great Watcher knows that other have suffered because of it. Now… now, maybe some good will come of it. If Carth sticks to her side of the bargain, then it'll be worth it."

"Haern—"

Haern pushed off the tree and shook his head. He flipped the knife a few more times in the air before sliding it cleanly into his wrist sheath. "Not going to talk me out of this, Rsiran. And Jessa can't come after me. You saw what Carth is capable of doing. If Jessa tries to come after me, or you foolishly think to come after me because she wants you to, then one or both of you will end up hurt. I'll take the punishment, and this time… This time there will be some good. We find the crystal, maybe we can even let Carth and the C'than take care of

Venass, especially if the Accords are no more." He sighed and nodded to himself. "Now. Time to get back to work. And you've got to check in with the guild, I would imagine."

CHAPTER 32

Rsiran held onto the hilt of his sword, letting the leather wrap press against his palm, and trying to ignore the rising frustration. The Elvraeth council had summoned him again, and he had grown tired of trying to determine if he should really answer the summons. This time, he would do so without Luthan present for support. The old man had simply disappeared on him, leaving them nearly dead at Isander's hand.

Ephram met him in the hall outside the council chamber. The alchemist guildlord wore a simple cloak today that left the serpent medallion—the mark of the guildlord—hanging free outside his shirt. His eyes had a weary expression, and the deep green seemed strangely faded.

"You answered the call," Ephram said.

"You don't have to seem so surprised," Rsiran countered.

Ephram smiled tiredly. "Surprise doesn't really fit, at least not with you."

"What is it?"

"This," Ephram said, sweeping his hand around him. "All of this is wrong. The Elvraeth do not summon us this often. That they would do again so soon tells me there is something that they plan."

"Do you think it has anything to do with Venass?" Rsiran asked.

"The Great Watcher knows that I hope it doesn't."

He considered telling Ephram what he'd done, and the fact that they had committed to Carth to work together, but decided it would be better for Ephram not to know. What would the Alchemist Guild guildlord do anyway?

They stopped at the door to the chamber, and Rsiran heard voices drifting out of the room. Sarah's was the clearest, and she was agitated. He hadn't seen her much of late since he'd been away with Haern and Jessa trying to find other allies to help in the fight against Venass.

"She doesn't sound too happy," Rsiran noted.

Ephram shook his head. "She is rarely happy, especially when it comes to the Elvraeth."

"Why?"

"There are many reasons, but she had a boy very close to her exiled. He died before she managed to discover what happened to him."

Rsiran clenched his jaw. He hadn't realized that Sarah had been close to one of the Forgotten. Wasn't that something that she should have told him, especially as they worked deeper and deeper into searching for Venass? Why would she keep something so important from those she worked with?

But then, he had kept secrets from them as well. He had been doing better, but he still didn't share openly, not as they would prefer him to do.

Ephram pushed open the door to the chamber. Gersh stood next to Sarah, his meaty arms crossed. The shirt he wore today had the sleeves either torn or cut off, exposing scarred and tattooed arms. His brow furrowed deeply as he glanced from Sarah to Naelm who stood on the other side of the long table leaning on clenched fists. Tia almost blocked Sarah from getting any closer.

As he looked along the line of the council, he noted that they were all there other than Luthan, leaving an empty seat. Rsiran's gaze lingered on it, knowing that the one person he could somehow count on within the Elvraeth council was missing—and there was nothing that he could do to find him.

"Sarah," Ephram said softly as he approached, laying a hand on her arm.

Sarah shook it off and didn't take her gaze off Naelm. "No, Father. The council in their wisdom thinks that the guildlords must grant immediate access to the crystals."

Naelm smiled, though it seemed a placating smile. "That is not the conversation at all, Ephram. The agreement is that the Elvraeth are granted access to the crystals while the guilds guard them. As the guarding of the crystals seems to have failed, the council has decided that we must maintain our access."

Ephram opened his mouth to argue, but Rsiran spoke up first. "Why only the Elvraeth? What about others in the city?"

"Careful with your questions, guildlord," Yongar said.

Rsiran glanced at him. The younger man had made it abundantly clear how he felt about Rsiran's presence among the guildlords. He was the type of man who wanted to keep things exactly as they were, not changing the fact that the Elvraeth were responsible for exiling hundreds—possibly thousands—from the city over the years. That practice had done nothing other than develop increasing dangers. A result so obvious and easily anticipated, it was almost as if it were something they had planned.

"And what question is that, Councilor? The one where I question the logic that only those born to the Elvraeth may be granted access to the crystals, or do you refer to where I wonder if perhaps others in the city shouldn't be given the chance to hold the Great Crystals?"

"The Elvraeth are gifted with the ability to handle—"

Rsiran's sudden laugh seemed to catch everyone off guard, including Sarah, who finally managed to compose herself and looked at him, a question in her eyes.

"Gifted? You are gifted because you maintain contact with the crystals. That is the only reason. What would happen if someone not so 'gifted' held one of the crystals? Would they develop the same gifts as the Elvraeth?"

That was a question that even Della hadn't been able to answer for him. Rsiran had a growing suspicion that the only reason the Elvraeth maintained their abilities was because of their connection to the crystals. There was something about the crystals that kept all of the people of Elaeavn powered, but it was something that faded the longer people were away from the city. He'd learned that from the Forgotten. They would likely do anything to regain that access, which was the reason that Rsiran thought they came after the crystals in the first place.

"Those of the Elvraeth bloodline are the only ones granted access to the crystals," Sasha said. "And now, you have changed even that."

"For the safety of the crystals," Rsiran said. "If I wouldn't have done what I did, what would have happened to the other crystals? Would we have lost another? All of them? And then what would the Elvraeth do without their precious crystals?"

None of the council spoke.

"What does it mean that *I* was able to reach the crystals? If I could do it, then it stands to reason that others could. Perhaps I should see how many others within the city could reach them, particularly those without the Elvraeth bloodline."

"Careful, Lareth," Tia whispered.

"You should listen to the other guildlord," Yongar said.

Naelm tapped his hands on the table, and the other councilors fell silent. "The Elvraeth are tested because it is most likely that our bloodline will be able to reach the crystals. If all were tested, it would be a waste of time. You are too new to your position to understand what has been attempted in the past, but if you took the time to try to understand, you would learn that the Elvraeth have held the rights to that power for centuries. But now the guilds presume to prohibit access. That is unacceptable to the council. We would have the access to the crystals restored."

Rsiran shook his head. "No. Not until we find the missing crystal."

Yongar started to smile, and Naelm shot him a hard glare. "Is that your position as guildlord?" Naelm asked.

Ephram raised his hand, as if trying to warn Rsiran, but he ignored it. The other guildlords continued to fear the Elvraeth, as if the Elvraeth would or could dictate to them how they would protect the crystals.

"That is my position," Rsiran said.

Naelm watched him and then nodded. "The council is not helpless here, Master Lareth. If you will not restore access to the crystals, then you will be stripped of your position as guildlord."

"I serve at the discretion of the Smith Guild."

"The Smith Guild exists at the discretion of the Elvraeth council," Naelm said.

Rsiran looked to the other guildlords, but none of them spoke.

He thought he understood the timidity that the others had around the Elvraeth. They still feared them, even though the guilds preceded the Elvraeth. They *believed* that the Elvraeth had a right to that rule, and that they somehow did so more righteously than anyone else would have done.

It was time for that to end.

Della had asked him to help bring some sort of unity to the guilds, but how could he do that if there was fear of the Elvraeth? For that matter, how could the rest of the people of Elaeavn ever manage to find the healing that they needed, the ability to stand up against the oppression of Venass, if he wouldn't even oppose what the Elvraeth attempted?

Were Luthan here, he might not have said anything, but the other council members here might not have said anything, either. The old man had a way of tempering the frustrations between the guild and the council, almost as if he knew that to be his role, something that he might actually have Seen.

"I think I am done here," Rsiran said.

Naelm nodded. "It is good that you see the sense. You will release the barrier you have placed on the crystals, and instruct the guild to choose another."

Rsiran took a step forward. "I think you misunderstand me. I am done here. I am not done as guildlord."

He faced the other guildlords. "You may have forgotten the role *our* ancestors played. The clans preceded everything else in the city, especially the Elvraeth. Without the clan, and now the guilds, the Elvraeth would never have discovered the crystals. We owe no fealty to them. They should recognize that we have as much a right to lead the people of Elaeavn as they do."

Sasha gasped. Yongar stood. Naelm watched him silently.

"Lareth—" Tia started.

Rsiran shook his head. "They have tried to disband the Sliding Guild. They marginalize Sarah as the Thenar Guild. The Great

Watcher only knows what they have done to the Miner Guild to keep Gersh from snapping. And the Smiths… the Smith Guild no longer will tolerate what the council proposes."

He turned back to face the council. "This is *my* decision. I *am* the guildlord of the Smith Guild, and the Elvraeth do not have the power or the authority to remove that title from me. You may disagree, and you may wish that I did not serve, but know that I do not fear you."

Rsiran turned away, and Naelm yelled after him.

"The council still rules the city."

Rsiran paused. "Is that a threat?"

"Do not make an enemy of me, Lareth," Naelm said.

"Try and exile me. See if that punishment holds. Know this: I will not release the protection around the crystals until I decide they are safe. Without me, there is no one else able to reach the source of power that protects them. Think on that as you determine whether to threaten me."

CHAPTER 33

Tension filled the inside of the Hall of Guilds. Rsiran stood in shadow along the wall, making a point of leaving the others alone. Ephram and the other guildlords were upset with him. Every so often, Tia glanced over as they spoke softly to each other, and Rsiran couldn't read the expression on her face.

Sarah stepped away from the others and came over to him. "Father is—"

"He's upset. I understand."

Sarah shook her head. "Upset, yes, but I don't think you understand."

Rsiran watched Ephram for a moment. The older man appeared agitated, and every so often, he rubbed a knuckle into his eyes. "Why didn't you tell me that someone you cared about was exiled?"

Sarah flushed. "Does that matter? The Elvraeth council decided what they did. There's nothing I can do to change it."

"It matters that you didn't share with me."

"There are more than a few things that you've never shared with us, don't you think?"

Rsiran chose not to argue, at least not about that. Doing so after everything that they had been through would get him nowhere. "I'm leaving the city again to try and find the crystal."

Sarah sniffed. "I think you're going to have to."

"What does that mean?"

"You're not safe here, Rsiran. With the way you spoke to the council… they're not going to let that drop. They might not have the authority or the ability to exile you, but don't think for a minute that the council is helpless."

"They didn't do anything when Venass attacked."

"And why is that, do you think? Why wouldn't the Elvraeth have defended the city when Venass attacked?"

Rsiran hadn't been able to come up with an answer other than a disinterest. The only other answer that he could come up with would mean that the council *wanted* Venass in the city, but that didn't make any sense, either.

"They wanted the guilds to take care of it," he said.

Sarah nodded, and leaned into him, lowering her voice. "The guilds. Do you think the Elvraeth care if the guilds are destroyed?" She hesitated, letting the words sink in. "The Elvraeth have always resented the fact that the guilds protect the crystals. They're given free access, but they fear a time when that might change. And now you come along and change it, just as they feared."

"I only did what was necessary to protect the remaining crystals."

Sarah nodded. "I think you did what you needed, but that doesn't make them any less fearful that their access could be permanently revoked. Especially Naelm. That man has lived long enough, and tried to force my father enough times to grant the Elvraeth access to the crystals, that I know what he wants."

Ephram's agitation made more sense. Rsiran had assumed that the guilds had never opposed the whim and will of the Elvraeth, but he was mistaken. Ephram had resisted, but had done so in the only way that he could. Rsiran understood that there was only so much that most people could do against the Elvraeth. Even as guildlord, Ephram was no different.

"Do you really think that the Elvraeth would allow Venass to enter the city?" Rsiran asked.

"Maybe not quite so conspiratorially as that sounds, but would they do anything to stop entry when they realized what might happen to the guilds?" She shrugged. "I don't know. But I can see the Elvraeth viewing this as an opportunity, and one that you made more difficult."

"Why do you think I would have anything to fear remaining in the city? The guilds serve as the constables in the city. As guildlord, I would be protected."

"Constables, yes, but the Elvraeth have their tchalit. They are not helpless. Father might know more about them, but we haven't been able to gain access to their ranks, despite how much we might have tried."

Ephram finished talking with Tia and Gersh and came over to where Rsiran and Sarah stood talking. "Well. Now that we have a more difficult path, I think you and I should have a talk."

"I'm not going to release access to the crystals until we find the fifth. And until we find some way to restore the Elder Tree to replace the protections for the crystals."

"I will not ask that you do. What I came over to tell you is that you have the support of the guilds, Lareth. All of them."

Rsiran glanced to Sarah. She seemed surprised by the comment. "Father?"

"Lareth was right. We have allowed ourselves to fear the Elvraeth for far too long . It is time that stopped. Now, I'm not convinced that disrupting them in the way that you did was for the best, but we have long suspected that they have no interest in maintaining the guilds. That must stop as well."

"Father—an uprising is not what the city needs."

"The city needs leaders who care about the people," Rsiran said.

"Don't tell me that you agree with him," Sarah said.

"I agree with your father that something needs to change. The Elvraeth care for nothing other than maintaining their power while the rest of us suffer. They have done nothing to deserve our loyalty. But I need more from you than words, Ephram. You've been holding back, refusing to share what you know about shadowsteel."

"Lareth—"

"Venass continues to attack with shadowsteel, Ephram. I need to find how they are making it, and stop them before they do any real damage."

Ephram looked at Sarah and sighed. "That's just the problem. In the quantities that you describe, the making of shadowsteel would require significant energy. The alchemists never managed much more than small amounts, and even then it was not stable. For the weapons that Venass has produced…"

"What do you think it would take?"

"I don't know. It's possible that they hide something in Thyr, but—"

"They don't," Rsiran said.

"How… You've Traveled there?"

He nodded. "I had to know."

"You were willing to risk detection by going to the tower?"

"They might have detected me, but it was worth the risk to know." And had he found anything, he wouldn't have been able to do anything, but at least this way, he *knew* that Venass had nothing in Thyr. That made it worse.

Where were they producing shadowsteel?

When they attacked the Elder Trees, he thought they had used the Forgotten Palace or maybe even someplace within Ilphaesn. For as much shadowsteel as they had found, he had expected to find *something* in Thyr that would give him a hint, but… there had been nothing.

Finding the shadowsteel was almost as important as finding the crystal. Without stopping the production of shadowsteel, Rsiran didn't know if there was any way he would be able to fully stop Venass if they attacked again.

"You found nothing?" Ephram asked.

"Not in the tower. Lorcith, some heartstone—" though not as much as he would have expected "—but no evidence of my father. No evidence that they manufactured anything like what we've encountered. And until we find the missing crystal—"

He didn't get the chance to finish.

He detected a stuttering against his senses, almost like lorcith, but not with the same intensity as the knives that he carried. It felt the same with heartstone.

"What is it?" Sarah asked.

Rsiran shook his head. "I don't know. There's something—someone—down here with us."

"Venass?" Ephram asked.

Rsiran didn't think so, but it was possible. Venass had proven willing to enter the city, and had come for him, attacking without fear, so there was plenty of reason to believe that they would come for the guilds now, as well. But what he detected was subtle, and didn't really remind him of what he would detect from Venass.

A voice echoed from down the tunnels, shouting with agitation.

"Tia?" Ephram said.

As he started off, Rsiran tried grabbing for his arm but the old man moved too swiftly. He wasn't able to reach him. Sarah's eyes widened in alarm.

"You know what this is?" Rsiran asked.

"This is the Elvraeth," she whispered.

Rsiran *pulled* on the knives with him, and Slid, reaching Ephram. He found him surrounded by three men, each carrying wickedly curved swords. A fourth stood outside the ring of the men, a flat expression in his gray eyes. Rsiran had seen a man like him before; he was a sellsword, possibly of Neeland, men deadly skilled with their swords. The Elvraeth hired them to guard the warehouse, so Rsiran shouldn't be surprised to find one here.

Where was Tia?

He found her in a heap on the ground nearby, chains wrapped around her wrists. Elvraeth chains.

Anger flooded him.

He had been attacked by the Forgotten, attacked by Venass, and now they would be attacked in their own city? Was that the kind of leadership the Elvraeth wanted?

Rsiran would not stand for it, not anymore.

He sent knives streaking from him. The sellsword managed to knock one of them from the air, but the second caught him in the throat, and he fell in a spray of blood. The three men surrounding Ephram turned to Rsiran, realizing the real threat. Something moved toward him, and Rsiran Slid, emerging in the shadows.

A hidden man lunged forward, and slapped chains upon Rsiran's wrists.

Rsiran glanced at them. Heartstone alloy.

Had the Elvraeth learned nothing from him coming to them? Did they really think that they could trap him so easily?

He slapped his arms around the attacker, and Slid, dragging the man with chains around his neck. Anger made his Sliding faster than he usually managed. Rsiran emerged briefly in Ilphaesn, and left the man, Sliding quickly back to Tia and Ephram.

The three attackers stared at him with their mouths agape.

"Did you think these chains would stop me?" Rsiran asked. He *pushed* on the heartstone that he detected within the clasp, and the chains fell free. He did the same to the chains on Tia, and they dropped to the ground. Rsiran *pulled* on the chains, wrapping them around his arm, and Slid to the nearest man.

With a quick flick of his wrist, combined with a *push* on the heartstone, the chains snapped into place on the man. He spun, catching the next the same way. The third man watched him warily, and Rsiran simply *pushed* the blunt end of a knife at him, catching him in the middle of his forehead so that he dropped to the ground.

"The Elvraeth attacked," Tia said.

"We knew it was a risk," Ephram said.

"They should not have been able to organize so quickly."

"This would have been planned for a while," Rsiran noted. "But how would they have reached the Hall of Guilds? They would have needed help…"

He looked around. "Where is Gersh?"

"He wouldn't have anything to do with this," Ephram said.

"Are you sure? The Miner Guild has not been all that interested in changing things," Rsiran said.

"They wouldn't risk the safety of the guilds," Ephram said.

"What if the Elvraeth promised them their guild could remain intact?" The miners wanted to pull the lorcith from the mines, and they wanted control. Rsiran didn't think they sought anything else. The Elvraeth would probably have even been willing to leave them untouched. Who else would handle the prisoners? Who else would recover lorcith?

"The Hall of Guilds is unsafe," he said. "We need to go."

"Where? Where can we go that the Elvraeth won't reach us?" Ephram's voice rose as he spoke, the anxiety in it making his voice screechy.

"I have a place," he suggested. "First, there's something I need to do."

Rsiran grabbed onto the three guards he'd chained, and *pulled* them in a Slide to the palace. When he emerged, Sasha sat alone in the council chamber, her eyes the same distant expression that Haern wore when he had a Seeing.

He *pulled* on the chains, releasing the men, and wrapped the chains around his arm. He would not leave them for the Elvraeth to use on them again. "Tell Naelm the attack will not work."

The woman blinked and turned to Rsiran. "I have already told him that it is a mistake to attack in this fashion. You could be an ally."

"An ally. If that is what you want, you have a strange way of approaching it."

"I would have you as an ally. The others…"

The door to the council chamber opened, and five men entered.

They started to surround him. Rsiran had the chains and a handful of knives, but not enough to protect himself from a full attack. Better to Slide away and hide from them.

The men surrounded him but made no attempt to get any closer. Two of them carried strange swords in their hands. The other two had crossbows. Rsiran had learned how crossbow bolts could be deadly to even him. He might be able to Slide quickly, but would he be fast enough to avoid a bolt catching him in the back?

Too late, he noticed a subtle pressure from the man coming in last.

Rsiran stared at him, noting the finely healed scar along both sides of his face. Venass. He pulled something from his pocket and flicked it at Rsiran.

A dark sphere streaked toward him.

Rsiran attempted to Slide, but was trapped in place.

He tried again, but again found himself unable to Slide.

The dark sphere almost reached him. If it was shadowsteel and like the one he had tested with Jessa, he feared what would happen if it touched him.

Rsiran had a few knives, not enough to protect himself from an onslaught, but he didn't dare risk letting the shadowsteel touch him. He had been so caught up in finding the forge to stop Venass, that he'd not had time to study the shadowsteel sword they had brought back, to try to learn how it affects his abilities. How this sphere might hurt him, or worse. That had been a mistake, and maybe one that Venass had intended him to make.

Using two knives, he *pushed* them at the approaching sphere.

It struck the sphere, deflecting it. Rsiran continued to *push*, increasing the intensity that he used, smashing the knives against the sphere. They flattened and wrapped around the sphere, the same way they had when he had been attacked in the streets outside of Thyr.

The lorcith in the knives became muted, but Rsiran continued to *push*, forcing the sphere away from him, and smashed it into the wall where it impacted with an explosive force.

He still couldn't Slide.

The man from Venass approached, walking around the outside of the others, careful not to cross through the ring of the four men surrounding Rsiran. "You made a mistake in coming here, guildlord."

Guildlord. That meant they knew about him. They knew what he could do, as well, and had prepared for it, figuring out some way to keep him from Sliding. Or so they thought. Rsiran had a trick remaining, one that even his grandfather wouldn't expect.

"The council made a mistake if it thinks that siding with Venass will help them achieve what they want."

"Do you really think you know the mind of the council?" the man said.

"I don't know the council. I know that you won't be able to reach the crystals."

The man from Venass smiled. Rsiran waited before doing anything else. He needed to know more about what they intended, and this was the best chance that he had. If he did manage to Slide away, he would lose his chance to find out what they wanted from him, if anything. It was possible that they only wanted him dead now.

"The crystals," the man said. "You have prevented access for now, but that will not stand once the rest of your Elder Trees fail."

So that was it. Venass thought to destroy the remaining Elder Trees. Rsiran didn't know if they could, but they had managed to destroy one of them, and damage another. The protections that he placed around them might not be enough for the trees to remain intact. The guilds would have to change their focus, and protect the trees.

"They will not fail. Venass thinks they understand power, but they do not. They know there is power in the world that they seek to possess, but what they don't understand is how to use that power, to have the wisdom to recognize that they are not all powerful…"

"You're a fool, blacksmith. You haven't the knowledge or the experience to stop what we have been planning for decades."

The attacker pulled another two spheres from his pocket and held them up.

Rsiran eyed them. He could stop one, but would he be able to withstand two?

If he couldn't manage to Slide, it wouldn't matter.

Rsiran *pushed* on the remaining knives that he had with him. Three were heartstone, and they streaked toward the men surrounding him. The others were lorcith. Rsiran managed to hit two of the men, but the knives didn't penetrate very far, managing only to catch them in the shoulders. None of the men winced; none of them even moved.

That left him out of weapons.

The man from Venass smiled. "Now, I think you are fully disarmed. Unfortunate. We thought so long on how best to trap you, but it became clear there would be only one outcome when it came to you. A shame. I still think we could have learned much from you."

He brought the spheres together.

These weren't like the other ones. By bringing them together, they would work like the ones Rhan had used when he had nearly killed Rsiran.

He tried Sliding, but they still prevented him somehow. Was it the spheres? Some secret of shadowsteel that he didn't know?

Rsiran *pulled*, drawing toward the place in between Slides, and felt himself begin to ooze away, but he would be too slow. They held him fixed in place, unable to move.

The spheres would reach him before he could get away.

Rsiran felt it as part of him managed to reach the place in between Slides. As he did, power began to flood into him, power that he drew upon from the Elder Trees. Awareness of lorcith flooded into him, combined with something that Luthan had once said about the stone in the palace.

The heartstone that was added to the stone for the building had become something different. Travelstone. Could he call on it as he did heartstone and lorcith?

He *pulled* on it, using the strength of the Elder Trees to fuel him. Chunks came free from the wall, and he directed them at the men surrounding him. Two of the men fell. The resistance to Sliding disappeared.

Rsiran finished his Slide, and stepped into the space in between.

CHAPTER 34

Rsiran paused long enough to let power flood into him. As usual, the power that filled him left him restored and strengthened, and wishing that he could use that power on the other side rather than only here.

But he had used it, hadn't he? He had paused in between the Sliding, pulled partway so that he could reach only a part of the Slide, with part of him on this side where he accessed that energy. Could he do that again? Could he be half in one part of the Slide and half in another? If he could, then he would have access to power that even Venass wouldn't be able to understand. He might even manage to contain shadowsteel and prevent the shadowsteel spheres from harming him.

How had he overlooked the possibility that the Elvraeth might be working with Venass?

He had wanted to believe that the Elvraeth wanted peace for the city, but what they really wanted was their power to be secured, and they viewed the guilds as a threat to their power.

He couldn't delay here for too long.

And he needed to return, but to where?

The palace. He needed to know who else in the palace might be a threat to him.

He hoped the guilds were safe.

Rsiran Slid back to the palace.

The halls were empty. Faint blue light glowed from the lanterns as well as from the heartstone set into the walls themselves. Restored by the Elder Trees, Rsiran felt the way the heartstone tugged at him. He could *pull* on it if he wanted. With enough strength, he wondered if he could bring the entire palace down.

Was that what it would take to keep the city itself safe?

Rsiran pushed the thought out of his mind, listening for anything that would make him think there were others from Venass here. He focused on lorcith and on heartstone, searching for them.

He Slid to the nearest source that he sensed and emerged in a small room. Three men looked up as he entered. One of them had a long scar of Venass. Hjan. Rsiran couldn't tell about the others.

The Hjan quickly pulled a black sphere from his pocket.

Rsiran started to Slide, but paused halfway in the Slide, so that he was partway across the threshold where he could reach the Elder Trees' power. He *pulled* on that strength and used it in a bolt of power that knocked the man back. He didn't risk using the power on the shadowsteel sphere, not yet certain whether it would harm the trees.

The Hjan hit the wall with a soft thud. The sphere remained in his hand.

"Pick it up," Rsiran said to the others.

Neither man moved. Rsiran used another bolt of power drawn from the Elder Trees and sent the nearest man flying back to the wall, where he crashed and landed next to the Hjan.

"Pick it up," he said to the one man standing.

"Who are you?" the man asked. His medium green eyes widened as he watched Rsiran.

"I'm the guildlord. Now. Pick it up."

"Why?"

"Because you're going to destroy it."

The man grunted. "You destroy it." He lunged for him, but Rsiran had been ready. Using the power, he sent a bolt of power through the man, and he dropped to the ground.

The sphere remained in the hands of the unconscious Hjan. He had to find some way to prevent the sphere from being used on him.

The heartstone in the walls of the palace was the only thing that he could think of, but using that would take strength and care so as not to destroy too much of the building.

Remaining partially through the Slide, he *pulled* on the heartstone in the walls. The connection to heartstone had once been weak, and then it had been slippery, but the more he worked with it, the easier it became for him to use. Now, heartstone felt little different from lorcith, though he still didn't have the same capacity to communicate with it.

The walls *pulled* away, slowly folding so that they reached the sphere in the Hjan's hand. Rsiran wrapped the heartstone around the sphere, and withdrew it into the walls of the palace. Within a moment, it exploded, but the heartstone and the stone itself contained it.

Without the connection to the Elder Trees, Rsiran wouldn't have been able to stop that sphere from damaging him—or possibly damaging others.

He listened for other senses of lorcith and heartstone, and Slid to the next that he detected.

Two men, neither Hjan and likely only the tchalit, waited in the hall.

Rsiran struck them down the same as he had the last.

The next room had another of the Hjan. Rsiran didn't even attempt speaking to him, and used the power of the Elder Trees to attack him. He Slid on, again and again, each time drawing upon the power of the Elder Trees.

Finally, he reached a room on one of the upper floors.

Inside, he found Naelm. Three Hjan were with him, and Slid toward him the moment that Rsiran had entered, almost as if waiting for him.

Rsiran Slid partway, *pulling* on the Elder Trees, and disabled them with the same pulse of energy he had used on everyone else.

"Was this your idea?" he demanded of Naelm while *pulling* on the walls, curling them out so that they pulled the shadowsteel weapons into the walls. The Venass attackers didn't move. They weren't dead—not yet—though he considered using the iron fire poker in Naelm's room to end them.

"Was what my idea?"

"Using Venass. Did you really think that you could use them to eliminate the guilds?"

Naelm's face twisted. "The guilds have had too much power for too long."

"The same can be said of the Elvraeth."

"We were chosen by the Great Watcher to rule in Elaeavn. The guilds had their time and it is over."

Naelm took a step to the side. Rsiran didn't have any weapons to hold him in place, nothing other than the Elvraeth chains still wrapped around his arm.

He Slid to Naelm and slapped the chains onto him. With them in place, Rsiran could control him somewhat, and keep him from going anywhere.

Sliding back, a tingle ran up his back. There was something else that he sensed, equally familiar. Heartstone. He had detected this particular piece of heartstone before.

Rsiran spun.

Danis stood across from him.

Arrayed around him on the ground were a dozen shadowsteel spheres. They began spinning in a steady circle around him. Danis watched Rsiran, an interested gleam in his eyes.

"I am impressed. You have grown far more competent than I ever would have believed possible. Before you were troublesome. Now… now I think I have had enough."

Rsiran *pulled* on the chains that he'd clasped onto Naelm. "I thought the Forgotten deserved their exile. Isn't that what you claimed?"

Naelm crashed into Danis, but the spheres spinning around him did not falter, somehow parting long enough for Naelm to slip between them and then circled both of them. As they did, Rsiran's connection to the chains disappeared.

He thought of Luthan, and the way that he had simply disappeared. Was the same trick used on him?

"What did you do with Luthan?" Rsiran asked.

Naelm pushed himself away from Danis and wiped his hands on his pants. "Luthan was a fool. Thought that he Saw something about you that benefited the council, and didn't believe me when I told him there was no way that he could have. How can he See anything with the damned ability to Slide protecting you?"

"And Danis?"

Rsiran suspected that he only had a few more moments before whatever Danis intended would be complete. Once the sphere released, and if they attacked him, he doubted he would be able to stop all of them.

But he could try to contain them.

He *pulled* himself partway in a Slide, barely enough that Danis would even know. With that connection, he still had enough access to the Elder Trees. He used that power and *pulled* on the heartstone all around him, drawing chunks free from the walls, and sent them flying at the shadowsteel spheres. As they struck, they fell harmlessly to the ground, as if the shadowsteel managed to create an impenetrable barrier that Rsiran couldn't reach beyond.

He *pulled* again, this time using the stone, dragging chunks free that he swung at Danis and Naelm. Again, they hit the barrier and failed.

Danis smiled darkly. "Impressive. But even your talents aren't enough against the wisdom of Venass. Now that the Elvraeth recognize what we can offer…"

"You were exiled."

"My *sister* was exiled," Danis countered. "I chose to leave."

Rsiran's breath caught. Could that be true?

What had Della told him?

But he remembered what Della had told him. Evaelyn had used her abilities against someone in the city, and had been exiled for it. Danis had wanted to help her and had followed her from the city, only… only it was likely that Evaelyn had not wanted his help, and he had instead gone to Venass where he'd learned their way of using metals and acquiring abilities that they should not possess.

"And now you think to return?"

"The guilds have controlled access to the crystals for long enough. And we now know how to bypass the barriers they have placed."

"Not all have been placed by the guilds."

"No. There is still the matter of your barrier, but I don't think that will pose as much of a problem as you believe."

Rsiran shook his head. "You still think the crystals are the key to power," he said. "That's been the mistake the Elvraeth have made for centuries. They have resented the fact that the guilds protect the crystals, when in fact, the guilds have possessed the real power all along."

"And soon, the guilds will be nothing more than a memory," Danis said.

The spheres were spinning more rapidly now, something like a blur around him so that he couldn't see anything more than streaks of black.

Rsiran wouldn't be able to stop them, which meant he wouldn't be able to reach his grandfather. All this time that he'd searched, and to be so close… only, were he to try anything else, he would risk the power of the Elder Trees. He refused to do that.

Danis watched him, that dark smile returning, almost as if he were Reading Rsiran, but the bracelets on his wrists made that impossible. Since putting them on, he hadn't been Read or Compelled by anyone.

"I See that you are finally coming to realize what you face. You cannot win here, guildlord. Elaeavn is lost to you."

He was right. If the council worked with Venass, and if Venass continued to place the shadowsteel spheres around the city, there was nothing that Rsiran could do until he discovered a way to remove them safely. That might involve using the power of the Elder Trees, but he didn't know how shadowsteel would affect the trees' power, and didn't dare attempt anything with it until he did.

That meant retreating.

Even though he was so close, he could almost reach Danis.

The shadowsteels spun even faster, and Rsiran felt a strange burning along his skin. He glanced down and realized that shadowsteel started to coat him.

His heart hammered.

Would he even be able to Slide?

He had to escape, which meant that he had to try.

"The city might be lost for now," Rsiran said quickly, "but the crystals will never be yours. And I will reclaim Elaeavn."

"You will die, grandson."

Rsiran shook his head as he *pulled* himself in a Slide. "Next time, grandfather."

CHAPTER 35

RSIRAN PAUSED ON THE OTHER SIDE LONG ENOUGH to draw the strength from the Elder Trees, *pulling* on so much of it that he filled himself, letting it pour out of him, spilling with bright white light as it burned away the taint of the shadowsteel.

He Slid, emerging in the Barth. No musicians played at this time of night, and the fire in the hearth had already started to fade. A few servers moved between the tables, cleaning up from what Rsiran suspected was the rush from earlier. Only a few tables had anyone sitting at them, mostly men gaming or sitting quietly sipping their drinks.

Brusus was there, and saw Rsiran's face. "What is it?"

"We need to leave the city. Now."

"But the Barth…"

"The Barth won't be safe. Get Alyse, and get out of here. Have someone you trust run the tavern until we can return."

"What happened?"

"Later, Brusus. Please, trust me on this. Anyone who knows us is in danger."

He paused, listening for Jessa. He detected her in the smithy, and that would be the next place he would go.

"Rsiran, there's something you should know."

"We'll have to talk about it later, Brusus. With what's happening in the palace, we need to move those we care about away from the city. We can go to the Aisl. I can keep us safe there, but first, we have to reach it."

Brusus nodded curtly. "And I'll get Alyse moving, but this can't wait." He nodded to a man sitting by himself at a table where the shadows of the tavern were thickest. "Ship came in tonight, Rsiran. I nearly killed him when he walked in, but he managed to convince me to let him live."

Rsiran *pulled* on the knives Brusus had on him, and *pushed* them toward the man. Firell sat watching him carefully.

"Why did you return?" he asked Firell.

"You came to me first, didn't you?" Firell said.

"Is Shael with you?"

"Not this time. Something happened, Rsiran. When you left, Jonas went searching for proof of what you said. We found something in Nalthin."

"Where is Nalthin?" he asked.

"South," Brusus said. "Far to the south. And inland. Firell wouldn't have been able to reach it by ship."

"Not by ship," the smuggler agreed. He hadn't moved, fixing Rsiran with a steady gaze, ignoring the knives that floated in front of him. "Shael heard rumors of something there, so Jonas Slid us to Nalthin."

"Heard rumors?"

Firell shrugged. "You'd be surprised to hear it, but the Forgotten aren't as destroyed as you might think. Oh, they don't have any interest in returning to the city, not like the others that I worked for, but they're keeping together for protection. Between the Hjan and…" He shook his head. "Doesn't matter. That's not why I came here. Wanted to tell you about Nalthin."

Rsiran frowned "And? What did you find?"

"The damnedest thing. Found a man with collections of lorcith that looked a lot like what you made, but none of them had your mark. Knives, a couple of swords, even other decorative items. Maybe not the same quality, but close."

"You returned to tell me that?"

"Not that." Firell swallowed. "Shael disappeared on me."

Brusus grunted. "Probably someone paid better than you."

Firell shot him a questioning look, then shook his head. "I'm not paying him this time."

"No? Seemed like Jonas had you pretty well controlled when I found you in Asador," Rsiran said.

"Jonas thought he could use us. Shael was pissed about what happened to him. Blamed you for a long time, and considered coming after you, but I think he knew that would have been a mistake. When I found him again, he decided that we needed to find out why the Forgotten used us."

"You were using Jonas?"

"Not so much using, as we wanted information. Damn, Rsiran, Shael almost died. I 'bout lost not only my life, but my daughter. We needed to know what all that was about."

Rsiran couldn't remain here for long. With Danis establishing a presence in the palace, they didn't have too long before the city became unsafe for them. "We can talk later. So Shael is gone. That's why you came. I don't think I can help you, Firell. Not right now with what we have going on."

Firell stood, trying to ignore the knives that Rsiran held in front of him. "Thought you might feel that way, but think on this, Rsiran. Who made those knives if it wasn't you?"

Rsiran glanced at Brusus, and he could tell from the way his friend's jaw clenched that he had the same thought as Rsiran. "You think my father did this?"

Firell shrugged. "Don't know. Nalthin is known to have mines. Not supposed to have lorcith mines, but not many really know. The city keeps it closed off from the outside, not letting anyone else get too close."

If it was his father, he might finally have a place to look. He'd thought him in Thyr, but what if Venass had moved him, thinking that Rsiran might go after him there?

But now wasn't the time to think about going after his father.

"Found this there, too." Firell pulled a small rounded shape from his pocket.

Rsiran recognized it immediately.

He *pulled* on the sjihn tree sculpture that he'd made for Brusus, and it flew to him from across the tavern. Holding it up, power surged from it the same way that it had when Alyse had somehow used it to confine the Hjan when they attacked, only this time, Rsiran used it to prevent the shadowsteel sphere from harming him.

"Damn, Rsiran!" Firell shoved the sphere back into his pocket. "What are you doing?"

"Where did you find that?"

"Like I said, it was in Nalthin. Man had it, said that he could get me others. Didn't think he was supposed to have them. They make a ton of this stuff there." Firell shrugged. "I thought you might know what it was. Help me know if it was valuable."

Rsiran looked over to Brusus. He hadn't had the chance to tell him about Danis and the shadowsteel throughout the palace. If what Firell told him was true, then he might have found the source.

But now, Venass was in the city.

Elaeavn had been lost… but Danis might be distracted as they secured the palace. That could give Rsiran time to Slide to Nalthin, discover if the shadowsteel forge was there, and then return. If he could disrupt the production of shadowsteel…

But he would have to move quickly. And he couldn't go alone.

He turned to Brusus. "How quickly can you reach the Aisl?"

"Rsiran—"

"I won't have much time to do this, Brusus, so I need to know that you'll be safe. Get Della. Haern. Send word to the guilds. Get them to the Aisl."

Brusus looked around the Barth. "I hate to leave this place."

"You're not leaving it for good. Just for now. We need to regroup. But trust me that it needs to happen now."

"It'll be done. You know I can do this, Rsiran."

Rsiran nodded. He *pulled* the knives away from Firell and handed them to Brusus. "Good luck."

"The same to you."

Rsiran grabbed Firell, and Slid to his smithy.

Jessa sat on their bed, sharpening her lock picks. When Rsiran emerged with Firell, she jumped up and unsheathed a long knife, holding it away from her.

Rsiran *pulled* it from her. "No time, Jessa. We're leaving the smithy and the city. I'll explain later. Grab what you need."

She nodded and quickly rolled the lock-pick set back up, stuffing it in her pocket.

Rsiran *pulled* on all the knives that he had remaining in the smithy. About half were lorcith and the other half were heartstone. He kept them separate, wanting to be able to easily determine which he had with him.

"What are you planning?" Firell asked.

"The council has allowed Venass to enter the city," Rsiran answered quickly. "The council thinks to destroy the guilds. But from what you told me, I think I can find a way to eliminate some of Venass's strength, but I have to act while they are occupied."

"I didn't tell you anything like that."

Rsiran nodded toward the pocket where Firell hid the shadowsteel sphere. "What you possess? That's what they intend to use. Pull it out."

Firell did, and Rsiran *pulled* on a lump of lorcith. "Set it on there," he told Firell when he'd positioned the lorcith on the ground in front of him. Firell did so, and Rsiran *pushed* lorcith around the shadowsteel orb, fulling encasing it.

It would hold, and hopefully long enough for him to return and deal with it fully.

Rsiran roused Luca from the cot near the back. When the boy sat up, he looked at the knives strapped to him, and glanced to where Firell stood by the bench and where Jessa finished her preparations.

"You're leaving."

"For a bit. I need your help with something. Can you gather all of the Smith Guild? Tell them the guildlord wants them to meet in the Aisl at the tree. All should go, including apprentices. The masters will understand."

"Why should they believe me?"

"Because I'm the guildlord," Rsiran said.

Luca's eyes widened. "I'll do as you ask, guildlord."

He scrambled away and raced out of the smithy. Rsiran watched, feeling a moment of amusement. "That's the fastest I've ever seen him move when I've asked him to do something," he said to Jessa.

"Stupid secrets. You could have told him you're the guildlord before now. Everyone else seems to know," she said. "What now?"

"Now we get the rest of our help."

CHAPTER 36

The Slide took them to a rocky expanse of barren landscape. A half moon shone overhead, giving enough light for Rsiran to see without the need of using any of his knives. He would have hesitated anyway, until he knew what they might face.

In addition to Firell and Jessa—she refused to allow him to leave her behind—he'd also recruited Valn, Sarah, Tia now recovered from the attack in the Hall of Guilds, and two other Sliders that Rsiran had met before, Marin and Hester. Both wore steel swords, though both carried lorcith knives with them at Rsiran's urging. They had served as constables, and had fought Venass during the first attack on the city.

"We should be back in the city helping with the evacuation," Valn muttered.

"The others are helping. Lareth is right in this," Tia said. "We can use this diversion."

Valn shook his head. "Yeah, Lareth might be right, but that don't mean I have to like it."

"None of us like this," Tia said. "The council actually thinking to attack the guilds. I would never have believed it."

"The attack is my fault," Rsiran said. "So thanks for coming with me."

"Yours?" Tia asked. "You might have been what prompted it, but the attack would have come, regardless. The council has resented our role for a long time."

"Still. Thanks."

"Just get this over with quickly," Tia said. "We need to return and ensure that the Aisl is safe." She looked over her shoulder, as if looking back toward Elaeavn. "Can't believe that we're returning to the forest after all this time."

"Who said we're returning?" Valn asked. "We're kicking the damn Elvraeth out of the palace. That seems like as good a guild hall as any, don't you think, Lareth?"

Rsiran smiled. "Do this first." He turned to Firell, who had been quiet since Rsiran Slid him from the city. The quiet made him uneasy, as if Firell hid something more from him. Did he intend to cross him again, or was it simply the fact that they were outside the city, and drawing Firell into a fight that he wanted nothing to do with? "Where now?"

He pointed over the rock they hid behind. "That's Nalthin. Not much of a city. It sits at a crossroads of sorts. Eshand Mountains behind it. To the north is Eban, but far to the north. South is beyond the mountains, but places that aren't profitable to sail to. Don't know those lands."

Rsiran focused on Nalthin, searching for any lorcith that he might detect within the city. Surprisingly, he discovered significant quantities, and as Firell had described. Knives and swords and dozens of other shapes. But there was something about the lorcith that was different, muted in some way, so that he couldn't clearly hear the song from it that he thought he should.

That change was important, somehow. Was it simply because it was mined elsewhere?

He Slid partially, so that he could access the power of the Elder Trees. As he did, he used that power and *pushed* on all the lorcith at once. Had he not managed to access the power of the Elder Trees, he doubted that he would have been able to do it all at once, but with that connection, he *could* use that energy. The *push* was soft, subtle, but enough that he had to draw on significant power from the trees.

The lorcith shifted.

Rsiran had no other way to describe what he felt as he *pushed*. The song changed with it, becoming clearer.

With that connection, he understood why it had been muted before; the lorcith in Nalthin was all tainted by shadowsteel. Or had been, before he used the power of the Elder Trees to burn it off.

"What did you do?" Jessa whispered.

"Why?"

"There was a flash of light around you. It's gone now."

Could she see it when he used that power? Had Danis seen it? If so, then he might not have been nearly as secretive as he had hoped.

"We need to hurry," he said.

"What of the lorcith?" Firell asked.

"I've restored it."

"What does that mean?"

"I don't know. But this is the place we needed to come."

Rsiran focused on the lorcith within the city, searching for something that sang to him the most clearly. He found it in the form of a strangely curved sword.

He *pulled*.

From the distance, he wasn't sure what would happen.

There was resistance, but he *pulled* even harder.

"Watch out!" Jessa said.

"Not an attack. That's me." Rsiran stood, and grabbed the sword out of the air.

He held onto it and listened to the soft song from the lorcith. He should be amazed by the fact that he had managed to pull it from the city from behind the rock, but he didn't have the time. They had to find and understand what Venass might have done, and destroy the forge if they could.

The lorcith in the sword told him its history. Rsiran knew how it had come from the mountain, and how the metal had been turned into something else, added to in a deep and angry fire, forced to take on darkness. Shadowsteel. Rsiran had somehow managed to burn away that shadowsteel, but the sword remembered it, and could tell him what had happened.

Where is the forge?

He posed the question of the metal, not certain that it would even know, but he had done a similar thing once before when trying to understand if he used the potential of lorcith, exhausting it by calling upon it. Then lorcith had given him a vision. Could it do the same again?

He waited, clearing his mind as he thought about what he wanted of the lorcith, much like he did when working at the forge, something that he hadn't done in far too long.

Slowly, a vision came into his mind, resolving into focus.

Not a city—so not Nalthin—what he saw reminded him of the Ilphaesn mines.

In the vision, there were massive amounts of lorcith, but other metals were there as well. Rsiran could tell iron and copper and precious metals like gold and silver, but there were others that he didn't understand.

Where would he find the forge?

The sword wasn't able to provide that to him, but he could use lorcith. Listening for it, he prepared himself for the possibility that it would be tainted by shadowsteel as well.

When he found it, Rsiran felt surprise.

A deep mine of lorcith, nearly as extensive as the one in Ilphaesn, stretched in the mountain near him. Why hadn't he detected it earlier?

Something obstructed his ability to detect lorcith. Probably shadowsteel, used in the same way that his grandfather had used it to prevent him from detecting the heartstone with him.

But focused as he was, he could reach past it.

Rsiran listened, searching for what seemed similar to the vision that he'd been given by the lorcith, and couldn't find it.

Straining, he Slid partway to the Elder Trees power before he realized what he even had done, and *pulled*.

Connected to their power, he extended his reach, stretching even farther from him, and found lorcith in the quantities that he expected from the vision. More than that, he detected something blocking his ability. Rsiran wasn't sure what it was, and sent a pulse of power through it.

Lorcith flared in his mind.

He looked at the others with him. They could follow—especially with Sarah guiding them—if he stepped into the Slides, but doing so opened him to Venass realizing that he was here, but then after what he'd already done, they might know he was here anyway.

Could he carry all of them with him? He'd never Slid with so many before, and would never have considered it, but he could use the power from the Elder Trees to restore himself, couldn't he?

"Gather around me," he said. "We won't have much time."

When they reached him, he *pulled* them into a Slide.

It went slower than any Slide Rsiran had ever attempted, but then he had never even considered trying to bring so many with him at one time. The colors that swirled around him were streaks of blue and white, and for the first time, he thought he saw and understood the connection to the metal, but then it was gone.

Pausing in the space between, he *pulled* on the power of the Elder Trees, replenishing his strength. Rsiran *pulled* on even more, drawing enough so that he could complete the Slide. And then they emerged.

The cavern reminded him of Ilphaesn, only the walls did not glow with the same steady light. The massive pile of lorcith did, giving more than enough light for Rsiran to see. Other metals were piled nearby. Iron as he had seen in the vision. Grindl piled next to iron as green bars. Smaller quantities of copper, silver, gold, and titanium. But no forge. Nothing that would make the shadowsteel.

"It's not here," he said softly.

"How can you see anything?" Valn asked.

"Lorcith lights the way for me," he answered.

"I see it," Sarah said. "Apparently, not as clearly as you, but I see it."

"I thought the forge would be here, but I don't find anything."

"Look around," Jessa suggested. "If it's here…"

They shouldn't spend too much time here. If the shadowsteel forge *wasn't* here, then he should return to the city and help with the evacuation, preparing the guilds for whatever Venass might have planned. Rsiran knew that he could use the power of the Elder Trees to protect the guilds—and that the trees might already protect the guilds without him doing anything—but if they could find a way to limit Venass, and prevent them from a future attack… that was valuable.

He focused on the lorcith. Now that he was in the mine, he sensed a much larger quantity than before.

Did shadowsteel use so much lorcith?

Ephram hadn't known. The alchemists once knew the formula, but it had been a long time since they had attempted to create it, and he hadn't remembered.

Rsiran *pulled* on the lorcith, moving it to the side.

When he did, another opening appeared, one that had been hidden by the lorcith before.

Light emerged from the opening, but this light was bluish, the same as the Elvraeth lanterns.

"What is that?" Valn asked.

"That's where we need to go," Rsiran said.

Jessa unsheathed her knives and took a step toward the opening. "Careful," she said.

Rsiran *pushed* on the heartstone knives that he carried with him. Here, with the connection to lorcith being what it was, heartstone might protect him more than lorcith.

They entered the opening. Stairs led down, with heartstone lanterns set along the walls. The stone was smooth here, and had no lorcith buried in it. If this had been a lorcith mine, it was no longer.

"Where do you think this leads?" Tia asked. She stood near his shoulder, the steel sword she carried unsheathed and reflecting some of the bluish light.

"Down," Rsiran said.

He *pulled* them down the stairs, emerging in a narrow hall. More lanterns lined the walls, but more than that, he noted doors along the walls as well. They were made of a dark metal—shadowsteel.

Rsiran considered the walls around him, realizing that *everything* appeared made—or at least coated—in shadowsteel.

What was behind the walls?

Shadows separated from the wall.

Rsiran jumped forward, *pushing* on his knives, using heartstone as he went.

Two of the shadows fell from the heartstone knives that he'd used on them. Two more remained.

Valn Slid behind them, followed by Tia.

They attacked, but the Hjan were quick.

Rsiran Slid partway, and *pulled* on power from the Elder Trees.

He sent it surging at the remaining shadows. Where it touched the walls, color burned through, as if he exposed lorcith hidden beneath. The remaining Hjan fell. Valn and Hester finished them off.

"How did you see them?" Jessa asked.

"Shadows."

"I can see that now, but before. How did you notice them?"

Rsiran shook his head. "I don't know. I saw them as shadows."

"Guess we're in the right spot," Valn said. "What do you think is behind the door?"

He stopped at the first one and stared at it. The entire door was made of shadowsteel, and appeared to be thick enough that he couldn't risk opening it. "I won't be able to open the door," he told Jessa.

She studied one of the nearest doors and nodded. "I'll do it."

They stopped at the nearest door, and she used her lock-pick set to open it. After she was done, Rsiran *pushed* on the lorcith in the door, burning away the taint from shadowsteel. *Pushing* on his lorcith knives, he held them out while Jessa opened the door, but the room was empty.

She did the same at the next door. Again, the room was empty.

"This is a waste, Lareth. Venass has left," Valn said. "We should return to the city. The guilds will need our help. You've said as much yourself."

They did need his help. And if there was no one here, then even this had been a diversion.

Rsiran glanced at Firell, but he remained tense, and his face neutral. Firell wanted to find Shael, but what if he wasn't here?

The next door was the same.

"There's only the one left," Jessa said.

They had come to Nalthin thinking to find the shadowsteel forge, but he had hoped that maybe he would find his father as well. Now it seemed they would find neither.

"We should return," he said. "Our time is better spent in the city."

"Let me open this door," Jessa said.

Rsiran nodded. "Fine. Then we go."

She crouched in front of the door and picked the lock.

When she pulled the door open, instead of an empty cell, there was another hall, this time stretching into blackness.

Rsiran *pushed* a knife into the darkness, and the light quickly faded.

Shadowsteel, and with enough strength that it overwhelmed his connection to the metal.

He couldn't go down there, not safely at least. Doing so risked his connection to lorcith.

Even without someone from Venass here, the shadowsteel would prevent him from going any farther.

CHAPTER 37

Danis's taunt hung in his mind. Venass had studied for generations. How could Rsiran have learned enough to overcome that knowledge?

"What is it?" Jessa asked.

"That's all shadowsteel. I think if I go down there, it'll affect my connection to lorcith."

Firell stood at the door. "I can almost see something."

Jessa stopped next to him. "What is it?"

"I... I don't know."

She spun him around so that he faced her and jabbed one of her slender knives at his neck. "If this is some part of a trick—"

Firell pushed the knife away from him. "No trick, girl. Had I wanted to play Lareth, do you think I'd have wanted him to bring all the help with him that he did? Look at this. Damn, you've got constables fighting with you now. The last time I was in Elaeavn, we were doing all what we could to avoid the constables. I want to find

Shael, and I want to find a way not to worry about Josun hunting my family."

"Jessa," Rsiran said.

She spun to face him. "We can't trust him."

"I don't. But that doesn't mean that he's lying to us."

"How do you propose getting down that hall?" Valn asked.

"I don't know."

"We can go," Hester suggested. The lithe man was soft spoken and had used his sword well. "You remain here, guildlord. We will do this."

If there were other Hjan, Rsiran didn't think he could rely on their ability to defeat them. He would have to go, wouldn't he?

Jessa rested a hand on his arm. "Let others do this, Rsiran. If it will damage you, then you can't—and shouldn't go."

"That's just it. I have no idea what it will do to me. What if it doesn't affect me at all?"

"Do you think that's the case?"

Rsiran tried reaching for the connection to the knife that he'd *pushed* into the hall, but detected nothing. If the shadowsteel connection was that strong here, what would he be able to do to protect himself?

"I could use the Elder Trees," he whispered.

"You could, but what if it doesn't work?"

He let out a frustrated sigh, hating that he would have to remain here, and that he would have to count on the others and let them risk themselves. "Fine."

She gave him a quick hug and started down the hall with Valn and Sarah. Hester and Marin followed, with Tia and Firell behind them.

Rsiran waited.

But he didn't have to, did he?

He might not be able to safely walk through the shadowsteel hall, but what if there was another way that he could help?

Traveling still felt odd to him, and he didn't use it nearly as often as he should, mostly because doing so left him weakened like Sliding once had weakened him. But this seemed a perfect opportunity to Travel.

Doing so would pose some risk. Without someone here to watch his body, if anyone came after him… he couldn't remain here. If the Hjan returned, he would be easy to attack.

Where should he go?

The Elder Trees.

He Slid, emerging near one of the trees. Dozens of people had already arrived, among them was Della. She hurried over to him, still limping.

"You've already returned," she said.

"Can you watch over me?" he asked.

Without questioning him, she nodded.

Rsiran closed his eyes, and Traveled.

He reached the inside of the mine outside Nalthin and drifted through the cavern until he reached the darkness of the shadowsteel hall. This was the part he wasn't sure about, but he would have to try.

Rsiran moved though the hall. Without his body and without anything of lorcith or heartstone around him, he hoped he would be able to travel without any restrictions. If it didn't work, he might be stuck here.

He felt nothing.

Relief washed through him. Venass hadn't perfected a way to prevent him from Traveling, at least.

He caught up to the others. In this form, he could observe them, but he couldn't speak to them. Watching made it seem almost worse.

They were little more than shadows to him. They paused along the hall.

"Here," Jessa said.

She slipped her pick into the lock and opened a door.

Rsiran wasn't sure what would be on the other side. Maybe nothing, much like what they'd found in the other rooms.

Instead, Luthan emerged.

When he saw them, he nodded. "About time he managed to find me."

"Who?"

Luthan looked past Jessa and seemed to stare directly at Rsiran. "Lareth. I thought he forgot about me."

"You disappeared," Jessa said.

"When I Slid to Cort, someone grabbed me. I think they knew I was going to be there. They pulled me here. I thought his tracker would allow him to find me."

"He can't see past the shadowsteel all around you," Jessa said. "And I hope that if Rsiran Traveled here, he was smart enough to leave the rest of him somewhere safe."

Rsiran nodded, uncertain whether Luthan could see him. If he could, would he be able to communicate on Rsiran's behalf?

"It seems that he did."

"There's another," Valn said.

Jessa moved down the hall and stopped in front of another door. When she opened it, Shael emerged.

She pulled out a knife and jabbed it at him.

Firell grabbed her wrist. "He's the reason I'm here," he said.

"You do be assertive, girl. Glad to see you, too."

"Watch him," she said to Valn.

Valn waggled his steel sword. "I'll watch him. What did he do to you?"

"Tried to poison us and leave us to the Forgotten."

"You do be escapin' so I don' know why you're so upset," Shael said. "Man has to earn a livin', and they paid well."

"Stab him if he tries anything," Jessa said.

Rsiran smiled. At least he didn't have to fear Shael while there was nothing that he could do to protect her.

Jessa started down the hall, her lock-pick set still in hand. Valn stayed close to Shael, his sword unsheathed, not giving the large man a chance to get too close to Jessa. "What else is down this hall?" she asked.

"Don' know what's down here. They be comin' with food once a day, an' never the same man, if you do be knowin' what I'm sayin'."

She turned. "I do be knowin', Shael."

"What you be lookin' for, girl? Maybe I heard somethin' that can help?"

"Rsiran says there should be a forge of some kind here. Not really sure what that would look like."

"You be with a smith an' you don' know what a forge be lookin' like?"

"I know what *his* forge looks like. Whatever we're searching for is to make this metal." She pointed to the walls.

"Somethin' like that would take heat, and with heat you got to vent."

He was right. Rsiran should have considered that before. The forge wouldn't be deep in the mountain, would it? Or if it was, it would need to have a way to vent the excess heat.

She knelt in front of another door, and worked the lock, quickly getting the door open. Before pulling it open, she paused and looked up at Shael. "Then where do you think it is?" Jessa asked.

"Don't know."

She stood up and pulled the door open. Her eyes widened slightly, and she took a step back. "Oh."

Jessa pulled one of her knives free and held it out from her.

"What is it?" Valn asked. "Hjan?"

She shook her head. "Not Hjan. This... this is different."

Rsiran floated into the room and nearly lost his connection to Traveling.

A thin, haggard man with a thick beard cowered in the corner. His arms wrapped around his legs. Wounds of various ages were scored on his flesh. In spite of that, Rsiran knew without a doubt it was his father.

"Neran. You need to stand," Jessa said. Rsiran was proud of how quickly she recovered. "We're here to rescue you."

His father looked up, and hollowed eyes seemed to catch Jessa and reflected confusion. "How do you know my name?" he said in a hoarse voice.

"You need to get up," Jessa said. "It's time to get you out of here."

As she entered the cell, he tried to scramble back. "I know you. You're with him!"

"What's he babbling about?" Valn asked.

Jessa shrugged. "Last time I saw Rsiran's father, I threatened to kill him."

"That's his father?" Sarah asked. She'd been relatively silent for most of the time they had been beneath the ground. "What happened to him?"

"Looks like Venass tortured him," Jessa said. "Can you walk? We need to get you out of here. Alyse is safe."

"Alyse?" He spoke her name in something like a whisper. "Don't harm her!"

Jessa shook her head. Rsiran could see the frustration level rising in her. She had little patience for his father, especially after everything he had done to Rsiran. "*We* haven't harmed her. We saved her. But you need to get moving."

Firell pushed his way into the room and took one look at Neran and hurried to his side. He slipped an arm around his waist and helped him to his feet, murmuring something that Rsiran couldn't quite make out.

They made their way to the door when Hester paused, tilting his head to the side. "Someone is coming," he said.

Panic flooded Neran's eyes. "They can't find me with you! The pain… the pain!"

"Damn, man, shut up!" Valn said.

"Can't you see he's been tormented?" Firell asked. "Take it from someone who has been there. This man needs our help, not you yelling at him."

"We still haven't found this damn forge," Valn said.

A harsh laugh echoed toward them.

"The forge? That's what you came for?" A figure stepped away from the wall, one that sent a chill through Rsiran. Danis.

And he wasn't alone. Six other men were with him, each with long lines across their face marking them as the Hjan.

"When we faced no resistance, I feared that I had misjudged. And now… now we have both my son-in-law and my grandson's favorite girl." He tilted his head and studied Jessa. "Strange that he would let you leave without him."

Jessa held her knife away from her. "Slide away," she said, though not to those from Venass. She spoke to Valn and the others. "Get free while you can."

"Oh, I'm afraid it is much too late for that," Danis said.

A gasp echoed from along the hall. "I can't Slide," Marin said.

Danis took a stuttering step toward someone at the end of the hall, and there came another gasp, and then the sound of a body crumpling to the ground.

"The time for holding you is over," Danis said. He stopped in front of Hester.

Hester swung his sword, but Danis swung a heartstone sword around, catching the one Hester used and knocking it away. His next slice caught Hester through the chest, and he fell.

Danis turned his gaze to Jessa. "Too bad he refused to come. And if he was foolish enough to Travel, he can watch as you all die."

CHAPTER 38

Rsiran had to do something, but what could he do? If he Slid to his friends, he would be powerless within the shadow-steel walls, and just as trapped as they. And in this form, he was equally powerless.

Wasn't he?

He'd tried *pulling* on power from the Elder Trees while Traveling and had failed before, but that was before he had learned that he could straddle the Slide, that he could exist in both places at once. He doubted that Danis would have discovered that secret yet.

But he had to act fast, or someone else would die.

Danis now stood in front of Sarah.

Rsiran couldn't return to his body and then Slide back, but could he *pull* his body toward him? He'd never tried it, and didn't know if it would even work.

Hopefully, Della would understand.

He *pulled*.

Rsiran paused the Slide partway, now existing in three places.

His mind split with pain, but the power from the Elder Trees was there. He could *feel* it.

Now, could he *pull* on it and use it?

Sarah fought his grandfather, but her sword was slow. As the next slice came, one that would take her head off, time seemed to slow.

Rsiran *pulled* on the power of the Elder Trees, filling with it.

Someone sucked in a sharp breath.

He directed the power at his grandfather.

The blow struck him in the chest, and he went spinning backward.

Rsiran didn't wait, attacking again, this time splitting the energy so that he could hit the other Hjan. Three went flying backward in blasts of light drawn from the Elder Trees.

To their credit, his friends lurched forward. Valn struck one of the Hjan, taking off one arm and then another. The man dropped. Sarah moved quickly, stabbing with her sword, and dropping another Hjan. As Rsiran surged another blast of power that hit the remaining Hjan, even Shael darted forward, moving more quickly than a man his size should be able to. He crushed one of the Hjan between his massive hands, holding him in place as the man tried to Slide.

"Rsiran!"

He jerked around at the sound of Jessa's scream.

Danis held her, his sword nearly to her back. "Interesting trick you've developed, grandson. As I said, I didn't think that you would pose such a challenge. Now that you have…"

As he slipped his sword forward, Jessa gasped.

Neran darted toward Danis, moving more quickly than he looked like he could in his condition, and grabbed the blade before it could penetrate too deeply. Years of working at the forge had made his father strong. Much of that strength had disappeared, wasted away as he'd been trapped, but Neran managed to throw Danis backward, likely out of sheer shock.

Jessa coughed. Blood spilled out from where the sword pierced her back, and she would need healing, but she had time. Rsiran's father balled his fists, and blood poured out from between his fingers.

Rsiran took a moment to note that the rest of the Hjan were all down, but so, too, was Tia. When had she fallen? Valn and Sarah approached carefully. Shael and Firell stood to the side, a dark and angry expression on Shael's face.

Danis merely smiled at them. "We have still claimed the city—"

Rsiran hit him with another blast of energy that threw him back. Before he could hit the wall, Danis disappeared.

"How are you here like this?" Jessa asked him.

"Traveling." His words came out strangely, filled with the power of the Elder Trees.

"We haven't found the damn forge," Valn said. "That was the entire reason for coming here!"

"All of it," Neran whispered.

"What?" Valn asked.

"All of this is the forge."

Rsiran's breath caught. Could Venass have used the entire mountain to create the shadowsteel forge?

But why couldn't they? He didn't fully understand the dark power of shadowsteel, only that it had nearly killed him multiple times, but forging it seemed as if it would take enormous energy, and where better to draw it from than a place filled with lorcith?

"Return to the Aisl," he said to Valn.

"What about the forge, Lareth?"

"Leave that to me."

Valn looked at the fallen forms of Hester and Marin before

kneeling next to Tia. He checked her for a pulse, and tears came to his eyes. Rsiran didn't need him to tell them that she was gone.

He slipped a necklace off her neck. The serpent symbolizing the head of the guild. He tucked it carefully into his pocket. "I can Slide two with me."

"I can take the others," Luthan said.

"You do be findin' that I'm harder to Slide with," Shael said.

Luthan eyed the large man. "Perhaps only one then."

"I need Jessa and my father," Rsiran said.

"You Traveled here," Luthan said. "Do you think you can Slide with them?"

He seemed genuinely curious as he asked.

Rsiran didn't know, and used energy to *pull* on Jessa. She Slid with a soft gasp. "Yes," he said.

Luthan grabbed Shael. "Where should we go?"

"The Aisl, if you are willing. The rest of the council has betrayed the city, allowing Venass access."

Luthan took a deep breath. "That… I did not See. I will meet you in the forest."

With that, he Slid, dragging Shael with him.

Valn nodded to Rsiran, grabbing onto Sarah and Firell. "Guildlord. Return safely."

"I will."

When he was gone, Jessa looked at him. "What are you going to do?"

"This has to be destroyed before Venass can use it again," he answered. He *pulled* Jessa and his father in a Slide, leaving them in the space between, before returning to the inside of the mountain. While there, he floated, insubstantial, but full of power from the Elder Trees. Would he be able to shut the forge down?

Even if he could, how would he do it?

He had no idea what it would entail.

Remaining as he was, he sensed the shadowsteel lining the walls as a pressure against him and his power. He had burned off shadowsteel before, could he do it again?

Would it take so much energy that it would damage the Elder Trees?

If he did nothing, and Venass remained in control of shadowsteel, there would be more risk to the trees than if he attempted to do this now.

Rsiran *pulled* on that power. It filled him, flooding him with a warmth that he shouldn't feel when he Traveled. He continued to draw upon it, and it radiated from him, flowing through him. Where it touched the walls, the shadowsteel disappeared.

He unleashed it, acting as something more like a vessel that allowed the power to flow through him. As it did, lorcith bloomed into his mind, released from the touch of shadowsteel. That lorcith lent power to him, somehow adding to what he could draw from the Elder Trees in a way that he had never experienced before.

Rsiran moved, untethered from his body, letting the power that he summoned fill the mountain. As it did, it spread, snaking away from him through the tunnels, and lorcith appeared, flaring in his mind, forming something of a map. Farther and farther he pushed the power, sending it deeper, until there was no more shadowsteel.

Lorcith in the walls gave a vision to him. Rsiran hesitated, before acting on the vision.

He *pulled* on lorcith.

Even filled with power, what he did should not have been possible.

The mountain groaned.

He continued to *pull*.

Cracks started to form in the ceilings. Debris fell through him, a strange sensation. Lorcith appeared in the ceiling where the shadowsteel had fallen away.

Rsiran *pulled* again.

Lorcith fell around him. The entire mountain began to collapse, the empty caverns now filled with lorcith. Still he *pulled*.

The mountain continued to rumble. Rock settled through Rsiran so that he was buried. He remained where he was until the sounds faded. Only then could he tell that the lorcith of this mountain was satisfied with what he had done.

Rsiran returned to his body.

Light from the trees surrounded him, four blindingly bright sentinels rising into the sky. The fifth remained dark, though was it as dark as it had been before?

He Slid back to the place between Slides where Jessa lay on the ground, blood seeping from her wound. His father knelt over her, shoving his hands down on the wound, but blood continued to leak. As Rsiran appeared, he looked up.

"I tried…"

Rsiran stepped in front of his father, and *pulled* on the power around him. With that power, he forced it into her, filling her as he had filled himself. There was a resistance, but he continued to *pull*, letting that energy wash around her until it overwhelmed the resistance that he detected. She took a shallow breath and looked up.

Rsiran turned the energy to his father and sent the healing power through him as well. If the sword had been poisoned—and judging by the way that Jessa bled, he suspected that it was—his father would bleed out next.

Neran gasped as the energy washed over him. Rsiran continued to *pull* on it until he no longer met any resistance within his father, and then released his connection to the trees.

Jessa sat up and kissed him on the cheek. "We found him," she said.

"And the shadowsteel forge is destroyed."

"Destroyed?" his father asked. "How were you able to destroy it?"

Rsiran shook his head. "Later. For now, I need to know if you want to return to Elaeavn. When I saw you last, you were content to die."

"There is nothing for me there."

"There is Alyse. There is your smithy."

"The guild would not allow it."

Rsiran laughed softly. "I'm not so sure about that."

"What of Kala?"

Rsiran shook his head. "I'm sorry. Mother is gone. When Danis attacked, she was caught."

His father only nodded, less emotion than he would have expected. How much had Neran known about?

"You protected Alyse, didn't you?" Rsiran asked.

"They wanted to use her. I would have done anything to protect her." He blinked. "And you, but you had more of my bloodline. You had not the same need."

"I know."

"You know?"

"I know about Danis. I know that Mother was born of the Forgotten. And I know the price you paid to return with her to the city. So yes, I know."

"What now?" Neran asked.

"Nothing has changed. You have to decide if you want to return to the city."

Neran looked around, and his eyes widened slightly, as if he could see the power from the Elder Trees. Maybe he could. "I will return and face the judgment of my guild."

Jessa met Rsiran's eyes, fighting a smile.

"Good. Because the guild will need all of us if we are to stop Venass for good."

He held out his hands, and Slid them to the Aisl.

EPILOGUE

When they arrived, Rsiran let out a slow and tired sigh. Time spent in the place between had restored his energy, but he had a physical tiredness that he couldn't recover from as easily. Seval found him first, with Luca walking with him.

"You made it. Were you successful?" Seval asked Rsiran.

"As much as can be done for now."

"Your apprentice shared with me what you told him," Seval went on. "Do you really think it's safest that we remain outside the city?"

"We'll know soon enough," Rsiran said. "If it doesn't matter, then we can return."

"But you don't know."

Rsiran shook his head. "I thought it prudent to be careful."

"What now?"

"Now we plan," Rsiran said. "Gather the others. The guild will have much to discuss."

Seval tapped his knuckle to his forehead and nodded to Rsiran's father. "Neran. Glad to see you returned."

When Seval left, his father looked at Rsiran differently. "What is this? Why does Master Seval address you that way? How is it that you have an apprentice?"

Rsiran patted his father on the shoulder. "You are a master smith, otherwise I could not share this with you."

"Share what?"

"I'm the smith guildlord."

"That… that's not possible."

"Believe it or not, but get used to the fact that the other smiths listen to me, and I speak for the guild. With what we're about to face, I will have to lead the guildlords as well, especially with the Sliding Guild guildlord now gone."

"There is a Sliding Guild?"

Rsiran nodded. "There's much you don't know. But if you want to know, I am willing to share with you."

Neran looked toward Seval talking quietly to Luca. A few of the other smiths were with him, and they occasionally glanced over to his father. "What will it cost me?"

Rsiran shrugged. "Your choice. Seval and some of the others have regained the ability to listen to lorcith. They've become more talented smiths because of it. A few have no interest, but recognize the value. Lorcith is plentiful, Father. If you want to listen to it, you can use it without worrying."

His father sighed. "I know that it's plentiful. When they held me, they… they forced me to listen until I could hear it again. The damned song fills me now. I had to tell them when it changed, when lorcith screamed. That was how they knew their damned weapons worked."

Rsiran shivered. "I'm sorry. It's my fault they held you."

"It is. But I drove you away."

"I can help you," Rsiran offered. "I can teach you to listen to lorcith the right way. You can learn to enjoy the song."

Neran shook his head. "I don't know. I'll think on it." He started to turn away when Alyse appeared from a small crowd. "Alyse?"

Alyse glanced from Rsiran to their father. "You found him?" she asked Rsiran. She pulled her hand from Brusus's and ran toward him. "Rsiran found you?"

His father started sobbing then. "I'm so sorry," he said to Rsiran. "For… for…"

Rsiran swallowed the lump in his throat. For so long, he'd wanted nothing more than his father's approval, but he'd grown past needing that. Now that his father was returned, he wanted to show him that he wasn't the foolish, undisciplined boy he'd thought, nor was he the petulant son who had stolen from his smithy. Rsiran wasn't sure who he was anymore, but he felt a part of something greater than himself now.

"I am, too," he said.

He left Alyse and his father alone, and moved to the center of the clearing. Della approached, relief on her face. Ephram was with her, and Sarah walked next to him. Luthan followed, every so often glancing at Della with a curious expression on his face.

"You should not have been able to Slide like that," she told Rsiran.

"I think there are many things I should not be able to do," he said. He looked to Ephram. "The shadowsteel forge is destroyed. They used an entire mountain to create it. We will have to protect Ilphaesn."

"I will have the miners begin work."

"Are you sure they can be trusted?" Rsiran asked.

"When Gersh realized what Naelm intended, he returned."

"This isn't the miners' fault. None of this is," Rsiran said. "But we must be the ones to end it."

Luthan turned his attention to Rsiran. "How do you intend to end this, guildlord?"

He didn't know, not fully. "We need the crystal. Venass doesn't have it—not yet—but that doesn't mean they won't go after it. The guilds must work together. We must drive Venass from the city. And the Elvraeth," he said, turning to Luthan, "can no longer rule as they did."

Luthan turned his cloudy eyes to him. "You would rule as guildlord?"

Ephram's eyes widened slightly, as did Sarah's.

Rsiran shook his head. "I don't think that's the kind of rule the people deserve. I'm not sure of the answer, but the first step is not depriving our people of their birthright."

"You would open the crystals to anyone?" Ephram asked.

"Anyone from Elaeavn would be allowed entry. So once we drive Venass from the city"—he made a point of saying *when* not *if*—"we will find the missing crystal. And then, we must find a way to rule the city fairly."

Della glanced to Luthan. "What do you say, councilor? Will his plan work?"

"I See… possibilities." Luthan sighed. "They are better than what I Saw when trapped by Venass. Then I Saw nothingness."

Della sniffed and looked to the trees. "Well then, we had better make ourselves at home until we succeed."

DK HOLMBERG is a full time writer living in rural Minnesota with his wife, two kids, two dogs, two cats, and thankfully no other animals. Somehow he manages to find time for writing.

To see other books and read more, please go to www.dkholmberg.com

Follow me on facebook: facebook.com/dkholmberg

Word-of-mouth is crucial for any author to succeed and how books are discovered. If you enjoyed the book, please consider leaving a review online at your favorite bookseller or Goodreads, even if it's only a line or two; it would make all the difference and would be very much appreciated.

CPSIA information can be obtained
at www.ICGtesting.com
Printed in the USA
BVHW041558060922
646324BV00004B/97